BRO DATE
The
BEST BROS FOREVER BOOK TWO

CHARLI MEADOWS

Copyright © 2025 by Charli Meadows
All Rights Reserved.

No part of this book may be reproduced in any form or by any electronic or mechanical means, including information storage and retrieval systems, without written permission from the author, except for brief quotations in a book review.

This book was created without the use of generative AI.

Editing by Katie at Between The Covers Editorial
Special Edition Cover by Caravaggia
Formatting by Charli Meadows

SYNOPSIS

Toby

For years, I've been pining after someone I can never have—my best friend, Shane. The thought of confessing my feelings and possibly losing him is so gut-wrenching that I've hidden my true identity from everyone, including myself.

Until now.

While staying with my grandparents for spring break—away from the testosterone-filled house I share with Shane and two other roommates—I decide I'm finally ready to pursue my attraction to guys. When I get back to campus, I download a gay dating app to meet people.

Shane's overprotective side flares to life, and he starts to stalk me on my dates, making sure I'm safe and swooping in to rescue me from disaster after disaster. When that protective streak turns into possessiveness, and he asks to kiss me, I have to pinch myself.

Is this the happily ever after of my dreams, or is Shane just leading me on to eventually rip out my heart when he realizes he isn't gay?

Shane

There's always been one ray of sunshine in my otherwise dark existence—my best friend, Toby. But when he returns from a trip to Florida and confides in me that he's gay and wants to start dating guys, irrational jealousy takes hold of me.

Stalking his dates may start by accident, but after the

first time, I willingly lurk in the shadows, watching him. *Protecting him*. None of these losers deserve Toby, and when he continues to get hurt by them, I can't take it any longer. I guess I'll have to be the one to show him how special he is and what he deserves.

When one heated kiss turns into a series of dates, I find myself falling for my best friend and questioning *everything*. Will this be the beginning of something beautiful, or am I doomed to lose the only good thing in my life?

The Bro Date is book two in the Best Bros Forever series, a collection of standalone contemporary gay romances. You can expect best-friends-to-lovers, bi-awakening, grumpy/sunshine, and forced proximity. This novel is intended for 18+ readers and touches on some sensitive subjects.

AUTHOR'S NOTE

Thank you so much for picking up book two in my new contemporary MM series—*Best Bros Forever*—and giving Shane and Toby's story a chance. Each book is a standalone, college age, and features some version of the best-friends-to-lovers trope.

I have to admit, I love writing grumpy/sunshine stories as much as I love reading them, so I really hope you adore these boys as much as I do! Sweet Toby has been in love with Shane and pining after him since high school, while Shane just wants to protect the one good thing in his life. Their love story is low angst, swoony, funny, and of course, spicy. In fact, my editor describes it as a warm hug.

Thanks for deciding to give my book a chance, and I hope you have as much fun reading about their relationship as I did writing it.

Content Warnings: Language, explicit sexual scenes, underage drinking, fighting, mild violence, narcissistic parents, and brief flashbacks to bullying and parental neglect.

PLAYLIST

Available on Spotify

Chokehold by Austin Giorgio
Sweet Love – Acoustic by Myles Smith
Ordinary by Alex Warren
DAISIES by Justin Bieber
LOVE by Kendrick Lamar and Zacari
Too Sweet by Hozier
Bad Dreams by Teddy Swims
Love Sick Doctor by Thunder Jackson
Pink Pony Club by Chappell Roan
Miles On It by Marshmello and Kane Brown
Diet Pepsi by Addison Rae
Sure Thing by Miguel
Moonlit Floor (Kiss Me) by LISA
Better by Khalid
Chasing Paradise by Kygo and One Republic
Falling by Iration
LOVE LOOKS PRETTY ON YOU by Nessa Barrett

*To my beta readers and dear friends, Jamie and Lane.
Thank you for everything, this one's for you!*

CHAPTER ONE
SHANE

The acrid smell of burger grease and deep-fried everything clings to my nostrils as I hastily clock out and untie my dirty apron, hanging it on a hook next to the employee lockers. Raúl has them professionally cleaned weekly, so at least I don't have to worry about getting the grease stains out at home. But that's about all I can say regarding my boss' character.

My locker is on the bottom row, and I'm certain Raúl did it on purpose, making my six-foot-four frame fold in half and squat down uncomfortably before and after every shift.

Prick.

It takes two tries for me to get the combination right, my oversized fingers slipping on the tiny dial while my knees dig into the cold, hard linoleum. I've been working as much as I can over spring break, and I'm exhausted, to say the least, but financial aid doesn't cover everything.

My best friend, Toby, was gone the entire time, staying with his newly retired grandparents in Key West to avoid going home to his overbearing parents. I don't blame him for wanting to avoid that shit, but the island they live on is pretty remote, so the cell service is spotty at best. We hardly kept in touch beyond a few emails. But Toby's finally back in town today. He sent me a text around lunchtime to let me know he landed safely, and he'll see me at home.

I've been looking forward to it all shift, instead of looking forward to another shitty day ending and the glorious reprieve of sleep.

I rifle through the ratty backpack I've had since high school, searching for my old-ass iPhone to check for new messages from Toby. I hate that I can't keep it in my pocket while I'm cooking, but it's *Raúl's kitchen and Raúl's rules*, as I'm reminded daily when he slinks around the place being a dick to everyone.

"Shane!" a loud and somewhat aggressive voice hollers from the kitchen.

Speak of the devil.

With a deep breath and loud exhale, I slowly stand up and turn around to face the asshole that I constantly have to remind myself is the one signing my paychecks.

His dark, bushy brows are drawn together, lips pursed like he's completely annoyed at me, even though I'm not on the clock anymore. "I asked you to reorganize the pantry two shifts ago. It's still a fucking mess. Why, Shane?"

I grind my teeth, hating when he curses at me like that.

Tonight was packed. The orders were steadily coming in, and it was hard enough to keep the kitchen clean and the food timely with just one other person on shift. But Raúl knows this, so there's no point in attempting to defend myself. "Didn't have time," I reply blandly instead.

Raúl glances at the backpack dangling by my side. "Lazy kids," he mutters under his breath.

THE BRO DATE

I don't correct him that I'm twenty-one and in college. I'll always be a kid in his condescending eyes.

"See to it that you make time next shift, or we're going to have a more serious talk," he threatens with his signature snarl.

"Copy," I grunt, ready to get the hell out of here. It's Saturday night, and Toby's finally home.

Seemingly satisfied with my response, Raúl nods and hustles back to his office, leaving me in peace.

I grab my jean jacket and rush outside to my beloved old pickup truck before I get ambushed again. A small smile tugs at my lips as I turn the key a few times until she starts, pulling out of the parking lot in a hurry. I'm so ready to relax with a cold beer and hang out with my best friend.

It doesn't take long to get home. The Salty Sandbar Café is located just east of campus, right on the Intracoastal Waterway. There's never too much traffic in Crescent Bay, even with the tourist season picking up.

Toby's Audi and Spencer's Jeep are parked in the driveway, so I park on the curb and hop out. It's first come, first served around here when we have four vehicles and no garage.

A refreshing gust of wind whips sweaty, tangled strands around my face as I hustle to the front door. When I step inside, I expect to find Toby and the rest of our roommates sprawled out on the couches, watching a movie or battling it out on the PS5, not a dark, empty living room.

Where the fuck is everyone?

Normally, I would be relieved by the peace and quiet, but I haven't seen Toby in over a week, and I miss him more than I'm comfortable admitting.

It's been us against the world since fifth grade.

I flip a light on and head to the kitchen for a glass of

water and to check the dry erase board for messages, since no one bothered to text me. Front and center on the refrigerator door, scrawled in Jake's chicken scratch, is the answer to my question.

Went to the Sigma Chi party. Meet us there.

It's not like Toby to go to frat parties, especially without me, so I jog upstairs and lightly knock on his door in case he's sleeping. When there's no answer, I peek inside, disappointed to find an empty bed that's still made up exactly the way it was a week ago. I gently shut the door, rest my forehead against the cool wood, and close my eyes for a moment. I'm fucking tired, but I guess I'm going to a party tonight.

With a resigned sigh, I drag my feet to the shared bathroom down the hall. I desperately need a shower. Can't show up smelling like deep-fried grease.

Loud, thumping bass fills my ears as I pull up to the frat party. Big Greek letters I can't read are spotlighted on the front of the baby-blue house with white trim. The front door is ajar, with people overflowing into the yard. I have no idea how campus security hasn't busted this yet, but I don't really care either. I just want to find Toby.

When I push through the crowd of drunk college kids on the front porch, I peer around the messy frat house, scanning the space for one of my roommates.

"Shane! Hey, bro! Want a drink?" some guy with a man bun shouts way too loudly before dapping me up.

I'm shit at remembering names.

"Nah. You seen Toby?" I ask.

"Oh, uh. Not recently. I heard he's back, though."

I grunt, not wanting to make small talk.

Before I can slip away, someone jumps on my back, wrapping their arms tightly around my neck and squeezing.

Fucking Jake.

I take two giant steps toward the sofa and in one lightning-fast move, I pry his arms loose, bend forward, and flip the asshat over my head. Jake lands on his back, laughing loudly like he just went on the tallest ride at the county fair.

Jake Tucker is that one high-energy, obnoxious, d-bag of a friend that you just can't seem to ever get rid of. *And* one of my roommates.

"Where's Toby?" I ask, not bothering to say hello to the drunk idiot who just tried to choke me out.

Jake sits up, brushing his dirty blond hair out of his eyes. "Just saw him go upstairs. He was *trashed*, dude. Did you know he's absolute shit at beer pong?" Jake chuckles as if he knows something I don't. His blue eyes sparkle with mischief like he's baiting me somehow.

I clench my jaw so hard, I swear I hear a crack. Without another word, I turn around and head for the stairs, taking them two at a time while I dodge the drunk couples making out.

"*Uh ohhh.* Someone's in *trouuuble*," Jake singsongs behind me, but I just ignore his usual shit.

I check the first bedroom I find, and my gaze immediately zeroes in on Toby talking to a group of random guys I've never seen before. Something sharp pricks my heart, but I ignore it, rubbing my chest and watching my best friend laugh and smile at them when I haven't seen him in over a week.

Some guy with neatly styled blond hair reaches out and tugs on one of Toby's curls, causing a blush to spread over his cheeks and an awkward giggle to escape his lips. A rogue wave of possessiveness washes over me. My nostrils flare like a bull seeing red, and I have to clench my hands to stop from charging. I glance down at the dull pain, releasing my fists and finding crescent-shaped indents in my palms.

Before I have a chance to make my way over there and do something I might regret, Toby turns around and finally sees me standing in the doorway. A huge, dimpled smile spreads from ear to ear like he hasn't completely blown me off tonight.

"You made it!" he shouts, ignoring Blondie and tripping over the corner of the rug on his way over to me. I reach out on instinct, gently grasping his slim biceps and steadying him. His skin is soft under my fingertips with a sun-kissed glow from his week in Florida.

I swallow hard, unsure why I'm even noticing.

When Toby peers up at me through a mop of golden-brown curls, I'm met with a pair of glassy, half-lidded eyes I barely recognize. *"Hello, Schwayne,"* he slurs, laughing loudly and gaining even more attention than he already had.

"You wasted?" I grunt.

"Just a little tipsy," he says with a hiccup.

I raise an eyebrow in question, and Toby rolls his lips inward like he's fighting a laugh.

"Toby . . ." I say sternly, glancing at the audience of fuckboys behind him and narrowing my eyes at them.

"So grumpy," Toby murmurs, reaching up to smooth the crease between my brows.

I guess I am because I'm tired, hungry, and I really don't

want to be here, but I came for Toby, and after seeing the state he's in, I'm not leaving without him.

"Tobes! We're about to start another round of beer pong!" the blond douchebag hollers across the room, exponentially adding to the irritation brewing inside me when he uses Toby's nickname like they're already best friends.

He's *my* best friend.

Toby attempts to slip his arm out of my grasp, as if he's actually about to leave me here and drink more with those assholes. I don't let go. I've witnessed too many people make poor decisions because of alcohol, and I won't let Toby be one of them.

I usher him out of the bedroom and down the hallway, away from prying eyes.

"*Hey!*" he yells indignantly.

I pin him against the wall with my larger frame, leaning forward and breathing my words into his ear. "What's going on with you, Tobes?"

"Nothin', Shane," he huffs. "I'm just celebrating being home, okay?"

"Without me?" It's barely a whisper, and for a second, I'm not even sure his intoxicated brain hears me, but then his smile drops.

His eyebrows furrow, confusion piercing through the haze of alcohol. "You were working," he says in defense, but he's never gone to a party without me before.

"Who were those guys?" I ask, an unfamiliar sort of jealousy gnawing uncomfortably at my gut.

"What?" His brows scrunch even further, but I'm not buying it.

"You heard me."

Toby sighs with resignation. "Just some guys from Sigma Chi. They were teaching me how to play beer pong."

Since when does Toby hang out with frat boys and play beer pong?

"I'm taking you home," I say firmly. I *hate* not knowing if he's safe.

"No," Toby retorts, his chin lifting in defiance.

I clench my jaw, weighing my options.

"Don't make me throw you over my shoulder and carry you out of here."

"You'd have to catch me first!" he shouts with a loud, drunk laugh, darting out of my grasp and running down the stairs.

Motherfucker.

"Toby!" I holler at his retreating back, ignoring the thrum of the party and the nosy people staring.

He doesn't stop, continuing to weave his way through the crowd in an attempt to get away, but I catch my prey, grabbing his wrist and spinning him around until he bumps into my chest. I stare down at him, scanning his face like I haven't seen him in a year rather than just a week. His eyes shimmer like molten gold, melting into my soul.

"Are you done now?" I lift an unamused brow, ready for him to volley back some smartass comment.

Toby hiccups, swaying on his feet. "Actually, yeah. I *am* done." He grimaces, holding his stomach like he might be sick.

I wrap a protective arm around his shoulders, steadying him. "Let's get you home," I whisper, my lips accidentally brushing his ear as I lead us to the front door. Toby shivers, and a strange little whimper escapes his lips, but I ignore the odd response, chalking it up to alcohol.

As soon as we step off the porch, an angry gust of wind slams right into us.

"Fucking hell, it's *freezing*!" Toby whines, hugging himself and rubbing his upper arms for warmth.

"It's sixty-two degrees out," I deadpan, glancing over and catching the sheepish look on his face.

"It was eighty degrees in Florida this morning!" Toby cries, defending himself. "And it's windy!"

Shaking my head, I shrug out of my worn jean jacket. It's at least three sizes too big for him, but I slip it around Toby's slim shoulders, allowing it to cocoon him.

"Mmm. Warm," he sighs, closing his eyes for a moment while we walk down the sidewalk to my truck. "Sure you're not cold?" he asks, nuzzling deeper into my jacket and taking a subtle sniff.

"I'm fine," I grunt, helping him into the passenger seat and buckling him in so he doesn't fall out and bust his drunk ass on the pavement.

"Thanks, Shane," he murmurs, sinking into his seat and staring out the window.

Neither of us speaks on the short ride home, and when I put the truck in park and glance over, I see why. Toby is slumped in his seat, head hanging to the side uncomfortably.

"Wake up," I whisper, gently shaking his arm. "We're home."

"Huhhh?" he groans, lifting his head and slowly blinking.

"*Home,*" I repeat in slow motion before getting out and walking around to help him down.

Toby is known to be a little clumsy, and that's when he's sober, so I'm not taking any chances. I've got half a foot on him, but it still takes some fumbling to get him out of my truck and into the house. With one arm around his shoulders, I guide him upstairs to his room and pull back the covers, helping him into bed and tucking him in.

Toby hums contentedly with a dopey smile on his face, snuggling the fluffy white comforter under his chin. "Can't you stay a little while?" he asks, blinking big, sleepy, puppy-dog eyes up at me. He pats the spot next to him when I don't answer right away. "*Pretty please?*"

I'm starving from skipping dinner, but I'm also so deadass tired from being on my feet all day, that even a short walk down the hall to my bedroom seems like a marathon.

I'll just stay for an hour, then I'll get up and make myself something to eat.

"Okay." I sink into bed next to my best friend. We've had sleepovers since we were kids, and I guess we never really grew out of them.

Toby rolls over, allowing me to settle behind him as the big spoon. "Missed you, Shane," he murmurs before his breathing evens out and a small snore escapes him.

"Missed you, too," I whisper, drifting off into the best sleep I've had in a week.

CHAPTER TWO
TOBY

Bright, unfiltered light flows through the open curtains in my room, waking me from a groggy sleep with an unwelcome, early morning wake-up call.

"Fuuuck," I groan, pulling the covers over my head because I'm too hungover to get out of bed and close the curtains. My head is pounding—flashes of hot frat boys, beer pong, and a hurt-looking Shane stomping loudly through my mind. I rub my throbbing temples, but it's no help.

What the hell was I thinking?

Shane is my best friend, and last night I treated him like he wasn't important. Like I wasn't dying to see him after a week apart. Guilt scratches at my aching brain. For blowing him off. For worrying him. And for adding to the burden of his already full plate.

God, I'm a jerk. An absolute freaking jerk.

I should make it up to him somehow, like maybe I should drag my sorry butt out of bed and go get us some greasy, delicious breakfast food. My stomach rumbles happily at the idea, but my body won't move.

Sighing in defeat, I close my eyes and drift.

If only we could hang out all day like we used to when we were younger. I wish Shane didn't have to work so much, but he's putting himself through college *and* paying for housing, whereas my parents pay for everything despite our many disagreements. But Shane and I have always had vastly different home lives, especially as kids.

Homeschooled through third grade, I finally convinced my parents to let me go to an actual elementary school when we moved across the country to South Carolina from Utah. My dad's prominent Salt Lake City real estate firm opened up a new East Coast office based out of Crescent Bay, a charming coastal town known for its breathtaking oceanfront properties, driftwood beaches, and quaint coffee shops and cafés.

My mom gave in to my request without much debate, easily abandoning the homeschooling lifestyle she grew up with back in Utah. I guess she finally realized she could sell houses, too, and make her own money. If she just sent me away for most of the day.

In the end, we both got what we wanted.

Turns out, I was way ahead of my peers because I had no life and no friends outside of church, so I skipped fourth grade and went straight to fifth. That's where I met Shane —who was much bigger, much older, and luckily, much tougher than me. He was held back a year, repeating fifth grade for *reasons*, making him two years older than me. Neither of us fit in, so we gravitated toward each other and became best friends pretty quickly.

A light knock on my bedroom door startles me out of the warm, sleepy space I was floating in. I tug down the

THE BRO DATE

covers and take a deep breath of fresh air so I can finally wake my hungover ass up.

"Y-yeah?!" I croak, not moving from my cozy bed.

"I made breakfast," a deep voice murmurs through the closed door. "Come down when you're ready."

Food. Thank God.

Even though I was sort of an accidental dick last night, I'm glad he's not that upset because I love when Shane cooks for me.

I really missed it.

I missed him.

Most mornings, we eat in the cafeteria using our meal plans, but I always look forward to the weekends when I'm graced with the pleasure of eating Shane's food.

A rush of dizziness hits me when I stand up too fast, so I perch on the edge of the bed and close my eyes for a moment, taking a deep breath before releasing it slowly.

Man, I fucked up last night.

In more ways than one.

I stand up slowly this time, grabbing the sweatpants and hoodie draped over the back of my desk chair and slipping them on. I spot Shane's favorite jean jacket in a crumpled heap on the floor, so I pick it up and press it to my nose for a quick second, inhaling the spicy, familiar scent of his cologne.

"Mmm," I moan, wishing I could wear it all day.

But that would be weird. Right?

I take one last sniff before folding it nicely and placing it on top of my dresser. I'll give it back later.

Padding down the hall with bare feet, I lock myself in the bathroom to freshen up before I make my way to the kitchen.

The rich, earthy aroma of freshly brewed coffee fills my

nostrils as I descend the stairs slowly, careful not to trip since I'm still a little dizzy.

Shane's back is turned, his attention focused on the skillet in front of him. He's standing there in nothing but a pair of plaid pajama pants, and I swear he's doing this to me on purpose.

I grab a mug and make myself a much-needed cup of coffee, adding plenty of creamer.

"Sorry about last night," I blurt, taking my seat at the island.

"How are you feeling?" Shane asks, ignoring my apology and plating up perfectly cooked, over-easy eggs on top of avocado toast.

"A little hungover, but I'll survive," I admit.

"You have to take better care of yourself," he says matter-of-factly, setting a plate in front of me and pouring a tall glass of orange juice to go with it.

I take a deep breath, releasing a dramatic sigh. "Don't worry, I'm never playing beer pong again," I vow, desperate to get some food into my belly to soak up any remaining alcohol and give me some energy.

"Good," Shane says simply, taking a seat next to me and digging into his food.

I smile at how easy that was for us to get over. Shane never holds a grudge. He's always been there for me, even last night when I was being a drunk idiot.

Scooping up a rogue spoonful of Shane's creamy avocado spread, I hum at the delicious flavor. "I missed your cooking," I admit, peeking at him out of the corner of my eye.

Shaggy dark hair hangs over his forehead, blocking intense brown eyes from view. His strong jaw flexes as he chews, drawing my gaze to perfectly shaped lips I've dreamed of kissing ever since I was in ninth grade and first realized I had a crush on my best friend. The thought of losing him terrified me so much that I locked up the possibility of being gay until recently.

Really recently.

While I was hiding out from the world down in Key West and hopelessly contemplating my sexuality, I decided I'm finally ready to pursue my attraction to guys. I can't continue living in the closet just because I fell in love with my straight best friend.

I need to branch out and take risks.

I need to date.

A couple nights ago, I downloaded one of those gay dating apps, but I've been too chickenshit to open it and make an account. I still count it as progress though because I've got to do *something* to stop thinking about how fucking hot Shane is—

"What're you looking at?" he mumbles, swiping his messy hair back and observing me with concern.

My cheeks flush, realizing I've been staring at him this whole time, and I've hardly touched my food beyond a couple bites.

A buzz in my pocket saves me from having to come up with an answer, because I definitely can't tell him I was staring at *him* for five minutes.

"Shit. It's my mom."

I've been avoiding her since before spring break.

> Aren't you going to say hello to your parents now that you're back in town? I'm starting to think you're avoiding us.

Maybe because I am.

I reply quickly since I can't get away with ignoring her anymore. Poor cell service is no longer an excuse.

> Sorry, Mother. Of course not. I've been getting ready for classes to start again.

School is usually an acceptable excuse for her, even if she's disappointed that I want to pursue music full-time and *not* sell real estate.

> Dinner at six sharp tonight. It's not a request, Tobias.

"Fuck me," I complain, knowing I don't have a choice, and texting her back like a good son.

> Yes, ma'am.

"What's wrong?" Shane asks, setting his knife and fork down and turning those dreamy fucking eyes on me.

"My parents are forcing me over for dinner tonight," I complain with a frustrated sigh.

I wish Shane could come with me as a buffer because without him, it's no holds barred. They will tell me exactly what they think of me, no matter how much it could hurt.

"Need a dinner date?" Shane asks, halting my building panic. "Maybe a bodyguard?"

More like a knight in shining armor.

"Yes," I breathe out in relief. "Please and thank you."

I swear he can read my mind.

"On one condition, though," Shane says with a smirk. "Finish your damn breakfast before I feed it to you myself."

I hate the way my stomach fills with butterflies, and my body desperately wants to let him. All I can do is laugh it off and finish the rest of my food like he told me to.

"*Thank you,*" I say, pouring as much heart into those two words as I can. "For breakfast, and for coming with me tonight as my emotional support Shane."

I hope he knows how much I mean it.

"I think I prefer bodyguard." He reaches over, giving the back of my neck a tender squeeze and sending shockwaves down my spine and straight to my dick.

Fuuck.

"What time should we leave?" Shane asks with a small smile, completely oblivious to my inner turmoil as he gazes down at me with affection. His rough palm continues to massage my neck, his long fingers snaking into my hair and causing goosebumps to erupt across my skin.

"F-five," I stutter, my cock involuntarily chubbing up. I bite my lower lip to stop an embarrassing moan from slipping out.

He finally lets go, and I don't know if I want to cry in relief or disappointment.

Good Lord, it is beyond fucked up to get a hard-on for your straight best friend.

What the hell is wrong with me?

"I gotta go to work now, but I'll be home before five. Promise." Shane holds his pinky out, and I wrap mine around his, accepting the unbreakable vow.

Shane is a man of his word. I'd never doubt him.

He stacks our plates and stands from the island, taking the dirty dishes to the sink, ready to wash everything like he's so used to doing at the café.

"I got those, bro," I say, trying to sound as normal as I can despite the boner I'm hiding under the counter.

"Thanks, Tobes."

"See you tonight," I add with what I hope isn't an awkward smile.

"Later," Shane mumbles, leaving me and the problem in my pants behind.

I wait another minute to ensure he's really gone, then rush upstairs, leaving the dirty dishes in the sink. I'm too horny right now, there's no way my dick's going down until I come.

After grabbing a towel from the linen closet, I lock myself in the bathroom and turn on the shower so the water can start to heat up. I slip out of my clothes, staring at my tanned and toned body in the mirror while I stroke my cock, unable to wait any longer.

Fuuuck that feels good.

I haven't come in over a week, having forbidden myself from jerking off in my grandparents' home long before this vacation ever started.

I pick up the pace, and it doesn't take long for me to skirt the edge.

A sudden knock on the door nearly gives me a heart attack.

Shit! Who's home?

"Toby? You in there?!"

At the sound of Shane's deep voice, adrenaline shoots through me, and I come instantly, slamming a hand over my mouth to muffle the embarrassing whimpers.

Ropes of cum—a week's worth to be precise—stripe the bathroom counter, my cock pulsing in my hand as I continue to fire load after load.

"Forgot my watch!" Shane yells over the running water.

My chest rises and falls rapidly, a fucked-up sort of thrill flowing through me.

"*Tobes!* I'm gonna be late! Just hand me the damn watch!" Shane hollers through the door, and I stare down at said hand completely covered in jizz.

"J-just a second!" I finally manage and turn the sink on, washing my hands thoroughly before I dare touch his watch. I crack the door, sticking my arm out to offer it to him.

"Thanks, bro." Shane takes the watch, and I quickly lock the door again before he catches a glimpse of the cum-streaked sink, and I have to leave town *forever*.

Slightly shell-shocked by what just happened, I'm frozen for a moment before a choked laugh erupts from the pit of my stomach at the absolute mess that is the bathroom counter.

That is fucking diabolical.

CHAPTER THREE
TOBY

Later that evening, Shane knocks on my bedroom door, showing up just like he promised he would. I open the door with a smile, stepping aside. "Hey, come in," I say, feeling a little awkward around him after what happened this morning, even though he's completely innocent and has no clue that I'm a raging pervert.

Shane brushes past me, a spicy wave of citrus and bergamot in his wake. He perches on the end of my bed, looking so fucking handsome in black slacks and a matching button-down with the sleeves rolled up. His monochromatic tattoos peek out, the lone wolf drawing my eye. It's the first one he ever got, and also my favorite.

I finish tucking in my baby-blue button-down, feeling like a Sunday school teacher in khaki pants and loafers. "How was work?" I ask lamely, all too aware of how sexy he is and how completely distracted I am because of it.

His stare is powerful, like the rest of the world stops moving when he looks at me. My cheeks slowly heat up, and I fight the urge to press my palms to them.

"It was okay," he finally responds in that deep, growly voice of his.

I nod way too many times, probably looking like a damn bobble head. "Good. Good . . . So, uh . . . I really appreciate you getting off early for me."

The thought of facing my parents alone right now makes me want to puke.

I haven't told anyone I'm gay, and the two of them sure as hell won't be the first to know, but I still feel on edge around them because they disagree with pretty much everything about me. I'm sure being gay will just be another thing added to the list.

"Toby," Shane growls, and I glance up from where I was picking at my nails, my breath coming out in short, little pants. We lock gazes, and his stare is so focused, my stomach decides to attempt gymnastics like we're trying out for the Olympics. "You okay?" he asks.

No. Nope. Definitely not okay.

I'm gay, Shane.

Gay!

The words ping-pong around in my head but never leave my mouth. Something deep down keeps telling me that as soon as he finds out I'm into guys, he'll automatically *know* I've been in love with him for years.

I mean, how could he not?

I shake my head, unable to get any words out while I attempt to calm my racing thoughts and shaky hands.

Shane stands from the edge of the bed, towering over me as he steps into my personal space. "Relax, okay? Nothing bad will happen. That's why I'm here." A lock of raven hair falls free, dangling in front of his eyes and tempting me to slick it back with all the rest. "Just take a deep breath." Shane breathes in through his nose, then out through his mouth slowly. "Come on, Tobes. Do it with me."

He's so earnest and so pure.

I do as he says, finally getting my breathing under control. "Thank you," I murmur, "and thanks for showing up." I stare off to the side, cataloging my messy desk and the trash can full of crumpled sheet music that desperately needs emptying.

Out of the corner of my eye, a large hand reaches for me, turning my head and tilting my chin so I'm forced to look him in the eye.

"I *always* show up."

There's no room for argument there.

I swallow hard as Shane stares down at me, my traitorous stomach flipping and tumbling, once again aiming for a gold medal floor routine.

Hiding anything from Shane is *hard*. He sees right through me. But now is *not* the time to come out to him.

"We should probably go," I say a little too breathlessly. "Don't wanna be late." Slipping out of Shane's orbit, I pat myself down, making sure I have my phone, wallet, and keys.

"I'll drive," Shane announces, and that's fine with me, so I toss my keys back on the desk.

I'm sure my mother will absolutely love the rusty old pickup truck parked in her driveway.

We arrive fifteen minutes early to my parents' house on the beach, which is right on time according to their standards. Shane hops out, jogging around to open the door for me. It kind of feels like we really are on a date, but then I remember it's only because the door is jammed and hard as hell to open.

My desperate brain needs to chill the fuck out. It's embarrassing.

Solar lights illuminate the small path from the driveway to the house, and beautiful palm trees dot the immaculately landscaped front yard. Three stories tall and built on stilts, the house I grew up in could be featured in the pages of a magazine, and honestly, that would probably be my mother's dream. The pale-yellow exterior is accented with white trim, porthole windows, a wraparound porch on the second level, and a giant, way-too-steep staircase that has plagued me since childhood.

"Need a sec?" Shane asks, handling me with kid gloves as I hauntingly stare up at the house that was never really a home.

I shake my head. "No, I'm fine. Let's get this over with."

Shane doesn't look convinced, but we climb the steps and ring the doorbell, nonetheless.

My mother greets us with a forced smile and tight eyes like she's already annoyed, and maybe she is, since I texted her last minute and said I was bringing a guest.

As if he can sense the spiders crawling under my skin, Shane steps closer, allowing our arms to brush and offering his silent support.

"Good evening, Mother." The words taste foul when I don't even want to be here, but what else am I supposed to say?

"Mrs. Livingston," Shane adds politely with a nod.

"Tobias. *Shane.*" I swear her lip curls a little when she practically spits his name like it's poison. She scans him from head to toe, lingering on the tattoos sticking out of his rolled-up sleeves. *Judging him.*

I fucking hate it, and I hate being here.

"So good to see you boys. Please, do come in," she says with false sincerity.

I'm sure my mother isn't happy I brought him, but tonight, Shane's offering to be my shield, and I'm going to let him.

"Say hello to your father in his study. Dinner will be ready shortly." Her high heels clink against the hardwood floor as she sashays back to the kitchen.

"Yes, ma'am," we say in unison, stepping into the large foyer, complete with an elaborate bouquet of fresh flowers and a giant, driftwood chandelier.

"This way," I murmur, leading him upstairs to the library as if he doesn't remember where it is. My parents have lived in this house since we first moved to Crescent Bay ten years ago.

I pause at the top of the stairs, speaking in a hushed whisper. "I'm sorry for dragging you along."

"Don't be," he murmurs, and I almost don't hear the next part. "I'd go anywhere with you, Toby."

My stomach bottoms out, and I tell my heart not to read too much into his words. Shane isn't gay. He doesn't even really like *girls*.

"I . . ."

I don't know what to say.

"Thank you," I whisper, feeling guilty that I'm hiding such a huge secret from him when he's been nothing but steadfast and loyal for ten years.

Shane reaches out, giving my shoulder a gentle squeeze and sending a lightning bolt straight to my dick.

"After you." He sweeps his arm out in front of us and holds it there.

I brush past him, leading us to the arched doorway of my father's study and lightly knocking on it.

"Tobias," he says in a bored greeting when we step into what has always been deemed *his* space and usually off-limits.

Matthew Livingston has thick brown hair that's neatly parted on one side and just barely starting to gray at the temples. His black-framed glasses compliment his strong jaw, and as always, he's wearing a fucking suit and dress shoes to dinner.

He's standing in front of the wet bar, sipping his favorite whiskey, while some nature show plays unwatched in the background. Not to mention, he's probably hiding out from Mom.

Silver moonlight shines through the skylights above, illuminating the wooden bookshelves lining the walls and the hundreds of books on them. If I didn't already know they were filled with nonfiction and religious texts, I might actually be impressed. Or even excited.

I prefer romance.

Taking a deep breath and steeling my resolve, I stroll over to greet my father with a strong handshake, followed by Shane.

"Shane, buddy. I didn't know you were coming," my dad says somewhat rudely before turning to me. "Tobias, when your mother told me you were bringing a guest, I thought you were finally bringing a girl home," he chuckles, trying to belittle me. "Shane's not your boyfriend, is he?"

My lungs freeze with panic. In fact, I think my brain does, too. I'm completely unable to voice any sort of comeback as all the blood drains from my face. Luckily, Shane swoops in and saves me with the perfect joke.

"Nah. Toby's outta my league," Shane quips with a smirk, giving me a subtle nudge with his elbow.

My dad barks out a loud laugh, ushering us over to the lounge area. "Take a seat, boys."

He sits in his favorite old wingback chair, while Shane and I take the sofa.

"So, tell me, son, how was Key West?" Dad asks, crossing his legs and resting his ankle on the opposite knee. "Your mother was quite upset you didn't come home for spring break when we've hardly seen you all year. You do know we live on the beach, too, hmm? You didn't have to go all the way to Florida."

"I wasn't out partying or anything. I was visiting family. *Mom's* family. It was Gran and Bo."

I knew I was going to have to defend myself.

"That doesn't make it right to ignore your mother this long, Tobias. Keep it up, and you can live at home for the summer."

"But, Dad—"

"I won't hear another word about it," he says sternly, completely cutting me off before taking a healthy swallow of his drink. "Just make sure it doesn't happen again."

"Yes, sir."

I hate when he makes me feel like I'm still a kid and can't make my own decisions.

"So, are you boys ready to get back into classes after a week off? It's important to finish the year strong."

"Yes, sir," I answer robotically, glancing over at Shane, who only nods.

"And you're still happy living in that run-down, old house with three other boys?" He narrows his dark brown eyes at me, almost as clueless as Mom is when it comes to how unhappy I was living here.

Neither of them can fathom why I don't want to continue living in my childhood bedroom and commute every day.

I mean, yeah, there are a few things that could be fixed when it comes to campus housing, and my room is pretty small, not to mention the bathroom is down the hall with *zero* privacy, but I wanted the full college experience with Shane, and I definitely got it.

"I am," I answer with more strength and resolve than I thought I had.

There was never any happiness here; I had to make my own as a kid.

With Shane.

My dad hums, not pushing the topic any further, and takes another sip of his whiskey. "Very well." He picks up the book on the end table and opens it, effectively dismissing us.

He probably only wants me to live here as a buffer between him and Mom, anyway. They don't get along and never really have, but they won't get divorced. They care too much about what other people think.

I shift on the couch cushion, feeling slightly uncomfortable with the prolonged silence.

"Dinner's ready!" Mom hollers from the kitchen, and I've never been more thankful to hear her shouting at me.

"You're excused, then," Dad murmurs into his glass before he tips it back.

I hurry from the room with Shane right beside me. Heat radiates from my face like burning hot asphalt in the summer, and I glance at Shane, whose jaw is clenched tightly.

Assholes are his trigger, and my dad is top tier.

"Would you like some wine, Shane?" my mother asks, pouring an expensive cabernet into Dad's glass. "You're twenty-one, right?"

Her innocent-sounding question is likely some sort of test, or maybe an insult. She damn well knows he's two years older than me.

"No, thank you," Shane replies calmly and politely.

She narrows cynical amber eyes at him, but before she can launch more questions, I interrupt with a dumbass joke. "I'll have some, Mom."

Crinkling her brow in distaste, she shakes her head like she's disappointed in me and serves everyone dinner.

Whatever.

Mom takes her spot at the head of the table, with my father at the other end. "Will you say grace, Matthew?"

"Of course, honey." My dad bows his head, and I honestly tune him out until I hear an *Amen*, and we all dig in.

The parmesan risotto is heavenly, but the sea bass steals the show. The food is delicious, just like it always is when the chef stops by and preps everything in advance, leaving right before my mother's guests arrive. She likes to pretend it's her cooking, but we all know it's not.

"So, have you thought any more about switching majors, Tobias?" Mom suddenly asks, immediately spoiling my appetite. I set my fork down and prepare to be lectured. "Violin is a wonderful hobby, but it's not a career, darling. It's time to grow up and choose something that will make you money. Like real estate. Right, Matthew?" She looks at my dad for backup.

"Yep. Finance or business is the way to go, not this fluffy music theory crap."

Fluffy what?

Something nudges my foot under the table, and I glance up from the spot I was staring at on my plate, completely disassociating from the conversation. Fathomless dark eyes meet my gaze, and I'm instantly pulled into the black hole that is Shane Carmichael.

My parents drone on and on about how important it is for me to choose something else—something they approve of—while I continue to get lost in Shane's intense stare. I feel safe with him, and that's the only thing getting me through this dinner from hell.

I was really hoping they wouldn't do this tonight.

"It's highly unlikely that you'll ever become a wealthy violinist, Tobias," my mother says brusquely, leaning back in her seat and finishing off the last of her wine.

"I'd say it's a long shot," Dad adds dismissively, placing his napkin on top of his plate like he's finished with dinner and the conversation.

"Be realistic, Tobias. You're not a child any longer." Mom rolls her eyes, and that's what finally bursts the dam of how much shit I can take.

I've had enough of them roasting me.

"Be realistic?" I huff, completely agitated by their asshole behavior before we even make it to dessert. "I've only got one chance on this Earth, just like you. So, why would I waste it on some soul-sucking job I hate? No, thank you. I'm gonna chase my dreams."

Fuck. I need to get out of here before the panic sets in.

"Your mother and I just want you to make smart choices for your future because it all starts now. Time to grow up, Tobias."

"Even Shane chose a respectable major. You can do so much with a business degree," Mom says matter-of-factly. "You really need to switch paths, darling."

That was the most backhanded compliment I've ever heard, and I can feel the embarrassment coat my skin like a glaze of shame. I glance over at my best friend, sitting stoically in his seat, completely unfazed.

"Mrs. Livingston," he replies evenly, as if she didn't just insult and compliment him all in the same breath. "With all due respect, Toby is the first chair violinist. It would be a blow to the entire music department if he left."

"Yes, well, be that as it may, it still doesn't change how I feel about the situation," she snaps before turning to me. "You're throwing away your future, Tobias."

"And my tuition money," Dad grumbles under his breath.

There's no point in arguing with them any longer.

I'm done. Checked out. Fucking finished.

Because if this is how they feel about my major, what are they going to think of me when I tell them I'm gay?

"Cheesecake, anyone?!" Mom suddenly asks with a forced smile, standing from the table like some sort of Stepford wife in her vintage flowered dress and soft blonde curls.

"Thank you for dinner, Mrs. Livingston. It was truly a five-star experience, but I think we're going to skip dessert and head home. Classes start tomorrow, so we need our rest."

My knight in shining armor.

Again.

I need to get out of here, and I'm so thankful Shane can recognize that.

We exchange hollow *goodbyes* and *see you soons*, but I

don't plan on it. Why would I want to be around people who don't support my decisions or even like me?

"Gah! They're absolutely infuriating!" I whisper-shout after we finally escape and step outside into the cool evening air. "And she wonders why I stayed with Gran and Bo for spring break." Desperate to leave, I rush down the steep stairs from hell as if the house itself exorcised me.

"Toby, slow down!" Shane calls out behind me.

I don't listen, missing the last step and rolling my ankle like a baby giraffe before falling to the ground.

"*Shit!*" I cry out, rough concrete tearing a hole in my khakis and scraping my knee.

Sonofabitch.

"Are you hurt?" Shane squats down next to me, his dark eyes slowly scanning my body for injuries and landing on my knee. "Let me see."

I squeeze my eyes shut, shaking my head no, and hoping I can wake up from this nightmare of an evening. Rough fingers encircle my wrist, gently removing the hand covering my knee. I hiss in pain when I open my eyes and see the damage.

Ouch.

"I've got a first aid kit in the back of my truck. Let's get you cleaned up," Shane says calmly.

Without asking if I can walk, he easily scoops me up, carrying my pathetic ass the rest of the way to his truck.

"I'm sorry you clocked out early for this shitshow," I mutter, shamelessly leaning my head against his hard pec and breathing in his familiar, calming scent.

Shane pauses, staring down at me for a moment, his intense gaze analyzing my face. "Work doesn't matter," he grumbles. "*You* matter."

"Shane..."

THE BRO DATE   33

Words elude me because everything I *want* to say would probably scare him away.

He carries me the rest of the way to his truck, opening the door and setting me in the seat sideways. "Be right back."

I nod, closing my eyes and resting my temple against the headrest. My knee stings and aches, so I focus on my breathing instead of the pain.

Shane comes back with what looks like a small tackle box, opening up a first aid kit instead. He pulls out a little spray bottle, and I see the word "antiseptic" on the side, immediately knowing this is going to hurt like a bitch.

"Do you want to keep these pants?" he suddenly asks, catching me off guard.

"No?"

Shane grabs hold of the hole in my khakis with two hands and yanks, carefully ripping it farther to expose my knee without having to take my pants off in my parents' driveway.

"This is going to hurt," he informs me two seconds before spraying the antiseptic directly on my scrape.

"*Fuck! Fuck! Fuck! Sonofabitch motherfucker!*" I holler like a complete heathen, gripping the sides of the seat for my life.

It feels like my knee is on fire, and someone tried to put it out with battery acid. I blink slowly, sweat beading on the back of my neck like I'm seconds away from passing out. I'm a complete baby when it comes to pain.

"Stay with me," Shane murmurs, his voice sounding muffled and far away. He squats down in front of me and blows on my knee, cool breath washing over my skin and soothing the burn.

"Better?" he asks, peering up at me from the ground.

I nod, mumbling a *thank you*.

Before I know it, I'm all bandaged up and buckled in. I lean back against the headrest and close my eyes, knowing I'm safe whenever I'm with Shane.

"What would I do without you?" I whisper, unsure if I even said the words aloud, or if they stayed inside my head where they belong.

"Good thing you'll never have to find out," Shane replies, and despite the burning pain in my knee and the emotional trauma from dinner, I smile.

I sure hope that's true.

CHAPTER FOUR
SHANE

I find Toby in the cafeteria the following morning, sitting at a small table next to the floor-to-ceiling windows. Sunlight pours in, casting a golden glow over him and illuminating his shiny curls.

Our early classes align most days, so we meet up for breakfast. I'd much rather cook, but there just isn't enough time. Besides, I paid for a meal plan, so I'm going to use it.

"Morning. Can I sit here?" I ask with a small, teasing smile, nodding to his backpack in one chair, sweatshirt in the next, and his violin case in the third. I stand in front of him, holding my tray while I patiently wait for an answer, like we're back in grade school, and it's the first day of class.

"Hey," Toby responds before a big yawn. "Yeah, 'course." He grabs the hoodie and tosses it on top of his backpack, leaving the chair next to him vacant.

An overwhelming sense of déjà vu hits me, and I quickly take a seat, being transported back to the very first day we met in the fifth-grade cafeteria.

"Hi. Can I sit with you?"

I set my square pizza back on the tray and stare at the boy standing next to my table. He's so much smaller than me and everyone else, with curly brown hair and strange gold eyes.

I shrug, scooping up a bite of the disgusting, watery corn and reluctantly chewing it because I know I need to eat, and I'll regret it later if I don't.

I can't sleep when I'm hungry.

"My name is Tobias. What's yours?" he asks, placing a purple lunch box on the table and sitting in front of me with a curious stare.

"Shane," I rasp, continuing to shovel food into my mouth, knowing the bell will ring sooner than we think, and I definitely want to get to the cupcake sitting on the corner of my tray.

It's not standard for free lunch, but Ms. Patricia, the lunch lady, always sneaks me one.

"Can we be friends, Shane?" Tobias asks, smiling at me like he hopes I'll say yes, even though we just met.

His question catches me off guard, but I shrug again. No one's ever asked to be my friend before.

"Okay! If we're friends now, then you can call me Toby."

"Toby," I repeat, testing the name out.

His smile widens further, causing dimples to pop out in his rosy cheeks. I'm not sure I've ever met anyone so excited before. I glance down at the butterfly on his shirt, realizing he's got to be a lot younger than the rest of us. Especially me, now that I'm a year older than everyone.

I adjust my stupid sling, grimacing when my shoulder throbs. I fell off my bike last weekend, and the doctor said I'm lucky I didn't break my arm. Mom wasn't happy because my urgent care visit cleared out her savings.

"Can I sign it?" Toby suddenly asks, and I stare at him a moment, creasing my brows and sipping my chocolate milk.

Huh?

Oh, he means like a cast.

"No one signs slings," I tell him matter-of-factly, watching his face fall and instantly regretting it.

"But you can," I blurt, nearly stuttering over my words because I'm not used to having a friend. I reach into my backpack and pull out a black Sharpie.

"Hey, Shane. Who's the new kid?" Adam sneers, interrupting us and eyeing Toby like he wants to start a fight.

Over my dead body.

The thought hits me out of nowhere, but it's strong.

"Toby," I answer, squinting my eyes at Adam and daring him to say something else.

"Why's he got a butterfly on his shirt and a purple lunch box?"

I stand from the lunch table, clenching my good fist, ready to knock him out if he says one more stupid thing. "So?" I ask. "What's it to you?"

"Isn't that for girls?" Adam asks with an ugly smile I want to punch off his face.

Toby stands up next, his face turning bright pink under the scrutiny, but he speaks his truth without faltering. "Purple's my favorite color, and butterflies are my favorite insect."

Adam sputters, not coming up with a sufficient response to those simple facts. "Weirdos," he mumbles before slinking back to his table full of cool kids.

I don't care, though. I'd much rather be a weirdo than a bully.

"So, what should I draw?" Toby asks with an innocent smile and sparkly gold eyes, completely unfazed by Adam's words.

"A butterfly," I tell him with a grin that feels foreign, handing him the Sharpie.

My phone buzzes in my pocket, startling me out of the daydream. I check my messages, seeing a text from my boss asking me to cover a shift tonight and being a dick all in the same sentence.

I can't deal with him right now.

Putting my phone away, I focus on Toby and the short amount of time we have together. "How's the knee?" Toby got dealt a shitty hand last night, and he didn't deserve any of it.

"Honestly? Hurts like a bitch and kept me up half the night, overthinking my entire existence," he admits with a self-deprecating chuckle. "I'll be okay, though," he adds, flicking his amber eyes to me for a quick second. "Thanks for taking care of me, by the way."

"You could have woken me up," I offer, the words flowing freely. The mere thought of him in pain and losing sleep doesn't sit well with me.

When Toby doesn't immediately respond, I set my fork down and glance up, taking a closer look at my best friend. Faint shadows cling to his under eyes, and his curls are more disheveled than usual, like he has too much on his mind.

I hate it.

"Talk to me," I plead, desperate to know every single thing that's keeping him awake at night and whether I can help.

He's been acting strange ever since he got back from Florida.

"Please."

Toby's anxious gaze darts around the cafeteria. "Not here. Not before class."

My brows crease, but I'll listen to him anytime, anyplace. "When?"

"Can you meet me at our spot at nine tonight?"

There's a lake on the edge of campus that has a nice walking trail and a beautiful sunset view. We found it freshman year when we were exploring, and Toby has since used it as a sort of meditation spot where he's free to play violin to his heart's content.

"I'll be there."

"I gotta go," Toby suddenly announces, standing from the table in a rush. "I need to get to the practice room early. Luke is gunning for first chair, and I can't let that happen." Toby slings his backpack over his shoulder, grabbing his violin case with one hand and the tray with his other, limping to the trash cans.

I clench my jaw, gripping the chair to keep myself from chasing after him and demanding answers right now.

How am I supposed to make it through an entire day of classes and a shift at the café without knowing what's wrong?

CHAPTER FIVE
TOBY

I've had heart palpitations all day, waiting to tell Shane I'm gay. He probably thinks I've been acting erratic since I got back from Florida, and maybe I have been, because I feel so fucking unsettled. I should have just blurted it out at breakfast, surrounded by a cafeteria full of people, because this is pure torture, and not the best idea for the first day back to school.

Despite the ache in my knee, I strap my violin case to my back and leisurely ride my bike to the lake in order to clear my head. I'm desperate for a reprieve from my thoughts, so I get there plenty early to practice my violin before Shane shows up.

Tonight is a really big deal for me. It'll be the first time I say the words out loud to another person, and I can't pretend I'm not a little scared.

Cypress trees surround the lake, beams of sunlight piercing through their tall, skinny trunks and casting a golden glow over everything. I wheel my bike off to the side of the trailhead and kick out the kickstand, following the path that leads from the parking lot to the sandy shoreline.

When I step out from the shaded trail, I smile at the sheer beauty of the sun setting over the water. Splashes of gold, pink, and magenta decorate the sky like a beautiful watercolor painting, creating the perfect backdrop to pour my heart out through my strings.

I make my way to the end of the small dock, setting my violin case on the wooden bench tucked against the railing. Wind whistles in my ears, and a chill seeps through my hoodie, but I don't let it stop me. I lugged my violin all the way out here, so I *need* to get some practice in before Shane arrives. The lake is one of the few places I can go without bothering anyone or anyone bothering me.

Music has always been my escape, ever since my parents forced me into piano lessons that I ended up loving, and even more so when I chose the violin in fifth-grade music class.

I pop open my case and carefully lift my pride and joy from its black velvet home. Tucking the chin rest under my chin, I allow my jaw to rest comfortably in the curved wood and assume proper posture. I warm up with some open string work, scales, and broken thirds before I jump into the fun part.

My bow glides against the strings like butter, and my body begins to move with the sounds of "Pink Pony Club," completely forgetting the pain in my knee. I give it everything I've got, releasing all of the anger and resentment building up toward my parents, and the fear of coming out. I dance and play my violin until I'm panting and out of breath with a huge smile on my face.

Damn. I needed that.

By the time I play a few more of my favorite songs, evening has turned to night. The moon reflects against the still surface of the lake, shining brightly and illuminating

THE BRO DATE 43

the surrounding forest. It's beautiful out here where the peace of nature brings a clarity my soul desperately needed.

Loud, slow claps startle me, and I nearly drop my bow into the water, spinning around to find Shane at the far end of the dock.

"*Shit!* You scared me!" I shout, clutching my chest.

The wooden slats creak as Shane makes his way to my end of the dock. "That was amazing, Toby," he says, standing in front of me with both hands in his pockets. "You were born to play. Don't listen to your parents."

"Thank you," I murmur shyly, setting my violin in its case as the anxiety starts to return. The anticipation of finally coming out to Shane is terrifying me right now. My heart starts to pound against my ribcage as if I'm being chased by a wild animal.

What if he knows I'm in love with him?

And what if he hates me for it?

My mind starts to spiral, and my breathing picks up.

What if I lose him?

Oh God. I don't know if I can do this right now.

"Toby, what's going on? You can talk to me," Shane urges, and my stomach fills with angry butterflies wanting to take flight. I *need* to tell him. I can't keep putting it off. It's not right to hide from the one person who's always been there for me.

"I . . ."

Why am I so scared to say the words to him?

"You what, Tobes?" His brows crease with concern. The moon reflects in his dark eyes, sparkling with pure intensity and a deep compassion. A connection that *I know* could never be compromised.

With a deep breath and shaky exhale, I steel my resolve

the best I can and speak my truth with my head held high. "I'm gay, Shane."

His expression relaxes slightly, the tension in his shoulders softening, but he doesn't move a muscle. My words hang in the air between us, the wind picking them up and carrying them away, leaving nothing behind but the sound of crickets chirping and gentle waves lapping against the pilings below.

"I like guys," I explain as if he doesn't know the meaning of the word. "And I've decided that I'm ready to explore that part of myself." I quickly shut up before I start rambling about how gay I am.

Say something, Shane.

Please.

He takes a step toward me and holds his palm out with a small smile on his lips. Relief washes over me, and I place my hand in his, electricity dancing along the surface of my skin where we touch. "I'm happy for you, Toby. *Really*. This changes nothing between us," he assures me, and his simple words relieve so much stress. "I hope you weren't scared to tell me."

A deep weight lifts off my shoulders, and I launch myself at him, wrapping my arms around his neck and squeezing tightly. I resist the urge to wrap my legs around his waist, letting them dangle instead. "You're the first person I've told," I whisper into his ear. "I was scared in general."

Shane returns my embrace before setting me back on my feet. "Have you . . . are you dating anyone?" he asks, seeming a little unsure to do so. This is unfamiliar territory. Neither of us has ever dated anyone, although I've heard rumors of Shane hooking up with tourists from time to time. We just never talk about it.

"Um . . ." I hesitate to answer even though he's straight and shouldn't care at all. "No, but I really want to." I chuckle awkwardly at how pathetic that sounds before pressing my palms to my eyes and slightly dying inside.

Big, cold hands wrap around my wrists, gently pulling them away from my flushed face. "Don't be embarrassed. You deserve to be happy, Tobes." Shane pulls out a paper swan from his back pocket, presenting it to me on his palm. "Just please don't get hurt, or I'm kicking someone's ass. Got it?"

My heart skips a beat at his words, and I take the swan, smiling with fondness. Shane has been into origami ever since we were kids. It was something his therapist suggested that actually stuck with him. I used to find them everywhere, and I mean *everywhere*. On the playground, in my backpack, locker, and all around my room. Sometimes the housekeeper accidentally washed them in my pants pockets.

But they're much rarer these days.

"I'll try not to," I whisper, holding it gently while the urge to confess my love for him threatens to claw its way out of my throat.

A single raindrop lands on my wrist, thankfully interrupting the moment before I blow up our entire decade-long friendship.

"*Shit! My violin!*" I quickly slip the swan into my pocket and scramble to clasp my violin case securely. I can't have another disaster like I did in tenth grade when it popped open, and my violin crashed to the floor right before the end-of-year symphony. I had to use an out-of-tune school rental while mine was in the shop, and it still haunts me to this day.

Shane ushers me toward his truck, opening the

passenger side and getting me and my violin to safety before running back for my bike. The rain is picking up, and his white T-shirt clings to his chest like a second skin. Hard nipples peek through the sheer fabric, along with each and every ab in his six-pack. I unabashedly stare while he wheels my bike over, turning around in my seat to watch as he lifts it into the bed of his truck. Shane's biceps bulge deliciously, but when I glance up, his smirk tells me I've been caught.

Shit.

I flush, spinning around in my seat and facing forward with wide eyes.

"*Damn!* That rain is cold," Shane exclaims, and my traitorous eyes dart to his nipples for a quick second, just begging to get caught again. "You hungry?" he asks, grabbing a hand towel from the backseat and rubbing it against his head, attempting to dry off the best he can.

"I could eat." It's been a while since dinner, and I worked up an appetite. Plus, I'll never say no to more time with my best friend.

"There's a new taco truck parked by the mall. I was gonna check it out if you don't mind a little drive? The rain should stop by the time we get there."

"I don't mind," I reply with a small smile, comfortably sinking into my seat as Shane turns the heat on low, making me feel cozy and warm and safe. "That sounds perfect."

Tonight couldn't have gone better, and ending it with tacos is just icing on the cake.

CHAPTER SIX
TOBY

The first week back at school flies by, but I've hardly seen Shane after coming out to him on the dock. Our only time together has been early morning cafeteria dates with rubbery eggs, soggy pancakes, and half-asleep conversations. I'm hoping we have an opportunity to hang out and talk more this weekend.

Since coming out to someone who cares about me wasn't so hard after all, I decided to tell my other two best friends—Tate and Daija—conveniently leaving out the part where I'm in love with Shane. I'm not sure how I feel about the fact that they weren't surprised at all, Tate claiming he can recognize his own kind.

When I admitted that I wanted to start dating, they squealed in unison and demanded that I come over to their apartment to set up my profile. I need a good push, or I might just linger forever, waiting on Shane like a ghost with unfinished business.

Now it's Friday afternoon, I'm done with classes for the week, and I'm at Tate and Daija's place, spilling my freaking guts.

"Alright," Tate exclaims, clapping his hands together in excitement.

His bleach-blond hair is even curlier than mine, with the bottom half shaved off and dark roots showing on top. He's definitely good-looking, but he's like an older brother to me. He's family. They both are. Tate and Daija immediately took me under their wing as a freshman last year. I was a *scared baby bird without a mother*, in their words, and they adopted me without question.

"Show me what we're working with, honey. I've got a party to get to after this, and by party, I mean a confused straight boy wanting to experiment." With an eye roll and finger quotes I could never pull off, Tate blows a bubble with his gum and pops it before chewing aggressively.

I can't help the blush that fills my cheeks. "*Experiment?*" I ask, knowing my friends won't judge me for being curious.

"Oh, yes, dear Toby boy. Experimenting with *dick*," Tate exclaims with a high-pitched cackle, like he's excited for what's in my future.

"Tate!" Daija admonishes. "Don't scare our baby boy away from team tryouts. You *know* I want him on our side."

"Tryouts?" I feel lost. *So* completely lost.

"Yes!" Daija shouts excitedly. "For Team Dick!"

They both burst out laughing, and my face heats even more.

"Okay, okay," Tate says, wiping his tears away. "Back to business. *Grindr*. What have you got so far?"

"I . . . um . . . I haven't even set up my profile," I admit sheepishly.

"*Oh my God!* This is going to be so fun!" Daija exclaims with the sort of excitement that scares me a little. Getting situated on her bed, she leans against the headboard comfortably and drapes a turquoise blanket over her lap.

She rips open a shareable-size bag of candy, smiling in anticipation. "Skittles, anyone?" she asks innocently, pouring some into her palm.

Daija is beautiful inside and out. Her makeup is perfectly applied after a long day of classes, including her lip gloss, and her long box braids are flawlessly twisted into a bun on top of her head. Most of the guys on campus would kill for the chance to spend a Friday night with her. Especially Jake.

I smile, sitting next to her and accepting a handful of colorful candies that I immediately pop into my mouth.

"Come on, tater tot," she coos at Tate, patting the bed on her other side.

With a half-smile and full eye roll, Tate crawls to his spot on the other side of Daija.

"So, Toby, I have to ask. Does Shane know you're doing this?" Tate suddenly asks, catching me off guard.

"Uh..."

My lack of an answer tells him enough, and they both erupt into a fit of giggles.

"Oh boy, you're gonna be in trouuuble," Tate singsongs.

"*What?*" I gasp, my brows creasing with worry.

"Like, *big* trouble."

"Oh, stop. Don't listen to him, Tobes. All he means is that Shane cares about you, and it's no secret that he's super protective of you," Daija explains with a soft expression.

My stomach does a backflip at her words, knowing it's true, but still feeling the flutter deep down.

"It'll be okay, babe. You like guys, and he'll just have to learn to deal with it and share you. *Now*, hand it over," Daija says with a stern smile, holding her palm out and wiggling her long, pointed nails. "Let's get this party started."

I reluctantly place my phone in her hand, and she starts tapping away, setting up my new profile.

On a gay dating app.

I almost can't believe it's happening.

"Girl, I don't know how you do that so fast with those talons," Tate chuckles.

"Oh, shut it. You're just jealous," she snaps back at her best friend.

"Yeah, bitch. I am," Tate laughs. "They're fab."

Daija smiles wide and kisses the air. "Thanks, babe. Now, let's focus. We've got a profile to slay, starting with the perfect pic."

She goes to my camera roll and begins scrolling through my photos, finding one of me on the beach in Key West that Gran took. I'm smiling in my short, flowered trunks, showing off my lean body while looking completely happy and carefree. I like it.

"Oh, yeah. The gays are going to drool all over you," Tate declares with glee. "You're a twink, honey."

"Mhm," Daija agrees, "and we haven't even gotten to his bio yet."

"They're gonna eat him alive," Tate says with an evil chuckle, like I'm not even here.

I swallow hard and bite my lip while my two best friends cackle like criminal freaking masterminds. I'm not sure if I should be terrified or excited for what's to come.

Well, it didn't take long for *Grindr* to work. It's Saturday, and I have a coffee date this afternoon. My first ever date with a guy.

I was flooded with messages as soon as my profile went

public last night, and I honestly had no idea there were so many local guys that were . . . *well*, into guys.

Andy, my date, goes to Crescent Bay University, too. He's a junior in Communications, but I've never seen him around before. When he messaged me the name of the coffee shop, I almost made up an excuse to bail when I realized that it's right across the street from The Salty Sandbar.

Shane reacted better than I could ever have imagined when I told him I'm gay, but that still doesn't mean I want him to see me *flirting* with a guy. But I also don't want Andy to think I'm some picky, whiny bitch, so I can't ask him to change the spot either.

I mean, Shane's always in the kitchen, so I'm sure he'll never see me anyway.

Ignoring the doubt in my gut, I quickly text Andy back, agreeing on the time and place. Excited butterflies swarm my belly even though I feel like I might throw up, too.

I need to choose an outfit that isn't screaming "desperate and trying too hard." My closet is pretty tiny, so I couldn't even bring a quarter of my wardrobe from home. And now, the other three-fourths are under lock and key, where I no longer feel welcome.

I decide on a soft cream T-shirt with my favorite light-wash baggy jeans. Comfortable yet trendy, I know Tate and Daija would approve. With a confident smile that I try so hard to fully embrace, I head to the bathroom to brush my teeth for the third and final time.

Guess I'm ready.

Squeezing the banister in a death grip, I descend the stairs *very, very carefully*. My knee is feeling a lot better thanks to Shane's strict icing schedule, but I'd prefer not to fall down steps again. I slip into my white sneakers lying haphazardly by the front door and lock up, jiggling the handle to make sure.

The fully loaded Audi Q3 my parents bought me for high school graduation two years ago is parked in the driveway waiting for me, but as I slip into the driver's seat, I find myself wishing I was curled up in the passenger seat of Shane's beat-up old pickup instead. Where I feel safe.

A sudden surge of nervousness wells up, making me pause.

Why does it feel so surreal to go on a date, and why is my heart galloping uncomfortably?

Something deep down screams Shane's name, but I ignore it, locking away those painful, unrequited feelings. *He doesn't like boys.* I need to move on.

I snap myself out of it, taking a deep, calming breath and starting the engine. A text pops up from Daija before I leave, wishing me luck and reminding me to send my location, so they can make sure I don't get kidnapped. The reassurance is perfectly timed, and I smile, doing as told before backing out of the driveway and heading to the coffee shop.

Time for my first date with a guy.

CHAPTER SEVEN
SHANE

"Hey, you know I'm not a gossip, right?" Jaycee whispers, and I immediately sigh, not wanting to chitchat with anyone while I'm working, even though she's always been nice to me.

"Yeah . . ." Never really thought about it. I wish she would just tell me whatever it is she wants to tell me.

"Well, I'm pretty sure I just saw your friend Toby walk into the coffee shop across the street with a guy I've never seen before. A pretty hot guy, actually."

"What?" I ask, not truly processing her words as I flip a burger and shake the fries so they don't burn.

"They just sat at a small table in front of the window," Jaycee says like she's announcing a sports game and giving me a play-by-play. "He just reached out and tugged on one of Toby's curls. Now he's holding his hand out on the table, waiting. Oh. *Oh!*"

"What?!" I repeat a little louder and a lot ruder. My heart drops into my stomach, and I nearly splash grease on my bare skin.

When Toby came out to me the other night, I can't say I

was completely surprised by the news. Growing up, there were some signs, and the fact that he never dated girls or even talked about them was one. I'm just glad he feels comfortable and safe enough with me to share that part of himself now. But I am a little worried about him dating. Toby is an extremely attractive person. I'm secure enough in myself to admit that. But he's also way too trusting, a little naive, and extremely new to the whole gay scene. And I know for a fact that he's a virgin.

A more intense urge to protect Toby flares to life inside me. Something... Primal.

"Sorry, babe. They're holding hands. Looks like your boy's on a date..." Jaycee says.

"Cover for me?" I rip off my apron, not giving a shit if I get in trouble or even fired. I will never let some douchebag take advantage of Toby.

Ever.

"I can't cook!" Jaycee cries, but I ignore her and rush out the back door so no one sees me.

I sneak down the tiny alleyway between the café and the clothing boutique next door, squatting behind the dumpster and peering around. I'm fully aware of the creep I've just become, and there's no going back now.

I watch Toby while he sits across from a guy with gold-framed glasses, neatly cut brown hair, and a way-too-tight baby-pink polo. Toby smiles wide, his dimples popping before he takes a sip of what looks like a cappuccino. He's raptly listening to something the other guy is telling him, using a lot of exaggerated hand gestures. Toby suddenly tips his head back, laughing enthusiastically. His curls bounce, and the other man's face lights up in accomplishment.

Unfamiliar jealousy roars to life in the pit of my stomach, and I look away, clenching my fists as I stare at the dirty pavement.

The door to the kitchen suddenly flies open, banging against the brick exterior and making me jump. Raúl steps out, sneering in my direction. "What the fuck are you doing out here?"

"Fresh air," I deadpan, refusing to let him fluster me.

"By the dumpster?" he retorts.

I just shrug.

"Crazy kid. Got a few screws loose," he mumbles under his breath.

I ignore his insults because if I don't, I'll be going to jail for a very, very long time.

"Break's over. Get back to work before Jaycee burns my kitchen down," Raúl demands, disappearing back inside.

I glance at Toby and his date one last time, weighing my options as the guy brushes Toby's hair off his forehead, most likely making him blush.

That should be me touching his curls and making his skin flush.

The thought hits me out of nowhere, putting me in a chokehold.

Fuck.

What?

I shake my head in confusion and retreat inside, leaving Toby to finish his date without me stalking him from a dark alley. I grab my apron and slip it back on, taking my position in front of the flat top and zoning out once again.

"You okay?" Jaycee asks, popping her head into the kitchen to check on me.

"Fine," I grunt, not wanting to talk right now.

She frowns and disappears back into the busy dining area.

My mind is spinning. I can't believe Toby's on a date and didn't tell me.

As soon as my shift ends, I check the *Find My Friends* app and sigh in relief when I zoom in and see that Toby is safe at home. I grab the rest of my stuff from my locker and rush out the door before Raúl can stop me.

The need to see Toby and make sure he's okay overcomes me, so I slip into his dark bedroom unannounced. He's been a vital part of my life for a decade, and as selfish as it sounds, I can't lose him to some random guy. It would kill me.

"Shane?" Toby murmurs groggily. "Is that you?"

"Yeah. It's me. Shh."

"What're you doing?"

"Just checking on you," I whisper. "Go back to sleep."

"Miss you," he murmurs before his eyes flutter shut and a soft snore escapes him.

The hallway light gently illuminates his delicate features, my eyes roaming his peaceful, sleeping face. I brush the curls off his forehead, standing there watching him sleep for longer than I probably should.

Before I go, I set a white paper swan on his nightstand. I made it on my break after witnessing Toby's first date. I'm not sure why it bothers me so much, and I'm not sure why I feel the need to make sure I'm not forgotten.

Sunday is my day to rest and reset, so I sleep in until eight-thirty, lounging in bed for another hour before I get up and take my time in the bathroom.

The kitchen is empty and quiet; everyone else is still in their rooms. The first thing I do is make a pot of coffee with the expensive coffee machine Toby's parents bought him as a housewarming gift. The rich, nutty aroma fills the kitchen and most likely drifts upstairs, waking my roommates so that I don't have to. I pour myself an oversized mug, adding a generous amount of hazelnut creamer to cool it down.

Slipping in my AirPods, I choose my recent playlist obsession and turn the stove on, ready to get lost in music and cooking. When I don't have Raúl breathing down my neck, I actually love it. I sip my coffee and wait for the skillet to get nice and hot before adding the bacon, filling up the house with more delicious smells. Today's menu is poached eggs with homemade hollandaise sauce and crispy bacon crumbles.

Jake wanders in first, his messy hair sticking up in every direction. He sits at the island in nothing but a pair of basketball shorts.

"Hey, morning breath," I tease, knowing he probably rolled out of bed and wandered down here with his eyes closed.

"'Sup, morning wood," he retorts, rubbing his tired eyes. "Is there coffee?"

I chuckle, grabbing a mug from the cabinet and pouring him a cup. I set it on the counter in front of him before getting the creamer out of the fridge again.

He fixes his coffee how he likes it, taking a sip and humming at the flavor. "Thanks, man."

Spencer strolls in next, freshly showered and ready for the day. His dark hair is shaved on the sides and long on top, and he's rocking a neatly trimmed five o'clock shadow.

"Jake, you bum," he laughs when he sees the state Jake is in. He makes himself a cup of coffee before sitting next to Jake and likely scrolling social media or checking stocks.

"Anyone seen Toby?" I ask. "Breakfast is almost ready."

The sauce is simmering, but I won't start the eggs until everyone's here.

"I heard him giggling like a schoolgirl in his room just now," Spencer says absentmindedly, still focused on his phone.

"Yeah, he's been acting weird lately," Jake adds. "I think he's talking to someone."

"You think?" Spencer says sarcastically before I shut this shit down.

"Enough," I interrupt with a loud bark. "I'll go get him, or no one eats."

Jake and Spencer hold their hands up in surrender.

"Sir, yes, sir!" Jake salutes me, and I leave the room before I knock him off his barstool.

I quietly make my way upstairs, stopping when I reach Toby's room and carefully pressing my ear to the door.

Muffled giggling meets my ear, followed by a playful, "Stop it!"

I swallow thickly, nearly choking on the lump in my throat. It's not even ten in the morning, and he's already talking to that guy?

I take a deep breath, steeling my resolve and knocking on the door three times. "Breakfast is ready," I inform him.

"Be right there!" he hollers, ignoring me to say goodbye to some asshole.

I stand there a moment, my mind racing with thoughts of protecting Toby.

"Yo! Toby!" Jake hollers from the kitchen. "Hurry up and finish jerking off! We're hungry!"

Rolling my eyes at my ridiculous roommate downstairs, I lean against the wall opposite Toby's door, propping one leg up and folding my arms across my chest. I can wait for him.

Quiet murmurs and more giggles escape Toby's room before the door suddenly opens, and he freezes when he finds me waiting.

"Hey," he says, smiling shyly, pushing his curls back, only for them to flop over his forehead again.

"Breakfast is ready," I repeat, continuing to stare intensely at him, making him squirm.

"How long have you been waiting there?" he asks hesitantly.

"Long enough," I murmur, pushing off the wall and taking one large step into his space. "Are you seeing someone?" I ask without hesitation because I need to know these things.

"Just talking," he admits. "Nothing serious."

"I want to meet him."

"*What?!*" Toby shrieks with panic written all over his face.

"You heard me."

"Absolutely not." He slips past me and scurries to the stairs in an attempt to avoid the conversation.

"*Toby!*" I whisper-shout.

I swear to God, he better not fall again.

Thankfully, he makes it down safely, turning the corner and casually strolling into the kitchen.

"About damn time, Tobias!" Jake shouts from the island as soon as we walk in.

I pop him on the back of the head as I pass him on my way to the stove. "*Hey!*" he shouts, rubbing the spot. "What was that for?"

"For always fucking yelling at people," I tell him, turning the burner on to start the water boiling. "It's rude."

"Yeah, yeah. It's also rude to hit people. But whatever, who's counting."

I ignore the comment, stirring the hollandaise sauce before I start the poached eggs. While they're cooking, I make the toast, buttering multiple rounds and placing two per plate. Once the eggs are done, I season everything nicely, adding slices of avocado on the side and drizzling hollandaise on top of the eggs. Last but not least, I add the bacon crumbles I prepared earlier and take everything to the island.

"Wow. This looks amazing, Shane." Toby smiles at his plate, then at me. "Thank you."

I nod, wishing we could have finished our conversation earlier, and take my spot across the island from everyone. I stand there and lean over, inhaling my food in a quarter of the time it took to make it.

"You did it once again, man," Spencer compliments, everyone else nodding vigorously while they finish their last few bites.

"So good," Toby sighs, rubbing his full belly.

"COD tournament, anyone?" Jake asks, pushing his plate away.

"First dibs!" Toby shouts before standing up and stacking everyone's plates, carrying them to the sink.

"What are the stakes?" Spencer asks with a dark brow raised.

"Loser has to do the dishes," Toby replies with an evil smirk, stacking the rest of my pots and pans in the large farmhouse sink.

Everyone groans, reluctantly agreeing to the bet as we pile onto the living room couch, starting up the PS5. After several intense rounds, Jake loses, shouting profanities and cursing loud enough to piss off the neighbors.

"Don't be a poor sport," Spencer teases, but Jake just scowls before disappearing into the kitchen to complete his punishment.

"I gotta pee, then we can start another round," Spencer says, leaving Toby and me alone in the living room.

Now's my chance to finish the conversation.

Toby's phone vibrates on the coffee table, cutting off that thought, but he grabs it before I can catch a name. His eyes scan the screen back and forth rapidly, a dreamy sort of smile slowly overtaking his face.

Who the fuck is making him smile like that?

Toby bites his bottom lip, abusing the soft flesh while his thumbs fly across the keyboard. Despite the desire to grill him right now, I sit in silence instead, waiting for our friends to come back, while Toby talks to someone else.

Five minutes later, Spencer wanders back in, plopping down on the couch and turning toward Toby. "So, you got a girlfriend or something?" he asks bluntly, instantly making me want to protect Toby.

"W-what?" he stutters. "No. What do you mean?"

"Oh, come on, Toby. You've been smiling at your phone and going missing a lot lately. Who are you seeing?"

"No one."

"Bullshit," Spencer retorts with a laugh.

"That's enough, Spence. Mind your fucking business," I growl, placing a protective arm around Toby's shoulders.

Spencer holds his hands up in surrender before zipping his lips with his fingers and picking up the controller. He goes to the online store and starts browsing the PS5 games on sale. No one says a word.

"Phew!" Jake shouts dramatically, strolling back into the

living room and cutting the tension. "I'm off dish duty for the rest of the week. Your cooking is amazing, Shane, but *damn* that was a steep price to pay, my man." When no one laughs, Jake glances around, trying to read the room. "What'd I miss?"

"Toby has a girlfriend," Spencer says teasingly, like we're still in fucking middle school.

I tighten my hold on Toby and narrow my eyes at Spencer, giving a quick shake of my head, hoping he gets the message to fucking *stop*.

"Really? Who is she?" Jake asks with an overexcited smile. "Do we know her?"

"That's what I'm trying to figure out," Spencer volleys back. "What color hair does she have, Tobes? You gotta give us some clues, bro."

"Yeah, man. What year is she?"

"*Just stop!*" Toby suddenly shouts, pushing my arm off his shoulders and jumping up from the couch. "Just shut up, okay? I don't have a girlfriend," he says before taking a deep breath.

I wish I could stand up and wrap my arms around him, but this is his moment.

"I don't have a girlfriend, because I'm gay."

The silence is loud, all of us seeming to be frozen in place.

My legs finally work, and I stand next to Toby. "Doesn't change anything," I say, and that seems to snap our roommates into motion.

"Of course not, man." Spencer looks remorseful for his teasing, but Jake starts to get one of those shit-eating grins that means trouble.

"So, then. Do you have a *boyfriend*?" Jake asks, and I twitch, damn near lunging for him.

Toby's warm hand circles mine, squeezing gently to let me know it's fine. "No. I don't."

It still doesn't explain the giggles and secret phone conversations, but I let it slide.

For now.

I also let Jake's rude question slide, because my roommates are actually pretty cool guys when they're not trying to give everyone a hard time. The four of us pick up right where we left off with COD, as if Toby didn't just come out. The rest of the afternoon is spent with a never-ending charcuterie board provided by yours truly, way too many multiplayer tournaments, and my best fucking friends.

CHAPTER EIGHT
SHANE

It's Monday night, and I've got thirty minutes left on my shift at The Sandbar. I'm painstakingly counting down the minutes until I can clock out and check my phone. After seeing Toby on a date and overhearing him giggling in his bedroom, I started opening the *Find My Friends* app way more often than I ever have. Even though we gave each other access years ago, I realize I'm invading his privacy by doing this. But I can't seem to care because I have to keep him safe.

"Hey, sweetie," Ms. Harriet says in greeting as she pulls a hairnet over her silver curls. "How you doin' tonight?" Her thick, southern drawl is always so sincere.

"Doing well, and you?" I ask my favorite coworker, happy to see her.

Ms. Harriet smiles. "Always so well-mannered you are, Shane. I'm doin' great. My arthritis is behaving, so that means this grandma can cook!"

I smile, glancing back at the flat top so I don't burn the chicken breasts. "Glad to hear it."

"Well, go ahead and clock out early if you want to.

You're a good-looking boy, I'm sure you've got all sorts of girls lined up and waitin' on ya. We're slow enough, so if the bossman's got a problem with it, he can take it up with me." She winks, holding up two wrinkled fists.

"Ms. Harriet, you're a lifesaver." I hug her very gently, and she chuckles heartily, shooing me out of the kitchen. I grab my stuff, sneaking out the back and down the alleyway.

As soon as I climb into my truck, I immediately open what's become my personal stalking app and feel a jolt of panic when I see that Toby isn't at the house. I zoom in closer, realizing he's at the movie theater. Fuck. He's probably on another date, and that bothers me more than I'm willing to admit to myself.

It doesn't take me long to get to the theater when I hit every green light along the way as if the universe itself is urging me there.

Monday nights are usually slow, so I walk right up to the ticket booth. "You seen this guy?" I ask, pressing my phone to the plexiglass window and showing the dude working there a photo of Toby.

"Why? You a cop or something?" he asks skeptically.

I slip him a twenty through the window. "Nah. Just looking for my friend."

The kid seems unsure, but pockets the money anyway and sells me a ticket to some rom-com I've never heard of, informing me it started close to an hour ago.

I sneak into the dark movie theater with my hood pulled up, hunching over to hide my tall frame. Picking a spot at the very back, I sit right under the projector, front and center with a bird's-eye view. I scan the half-full theater, searching for Toby's curly head and finding him a few rows down on the left, holding hands and sharing popcorn with a different guy than the one from the coffee shop. My gaze narrows, and I grip the armrests like I'm about to Hulk out and rip them off.

I don't like this.

At all.

Seeing Toby hang out with strange men doesn't feel right. In fact, it feels downright shitty. He should be spending that time with me. If I knew he wanted to go to a rom-com, I would have taken him myself.

I alternate between staring at the back of his date's head and whatever the hell is happening on the big screen. After a long day of classes and then work, I start to doze off. My head nods, and I jolt awake, blinking rapidly while I attempt to refocus on my target. The guy has his arm around Toby now, rubbing his bare skin back and forth. I fight the urge to catapult down there, pry his grimy fingers off my best friend, and bend them backward until he screams for mercy.

I don't know how much more time passes before the movie ends, but if my eyes had lasers, this fucker would have a hole through his skull. The credits finally roll, and I slouch down in my seat, waiting for the theater to clear before I sneak out after everyone. Under no circumstances can Toby see me here. He just wouldn't understand.

I'm not stalking him.

I'm *protecting* him.

When I step outside, I immediately spot them and dart behind a freestanding movie poster, crouching down to pretend like I'm tying my shoe.

Shit.

They're right fucking there.

"I had fun tonight," Toby says so sweetly that my stomach aches.

I peek around the sign, unable to stop myself from looking. Toby smiles up at his date, who's nearly as tall as me, with a buzz cut, ice blue eyes, and some lame-ass fraternity hoodie.

He doesn't deserve Toby's smile.

The fucker leans in, caressing Toby's jaw and puckering his lips. I grip the edge of the metal frame, trying to stop myself from jumping up and karate kicking him in the face.

He certainly doesn't deserve Toby's kiss.

Thankfully, Toby dodges the unwanted advance, stepping back a clear three feet. "I don't kiss on the first date, Tristan," he says matter-of-factly with more respect than this asshole deserves. "I told you that."

"Are you serious right now?" Tristan scoffs. "Whatever. I'm not wasting any more of my time with a *virgin*. I'm only here to fuck, and if that's not gonna happen, then you can *walk* home."

My jaw clenches painfully as I watch Toby sputter, standing there in complete shock while his date stomps off to the parking lot.

Blowing my cover in an instant, I jump out from behind the movie poster like a real-life superhero to confront this asshole who thinks he can talk to my best friend like that and just abandon him on the street.

"Hey fuckboy!" I yell at his retreating back, smirking when he responds to the name by stopping and turning around. "If I ever see you around campus, you better fucking *run*."

"And who the hell are you?" he asks, glancing between me and Toby with a creased brow.

"I'm the guy who's gonna kick your ass and drive your date home, you piece of shit," I growl.

"*Whatever.* I don't need this," he sneers, power walking

the rest of the way to his car and peeling out of the parking lot like the pathetic loser he is.

During the confrontation with Tristan, Toby wandered away and started walking down the sidewalk, like he's on autopilot.

I rush to my truck, slowly rolling up next to him and cranking the window down. "Hey, stranger. Need a ride?" I joke, leaning an elbow out of the open window. I'm trying to make light of a shitty situation that could have ended way worse.

"What are you doing here, Shane?" Toby asks skeptically, his big, watery eyes staring up at me. "Did you *stalk* me?"

"I... No. 'Course not."

Fuck, that's a lie. An absolute lie.

"I mean, *technically*, maybe a little."

Toby huffs, folding his arms across his chest. "I didn't need your bodyguard services tonight, Shane. Thank you very much."

"Actually, you did," I counter, leaning over to unlatch the door for him and pushing it open. "Now, get in."

"No." He turns away and starts walking down the sidewalk again.

I ease my foot off the break, rolling next to him like I have all the time in the world. My tires slowly crunch over the sandy asphalt. "You're not walking home. *Get in,*" I repeat with more force.

"Stop following me!" he yells, and I glance around, making sure no one's going to call the cops on us.

"Now is not the time to be stubborn," I growl. "Please. Just get in the truck, Tobes. You know I can't leave you here."

"*Ugh!* Fine! I don't feel like walking five miles home

anyway," he concedes before climbing into the passenger seat, buckling himself in, and crossing his arms with a pout.

We drive in silence for a while, neither of us knowing what to say. I don't ask him what happened, since I clearly witnessed it for myself, and I'm not sure what to say to soften the blow. But I need to cheer him up.

A little shop with a giant, lit-up ice cream cone and a blue and white striped awning grabs my attention, sparking an idea that might put a smile on his face.

"I'm in the mood for ice cream. Want some?" I ask casually, pulling into Coastal Creamery, known for its elaborate milkshake concoctions. "My treat."

Some of Toby's light sparks back to life, and he perks up a little. "Hell yeah."

We step inside and seat ourselves according to the sign. It's decorated like a nineteen-fifties soda shop, with black and white checkered floors, a long counter, and cozy booths along the windows. I choose a secluded booth in the corner, and we quietly browse the selection of over-the-top milkshakes.

Soon, a girl around our age comes over with a bright, welcoming smile. "Hey, guys! I'm Hailey, and I'll be taking care of y'all tonight. What can I get for ya, or do you need another minute?"

"You ready?" I murmur, and Toby nods.

"I'll get the Candy Crusher, please," he says with a small grin, knowing his milkshake is going to be piled high with peanut butter cups, mini chocolate bars, and sour gummy worms.

"And for you?" Hailey asks, winking at me.

I ignore her flirtation, never having been interested in dating, just the occasional hookup with a tourist I'll never see again. "Double Cookie Crunch."

THE BRO DATE

"Mmm," she hums. "Good choice. That one's my favorite."

I nod politely. "Cool."

Hailey beams at my one-word answer. "Be right back." She spins on her heel, darting into the kitchen.

Toby is staring out of the window, completely zoning out and likely replaying his horrible date over and over in his head, overthinking like always.

I can't confront him as if he's done something wrong, but I just wish he would talk to me.

I want him to *choose* to open up.

Everything he's going through can't be easy, and all I want to do is be there for him like he's been there for me my whole life.

I stare at my empty lunch tray as if it will spontaneously regenerate more food like one of the cool science fiction books Mom got me from the free book drive. Ms. Patricia, my favorite lunch lady, retired last week, so I'm back to one scoop of mashed potatoes and no dessert.

A shiny red apple suddenly appears on my tray, and I blink at it, confused as to whether my mind is playing tricks on me or not. A chocolate chip cookie appears next, along with a small hand darting away.

I peer at my new friend, wondering why he's sharing his food with me.

"Wanna try my turkey wrap?" he asks with a genuine smile I'm unfamiliar with.

Mom and I moved here last year from New Jersey, and I haven't made a single friend until now. I cut school a lot when we first got here, 'acting out after my parents' divorce,' as my guidance counselor declared in my school records. The transition wasn't easy for me, I'll admit, but it's still better than listening to constant arguing and having to stay up all night in case I needed to protect my mom.

My dad is a drunk, and I hope I never see him again.

I had to repeat fifth grade again this year, but at least all the kids leave me alone since I'm bigger and older than them now.

Toby hands me half of his wrap, and I take it, biting into what tastes like Thanksgiving Day turkey.

"Thank you," I mumble around a mouthful.

"You're welcome! I can bring more food tomorrow."

I stare at him, never having met someone so kind and generous. Money has been tight for Mom since she left my dad, and I'm not old enough to get a job yet. Free lunch only fills me up so much, so I won't say no to the offer.

"Oh! I could ask my mom if you can come over after school on Friday and have dinner with us?" Uncertainty creeps into his expression. "If you want . . ."

I'm not great at talking to grown-ups, but I'll do it for a chance to hang out with Toby and eat some good food.

Although I have learned to make a pretty tasty bowl of ramen.

"Why are you being so nice to me?" I ask, completely unaccustomed to it. I only met him a week ago.

"Because we're friends, silly, and that's what friends do. They help each other out." His teeth sparkle, and his dimples pop out again.

He looks so much younger than me when he smiles like that.

From here on out, I vow to always protect him and always be his friend.

No one's going to hurt Toby as long as I'm around.

"Here ya go!" Hailey exclaims, carefully setting our giant milkshakes in front of us.

"Whoa," Toby whispers in awe. "I can't believe I've never been here before."

"Well, we just opened last summer, so we haven't even been here a year," Hailey informs us. "Enjoy!" She disappears again, and we both stare at our desserts for a moment, unsure where to start.

Toby picks off a peanut butter cup and dips it into the whipped cream, pulling a gummy worm out next.

I take a spoon and scoop up a chunk of cookie dough ice cream, then dip it in the whipped cream and cookie crumble on top, holding it out for Toby. "Wanna try mine?" I offer him the first bite before I destroy it.

Toby nods, pushing his milkshake to the side and leaning forward. My gaze automatically zeroes in on his mouth. His soft pink lips part slowly, his tongue poking out as he takes the spoon into his mouth. He sucks on it, and I pull it out clean.

"Mmm," he moans, closing his eyes and making me swallow roughly.

Shit.

What the fuck was that?

I shouldn't be turned on by my best friend eating a bite of ice cream.

"Try mine," Toby insists with an innocent smile, completely unaware of my thoughts. He pushes his Mason jar across the table, and I scoop out a spoonful of rainbow ice cream. "Make sure you get a gummy worm," Toby insists, and my lip quirks.

His shake isn't bad, but I definitely prefer something with chocolate.

We continue to enjoy our desserts in a comfortable silence.

"You've got some whipped cream right there . . ." Toby says, tapping his bottom lip.

I wipe the corner of my mouth, but Toby laughs and shakes his head. "Let me help you." He reaches out and swipes at my bottom lip with his thumb, tugging on the sensitive flesh. "There. All gone."

My gaze once again zeroes in on his plush mouth before I shake my head, snapping out of it. "Thanks," I mumble, continuing to suck down my half-melted milkshake, hoping I don't give myself a brain freeze.

We finish our shakes, and I throw some cash down on the table, not wanting to wait for change and further engage with Hailey. "Ready to go home?" I ask my best friend, hoping I helped him forget about his shitty date. Even just a little.

"Yeah. Let's go," he replies with a small smile.

I hold the door open, and he slips past, stopping me before we step off the sidewalk. "Thank you for tonight," he murmurs, resting his hand on my chest and sending goosebumps sprawling across my skin. "Seriously."

So many unspoken emotions pass between us, threatening to knock me off my axis. With an understanding nod, I place my palm on the small of his back, guiding him to the safety of my truck.

CHAPTER NINE
TOBY

"We're doing this tonight, honey," Tate says, flipping through my closet, looking for something to wear out. "I won't hear another peep about it."

After I got dumped on the curb by my last date, Tate decided to cheer me up by forcing me into another new experience.

A gay bar.

"You've got nothing suitable," Tate declares, pulling out a bulging tote bag that I didn't even notice he brought. "Good thing I came prepared!"

Tate starts pulling out all sorts of shiny shorts and leather harnesses that I would have no idea how to put on. "Uh... I'm not sure about this part, Tate. Can't I just wear a button-down?"

Tate throws his head back, barking out a loud laugh, and I scowl at him. "Oh, honey. Just think of it as another round of tryouts for Team Dick. Now, put this on." Tate tosses me a pair of leather shorts, a tiny black thong, and a harness, nearly smacking me in the eye with a buckle.

"Before you make a fuss, the underwear is new, and I washed it for you."

"Tate . . . I don't know about this," I say, holding up the scrap of fabric with my index finger.

"Yeah, because you never know until you try, Toby boy," he retorts.

"Okay, but I'm not going to start wearing lingerie every day." I gather the tiny pile of clothing and hold it to my chest.

"Oh, honey. *That* is not lingerie. That's just underwear. When you're ready for that round of tryouts, you let me know. I'll show you leather and lace that'll make you blush for a week straight."

As if on cue, I feel my cheeks heat, making Tate chuckle and shake his head. "So innocent. So sweet," he murmurs.

Ignoring his teasing, I turn my back so he can't see the radioactive color of my face. "I'm gonna change in the bathroom," I mumble, peeking my head out of the bedroom door and peering side to side.

Coast is clear.

Sneaking down the hall to the shared bathroom, I lock myself inside and undress, slipping the thong on and adjusting my package in it. The fabric is soft and silky against my junk, and I stare at myself in the mirror for a moment before turning and looking over my shoulder.

My ass looks phenomenal.

Maybe Tate's on to something.

I step into the shorts next, and they hug my hips just right. But there are too many straps and buckles on this harness-thing, and I give up after a couple of minutes trying. Guess I'm going to need Tate's help on this one.

I scurry down the hallway, quickly knocking on my bedroom door and waiting for Tate to open it, just in case he's naked. My head is on a swivel, paranoid that someone's going to suddenly pop out and see me.

The door swings open, and Tate is standing there in metallic silver shorts and a black patent leather harness that's way more elaborate than mine. He pulls me in and shuts the door behind us. "Oh, honey. Let me help you."

"Can't I just wear something else?" I plead. "We don't want to attract any creeps."

"Speak for yourself," Tate laughs, opening up the harness, guiding my arms through the correct holes, and securing it in the front. "Now, there. Look at you," Tate coos, "like a *real* gay. Mama is *so* proud." He opens his arms, and I step into them, accepting his embrace while I roll my eyes. "Last thing is black eyeliner and a little bronzer, then you're ready to party!"

Old Downtown is bustling tonight; the cobblestone streets are filled with locals and tourists alike. A hot pink neon sign lights up the front entrance of Stick Shift, the best gay bar in town, according to Tate.

The bouncer eyes us up and down, salivating like a snake ready to strike. I use the fake ID that Tate and Daija helped me get last year, and the creep easily lets us in without even paying the cover.

Half the bar turns to stare when we walk in, and with all these eyes on me, I instantly wish I had my bodyguard standing behind me. Tate and I are the same size, so if I'm a twink, then so is he.

And I think we may have just wandered into the lion's den.

"Let's go sit at the bar for a minute," Tate suggests. "*And get a drink,*" he says way too loudly.

I frown at him, confused as to why he's yelling until we sit at the bar, and two men sit down on either side of us. Tate winks at me, and I have to fight a smile when they offer to buy us drinks. We accept the screwdrivers and keep the conversation short because these guys are way too old for us. After ten minutes of small talk, I make eye contact with Tate, pleading for him to get us out of here.

Luckily, the DJ decides to unknowingly help us out. "OHMYGOD!" Tate screams when a new song comes on. We look at each other and shout, *"Pink Pony Club!"* before chugging our drinks and using it as our getaway.

"Thanks for the drinks. It was nice to meet you," I politely say to the two older men as Tate tugs me away to the dance floor. I ignore their frowns, because we don't owe them anything for a five-dollar drink.

Tate and I jump and sing on the dance floor until we break a sweat, and the song changes to something a little more sexy.

"Turn around!" Tate shouts with a crooked smile. His curly blond hair glistens under the flashing lights, and I can only imagine mine is doing the same. He grabs my hips and spins me around, tugging my ass to his groin. "Twerk on me, honey!" Tate and I let loose and grind on each other like no one's watching, but I guess they are because guys start coming up to us. We dance with a few of them before we meet two cute CBU boys in linen button-downs and cargo shorts, like they just came from a dinner cruise on the harbor. It's actually kinda cute.

After rubbing my ass on the dude's semi for three songs, I finally spin around and introduce myself. "Hey. I'm Toby, by the way." My smile falters when I realize he looks familiar, with short brown hair and a diamond nose stud.

Oh my God. I think I saw him on Grindr.

Recognition flashes in his baby-blue eyes, and his smile widens. "Hey. I'm Landon, and this is my friend, Alex."

His friend is pretty hot, with chin-length black hair and bright green eyes, but the way he's staring at us is making me uneasy. Although Tate doesn't seem to mind.

"Hey. I'm Tate," he says, eyeing Alex up and down.

"Toby," I add breathlessly, trying to fan myself with my hand. There are too many bodies jumping and grinding on each other out here, and the music is so loud we can hardly talk. I need a break.

"Wanna get out of here? It's getting a little claustrophobic," Landon says, noticing my discomfort.

I nod, needing some water or maybe another screwdriver.

Landon places his big, warm hand on the small of my back, leading me from the dance floor to the bar.

"Uh, uh, uh. Not without me!" Tate hollers, following us with Alex hot on his heels. "We're a package deal tonight," he says with a teasing giggle.

"Fuck. That is so hot!" Alex hollers behind us all, and I can practically feel his eyes roaming the back of my body and lingering on my ass.

We all sit at the bar, waiting for the bartender to make his way over. A giant glass mirror stocked with liquor bottles lines the wall behind the bar, giving me a front row view of just how drunk I am.

Flushed cheeks, messy curls, and a leather harness that looks like some sort of sex thing. I have to admit, now that the shock's worn off, I feel pretty sexy.

"Are you on *Grindr*? You look familiar," Landon suddenly asks me, and I tear my gaze away from the mirror, blinking up at him.

I was hoping he wouldn't ask me that.

"Oh. Uh. Yeah."

"You guys ever message each other?" Alex inquires. "I'm sure Landon swiped right for you." He eyes me up and down with his arm around Tate. "I know I would. You're hot as fuck. Both of you."

Yup. Just the creep Tate wanted.

Tate giggles, whispering something into Alex's ear that I definitely don't want to hear, judging by the hungry look on his face.

"Pretty sure I swiped left," I blurt the truth, making Landon scowl when Tate and Alex burst out laughing.

Oops.

"Sorry!" I shrug, turning my back on them to face Landon. "Does it really matter now that we're here having fun?"

"No, guess not. So, does that mean I can get your number?"

Dating apps haven't really worked out for me, and I'm having a great time tonight, so I figure there's really no harm. And I also have a really hard time telling people no.

"Sure. Yeah. Okay," I say with a small smile, taking his phone and adding myself to the contacts.

Landon wraps his arm around me when the hot, surfer-looking bartender with long blond hair comes over, ordering for me without asking. "A screwdriver for my friend. Make it a double."

"Actually, can I get water instead?" I whisper into his ear. I should probably pace myself.

"Oh, shoot, the bartender just left, and I already ordered you a double. Tell you what. Next round we'll do water, yeah?" Landon ducks his head, giving me a wink that makes me a little uneasy.

"What about you?" I ask.

He holds up a nearly empty glass of clear liquid and ice. "Still sippin'," he says with a big white smile.

I glance over at my friend having a great time doing shots with Alex, and I don't want to ruin his night, so the moment the bartender sets my drink down, I grab it and chug half the thing. Time to let loose and stop worrying so much.

"Fuck yeah! *Chug! Chug! Chug!*" Alex shouts, but I set my glass down before I throw up all over the bar top.

By the next round, I'm no longer thirsty for water, so Landon buys me another drink. This time, a vodka cranberry, but I still don't see him order one for himself.

Oh well. I'm too drunk to care anymore.

As soon as my drink is gone, Tate grabs my hand, hauling me off to the dance floor with Landon and Alex hot on our heels.

"Shake what ya mama gave you!" Tate shouts before dropping it low and twerking.

"My mother would have a heart attack if she knew she gave me any of this!" I laugh before joining him in shaking my ass.

After another song, Tate wiggles his phone back and forth in front of my face. "Story tiiime!" he singsongs, drawing the word out. "Before we get all sweaty and gross."

"I'll show you sweaty and gross," Alex growls like the creep he seems to be.

Tate throws his head back, laughing obnoxiously. "You wish, baby." Alex scowls at that, but Tate ignores him, talking to me instead. "Put on a show for the camera, honey."

I'm drunk enough to listen, putting on a pretend strip tease even though I've got nothing to take off.

"So hot! You're going to have all the straight boys on my Insta jerking off tonight!"

Tate and I laugh loudly, but Landon does not look happy.

Whatever. We just met.

"Your turn!" I hold my hand out and Tate passes me his phone, so I can record him shaking his ass.

He takes things further than me, wiggling his thumbs into the sides of his shorts and tugging them down to show his thong and the swell of his ass.

I giggle, too drunk to stop him, and instead switch to Live. "Let's see that sexy ass!" I holler, encouraging him when I probably shouldn't.

"Alright. Alright. That's enough," Alex says, attempting to pull my friend off the dance floor when he clearly doesn't want to.

"Shots, anyone?!" Landon shouts before walking off and whispering something to the hot surfer guy behind the bar.

"*Woohoo!* Shots!" Tate shouts, tugging up his shorts and grabbing my hand, pulling me back over to the bar.

The bartender brings out a tray of shots, and Landon hands each one out specifically. Not thinking anything of it, I toast to new friends and new experiences. At least, I do in my head.

"Cheers!" I shout, and all four of us clink our shot glasses together before tipping them back.

CHAPTER TEN
SHANE

I'm on edge tonight, worried about Toby going to a popular gay bar known for some pretty wild nights, so I snuck my phone into Raúl's kitchen. Glancing over my shoulder, I make sure the coast is clear before reaching underneath my apron and slipping my phone out of my front pocket. I quickly scroll my news feed to see if either Toby or Tate has posted.

Sure enough, Tate's profile picture is lit up, so I tap on the tiny circle and a dark, shaky video fills my screen. Loud club music blares from my phone, and I curse under my breath, quickly turning it down. Toby's smiling face comes into view, and he blows a kiss to the camera before it zooms out to show him dancing and putting on a show for half the bar.

I can't seem to pry my eyes away from his body and that fucking outfit. Or lack thereof.

I swallow the uncomfortable lump in my throat and adjust the slight bulge in my pants.

What the hell is he wearing?
And why is my body reacting this way?

I'm not gay, but I think I might be crushing on my best friend, and I have no idea how this even happened.

"Holy shit," a soft, surprised voice murmurs next to me, and I immediately click my phone off, slipping it back into my pocket.

"What are you doing peering over my shoulder, Jaycee? Thought you weren't a gossip?" I ask, flipping the burgers I almost burned while I was watching Toby and Tate drinking, dancing, and being the centers of attention at Stick Shift.

"First of all, I'd have to be like seven feet tall to peer over your shoulder, and second, I already saw your bestie on a date with a guy, so this isn't a big shock. He looks hot as hell, though, but you know I would never say anything."

"Fine. Thanks, or whatever," I mumble.

I have more important things to worry about.

When Jaycee leaves the kitchen, I click on Tate's Live and find him showing half his ass on the dance floor while Toby giggles behind the camera. Two guys much bigger than them enter the screen, and they share a look I can't decipher before one shouts that it's time for shots.

Over my dead body.

Quickly untying my apron, I rush out of the kitchen with Jaycee hot on my heels. I fully empty out my locker, stuffing everything into my ratty old backpack. Consequences be damned.

"Shane! Don't do this," Jaycee cries, stepping in front of me. "I can't cover for you in the kitchen. Raúl's going to be pissed if you disappear again."

"Don't care." I've always said Toby is more important than some job, and I stand by it.

"*Hey!*" Raúl shouts at us, and her sad eyes slowly close as she takes a big breath.

THE BRO DATE

"Shane, please," Jaycee tries one last time.

"I gotta go." There's no changing my mind. She'll be fine here. Raúl doesn't treat her like garbage. "See you 'round." I step past her, ignoring the commotion behind me.

"Where the hell do you think you're going, Shane?" Raúl yells at my retreating back, but I don't answer, especially when he's shouting at me in front of everyone.

Raúl grabs my shoulder, spinning me around and yelling directly in my face, nearly triggering me into a flashback of the years leading up to my parents' divorce, and all my mom's shitty boyfriends since. I take a deep breath, knowing it's even worse if you give someone like him a reaction. I stare right through him instead and speak calmly. "Take your hands off me."

He immediately lets go and takes two steps back. "You can't just leave during a shift whenever you feel like it. This is the second time."

"It's an emergency, and I have to go," I say matter-of-factly. The details are none of his business.

"You're fired if you leave," Raúl sneers, throwing the ultimatum at me like a live grenade and not giving two shits about me as a human being.

My jaw clenches, even though I knew this would happen.

Raúl smiles like an evil fucking villain thinking he's got me right where he wants me. But I'll figure out something else. I *have* to. Because right now, Toby fucking needs me, and he will *always* be more important than a job.

"Guess I quit."

I pay the twenty-dollar cover and walk into the first gay bar I've ever been to, searching for my best friend. It isn't hard to find him on the dance floor, grinding against a guy who looks like he just won a spelling bee instead of someone who's humping my best friend's ass in front of a packed house.

My jaw clenches. Toby is pretty drunk and almost naked. A tight leather harness crosses his chest and hugs his shoulders, accentuating his slim yet toned build. Tiny leather shorts reveal his entire upper thighs, drawing every pair of eyes in this fucking club to his ass.

Fuck me. His outfit is even hotter in person.

Mr. Spelling Bee Champion slips away from the dance floor and goes up to the bartender with a slimy smile on his face. He orders another drink for Toby and water for himself.

Not fucking happening.

I weave through the crowd until I reach Toby, who's dancing by himself, completely unaware of his surroundings. I sneak behind him, but he catches me off guard, sticking his ass out and pressing it against my crotch.

Stilling his hips, I stop him from grinding against me further. My hands slowly slide up his sides, caressing his bare skin before bracing his upper arms. I spin him around, peering down into golden eyes that sparkle like glitter in the flashing club lights. The unique color is heightened by black eyeliner and shimmer on his cheekbones.

It's striking.

"Shane?" he asks in confusion, his brows creasing in the center. "What are you doing here?"

I shake the strange lust from my brain, focusing on my mission and getting Toby the hell out of here.

"You're coming with me," I demand calmly. "Where's Tate?"

Even though I'm pissed at our friend for encouraging all of this, I'd never leave him behind. Tate's coming with us whether he wants to or not.

"Coming with you?" Toby asks, blinking up at me.

I nod, not wanting to make a scene. We can talk at home.

"Oh my God, Shane!" Tate suddenly shouts, pushing his way over to us where we're standing still in the middle of the crowded dance floor. "What are you doing here?!"

"Taking you home."

Tate tips his head back, laughing loudly and drawing more eyes than I'm comfortable with. He's dressed similarly to Toby, with a shiny leather harness and matching curls, only blonder. I'm not into guys, but I can't deny they look good standing next to each other.

"I'm deadass serious," I inform him. "Let's go." My gaze darts to Toby. "Both of you."

If I have to toss them over my shoulders and carry them out of here kicking and screaming, then so be it. It's for their own good.

I'll always protect my friends.

"What's going on over here?" Mr. Spelling Bee Champion suddenly appears behind Toby, wrapping an arm around his midsection and splaying a large palm across his bare belly.

My nostrils flare, and I clench my jaw, but I won't let this fuckboy know that he's getting under my skin. "Toby," I say, ignoring the rando who thinks he has a claim over my best friend. I hold my hand out, silently asking him to come with me.

Toby grabs Tate's hand, then places his other hand in

mine. "It was nice meeting you, Landon. I'll text you later!" he says sweetly, because he is too nice for his own good.

"No, he won't," I inform Landon, tugging both Toby and Tate away from the dance floor.

"Hey! What the fuck?!" Landon shouts at our backs. "I just bought you drinks all night! You're seriously gonna leave with some other guy?"

I pause in my tracks, seeing red. This fucker thinks he's entitled to *something* over a few free drinks? Pathetic. Reaching into my back pocket, I pull out my wallet and slip two twenties from it before spinning around and throwing them at Landon's feet. "Cry me a fucking river."

Tate bursts out laughing, and Landon lunges for me, but his friend grabs him and holds him back. I smirk, making him struggle to get free. He's lucky his friend's smart enough to stop him. It wouldn't be a fair fight.

"Tate, call me!" The friend yells as we start to walk away.

"That won't be happening either!" I holler, not bothering to look behind us again.

"Why am I being dragged into this love triangle?!" Tate laughs as we weave our way through the cocktail tables that line the dance floor. "Or is it a pentagon now?"

"There is no triangle or any other shape," I growl, completely appalled by the idea of fighting for my best friend's attention with some fucking douchebag stranger. "I don't want you to ever see that guy again, Toby."

Tate snickers, whispering something to Toby that I can't quite hear. I push through the exit with two harness-clad twinks under my arms, completely aware of how this situation looks.

As we step off the curb, we draw the eyes of the bouncers working the door. "Drive safely! That's some precious cargo you got there, buddy!" the burly older man yells.

I look over and give him a death glare, leading my drunk friends around the side of the building where I parked. Opening the passenger side door, I fold the front seat down and help Tate up first. He climbs into the small back seat, and I adjust the front seat into an upright position. Toby climbs into the passenger seat, and I shut the door, running around to the driver's side.

"Can we stop for burritos?" Tate whines from the backseat once we get buckled in. "It's right down the street before the highway."

"Fine," I grunt, glancing over at Toby, who's resting his head back against the seat with his eyes closed. I unzip my hoodie, shrugging out of it and draping it over his exposed body. Feeling someone watching me, I glance at the rearview mirror and find Tate smiling back at me.

I immediately stop fussing with Toby and start the engine. "What's the name of this burrito place?" I ask, ignoring the knowing look in his eyes.

I drop Tate off at his apartment, helping him out and giving a small wave to Daija, who's standing outside in a fuzzy robe with her arms crossed like a disappointed parent. I texted her a heads-up before we left the club that she needed to help her best friend get inside safely.

When we finally get home, I wrap my hoodie around Toby's shoulders and sneak him upstairs just in case Jake or Spencer is home. I'm on edge, and I'd probably punch them in the face if they had something to say.

"Your room or mine?" I murmur, having to stop myself from picking him up and carrying him there.

"*Mine,*" he whispers, and as soon as I lock the bedroom door, Toby begins to struggle with his harness. "Get. This. Fucking. Thing. Off of me," he growls cutely, his lean muscles twisting this way and that.

I bite back a smile and set the bag of burritos down on his desk, approaching him as carefully as I might a wild animal. "Let me," I insist, grabbing hold of his biceps to settle his squirming. I carefully undo the buckle between his pecs and loosen the shoulder straps. "*Arms up,*" I breathe into his ear, sending a shiver down both of our spines.

Toby complies, raising his arms and allowing me to slip the harness up and over his head. "Thank you," he murmurs, surprising me by bending over and wiggling out of the leather shorts.

I suck in a sharp breath of air, unable to tear my eyes away from the tiny black thong he's wearing underneath. His package bulges against the silky fabric, stretching it out and showing the imprint of his cockhead. He spins around next, showing off his firm, toned ass that's paler than the rest of his body.

Fuck me.

What is going on with my head?

Clearing my throat awkwardly, I look away until I hear him crawl into bed.

When I glance back, he's sitting up, leaning against the headboard and staring at me innocently, like he has no clue what he just did. I glance down at the comforter settled around his lap, knowing what's underneath and honestly wanting another peek. Shaking the inappropriate thought away, I grab two water bottles from his mini fridge and the brown paper bag, handing him a foil-wrapped burrito and cold water. The bottom of the bed seems like a safe place to sit, so I take a seat and dig in.

"*Mmm,*" Toby moans, and I glance at him out of the corner of my eye, watching as sour cream drips down his chin and onto his bare chest.

I nearly choke on the giant bite of burrito I just took, my mind going to dirty, inappropriate places.

"Thanks, Shane," he says, closing his eyes and chewing with pleasure. "It tastes so fucking good right now. I needed this."

More creamy white sauce plops onto his chest, and I glance away, unsure why my dick seems to be getting more and more excited by this.

"You're welcome," I mumble around a mouthful of beans and rice, letting us enjoy our food and allowing Toby some time to sober up before I say what I need to say.

"So good." Toby burps, finishing off the last of his water.

When I'm done, I wad up the foil and toss it into the trash can. "So, Toby..."

"Hmm?" he hums innocently, sinking further into the bed.

I grab a napkin and scoot closer, dabbing the corners of his mouth and wiping his chest clean. "What the fuck were you thinking tonight?"

My tone seems to perk him up a little. "What do you mean?" his sleepy eyes stare at me, confused.

I grab another napkin and go over the spot again. "You're *nineteen*, Toby. You can't just go out and get wasted with guys you don't know."

He shoves my hand away. "I can make my own decisions, Shane."

"Clearly some pretty poor ones, letting guys you don't know buy you drinks all night. What if someone slipped you something? You can't be so trusting all the time, Toby." I never lecture him like this, but he's got me riled up when it comes to his safety.

"*I was with Tate!* And Landon isn't a stranger. Besides, nothing happened!" he shouts in defense, sitting up straight and staring me right in the eye. The blanket pools around his lap, hiding his distracting underwear from my gaze.

"But it *could* have. Bet you didn't know those assholes gave you alcohol while they had water."

Toby's brows crease. "I . . . That's . . . That's not true."

I lean closer. "I was there. Watching. And you better be glad I was," I growl.

"I don't need a shadow," he scoffs, turning his head to the side. "Everything's fine. Stop stalking my life!"

"Where have you been meeting all these guys anyway?" I ask, remembering the nerd in the coffee shop, the asshole at the movies, and now Mr. Spelling Bee Champion.

Toby hesitates, like he knows I won't like the answer.

"Just answer the damn question," I demand.

"I need to brush my teeth," Toby blurts suddenly, completely avoiding the conversation by jumping out of bed, slipping into a pair of silky basketball shorts from his floor, and darting out of the bedroom.

Hot on his heels, I push Toby into the bathroom, breathing in his ear like an annoying mosquito. "*Tell me.* Where the *fuck* are you meeting all these guys?"

"No," he retorts stubbornly, and I'm getting impatient.

"Toby."

"Fiiine," he whines. "*Grindr*."

Jealousy bubbles to life inside of me like a vat of acid threatening to spill over.

You can't trust anyone in today's world.

"Please don't do that anymore, Toby."

"Well, I have another date this weekend," he counters with sass, like he's been around Tate for too long.

"No. You do not," I say matter-of-factly.

Over my dead body will he meet up with another horny asshole from *Grindr*.

"Yes. I do," he insists with a defiant sparkle in his golden eyes, folding his arms across his bare chest.

"Then, I'll be there, too. Wherever you go. I will follow." I raise an eyebrow, daring him to challenge me.

His resolve waivers. "You can't. You're working."

"Nope. Just got fired," I say calmly, grabbing my toothbrush out of the drawer and squirting some toothpaste on it.

Toby gasps. "*What?* Why? What happened?"

I don't answer, turning the sink on and getting my toothbrush wet before shoving the thing in my mouth and pressing the button. Toby follows suit, and we stand there staring at each other in the mirror while we brush our teeth. I spit, rinsing out my mouth and drying off with my designated hand towel.

Toby does the same, asking me his question again. "Why did you lose your job, Shane?"

"I've told you before, Toby. You're more important than any job, and tonight was proof of that."

His head tilts like a confused little puppy.

He still doesn't get it.

"I'm going to sleep," I say tiredly, opening the door and stepping into the hallway. "In my *own* bed."

"Shane, wait. Can't we finish our conversation? Tell me what's wrong. *Please.*"

I spin around, pinning him against the wall and throwing out my own question since he wants to talk about our feelings so badly. "What are you searching for, Toby?" I scan his flushed face before focusing on bright amber eyes. "Hmm?"

This reckless behavior isn't like him.

"I've accepted that I'm gay, if that's what you mean," he says defensively, staring right back into my eyes.

"Of course that's not what I mean, but you've been putting yourself in unsafe situations, and I'd be a shitty friend if I wasn't looking out for you, Tobes. I saw Tate's stories."

His face pales. "Can we go back to my room and talk about this?" He slips under my arm, tiptoeing down the hallway and glancing back at me. *"Please?"*

I nod, giving in and following him back to his room, where I take my spot at the end of the bed.

Toby leans against the desk, his tight abs flexing naturally. "I'm not doing anything wrong or dangerous, I'm just dating and going out for once in my life," he huffs. "Just like any other guy my age."

"You're nineteen," I deadpan. "You haven't even hit the legal drinking age yet. You actually *are* doing something wrong."

Toby purses his lips. "I don't want to argue with you, Shane. You're just gonna have to get used to me being with guys."

His words are a solid punch to the gut.

I don't want to get used to that. *I can't.*

THE BRO DATE

"Are you looking for a boyfriend?" I blurt. The question tastes sour on my tongue, like bile rushing up a tender throat, ready to choke the life out of me. I don't fully understand the feelings growing inside me—the jealousy at seeing him smile and laugh with another man—but it makes my skin crawl so badly that I want to peel it from my bones.

"Hmm." Toby taps his finger against his bottom lip as if he knows it's torturing me. My gaze zeroes in on the soft, plump flesh, staring way too intently while he speaks. "I'm not sure about a boyfriend, but yes, I think I'd like to be kissed by a boy. Experiment a little. I'm just having fun, Shane."

Then have fun with me.

My heart gallops a million miles a minute like a herd of wild horses running toward the edge of a cliff and diving off, plummeting into the pit of my stomach. I press a hand to my abdomen as if I can feel it beating.

He could get hurt experimenting with people who don't care about him. *That can't happen.*

Something deep within me knows that would fucking destroy me forever.

"No," I growl low.

"I'm sorry?" His question is breathy and weak.

I stand up from the end of the bed, stepping into his space and staring down at him. An unbreakable, decade-long bond links us together, transcending mere friendship. And *no one* can get in the way of that. Especially not some random guy.

Without taking my eyes off of his, I reach out, gently cupping his jaw and rubbing my thumb along his cheekbone. "I can't stand to see another man touching you. It doesn't sit well with me, Toby. I can't let anything happen to you. If you want to kiss a boy... then, kiss *me*," I whisper, our lips only a breath apart.

He sucks in a sharp breath of air, his pupils dilating. "W-what do you mean?"

"Can I kiss you?" I ask him.

His cheeks flush a beautiful shade of pink that I swipe my thumb along.

"Yes," he breathes out, closing his eyes and parting his lips. "Please, Shane."

I slowly and cautiously lean forward until my lips gently press against his. They're soft and plush and so fucking nice that I kiss him deeper, allowing my tongue to sneak out and lick at the seam of his mouth. Toby lets out a whimper, and I seize the opportunity. His tongue meets mine stroke for stroke. With the adrenaline flowing, I don't have time to think about any possible consequences this kiss might have on our friendship, but I don't regret it.

I could never regret it.

Stubble scrapes my cheek, and something hard pokes my thigh, startling me for a moment before my own cock starts to respond, thickening in my jeans.

What the fuck is happening?

I'm not gay.

I like girls.

But holy fuck, I can't stop kissing my best friend, and I'm about five seconds away from slipping my hands into his shorts and grabbing two handfuls of bare ass.

"*Shane,*" he moans into my mouth, grinding his erection against my thigh.

"Toby—"

A sudden knock on the bedroom door has us jumping apart, panting and staring at each other with wide, shocked eyes as if we had no control over our own bodies just now.

"Hey, buttholes! Are you in there?"

Great. It's Jake.

"Go away!" I shout, my voice slightly hoarse.

"Oh, good! Just the person I was looking for. I'm hungry, dude!"

"*Fuck off!* I'm not your personal chef, Jake," I holler through the door, unwilling to face him right now.

"Then come with me to go get some food," he whines.

"Nah. I'm going to bed."

"Dude, you're like an old man with an early-ass bedtime. *Boring.*"

"It's not that early. Now, keep your fucking voice down," I scold. "Toby passed out, and I'm keeping an eye on him."

Toby mouths the word *hey*, folding his arms across his chest in a faux-pout.

"Of course he did. The lightweight," Jake chuckles, and I nearly laugh when Toby's eyes narrow. "Well, goodnight then."

"'Night."

I press my ear to the door and wait for the sound of Jake's heavy footsteps to disappear down the stairs before turning back around. Toby's under the covers, and the silky basketball shorts are lying on the ground again.

Shit.

I swallow thickly, unsure how far we should take this.

"I'm not gay," I blurt with absolutely no tact. "Or bi."

Toby's dimples make an appearance. "Oookay. So, if you're not gay or bi, then what was that?"

I shrug. "Don't know. Does it need a label?"

I just want him to be careful and safe. And if that means kissing me, then so be it.

"Of course not, Shane. But can we still have sleepovers?" Toby pulls the covers back, showing off his toned, tanned body in nothing but a black G-string and a pair of dimples.

Fuck me.

I groan, scrubbing a hand down my face in exasperation. He's going to be the death of my straight card.

CHAPTER ELEVEN
TOBY

L ast night was a literal dream, and I somewhat question whether it actually happened, but then I roll over, bumping into a hard body that smells like citrus, bergamot, and sweat.

Shane.

He kissed me last night. Actually fucking kissed me. And not just in my dreams. My morning wood thickens, poking his leg before I quickly pull my hips back.

Whoops.

I glance over and make sure his eyes are closed before carefully pulling the covers back and crawling out of bed. My mouth feels like I passed out on the beach and swallowed a gallon of sand. I'm desperate for one of the water bottles I keep in the mini fridge by my desk.

Twisting the cap off, I close my eyes and chug, loudly crinkling the plastic as I suck the water down. I can't help it, I'm dehydrated.

"Ahh," I exhale, tossing the empty bottle into the trash.

A throat clears behind me, and I nearly jump out of my

skin when I spin around to find Shane sitting up in bed with a smirk and a raised eyebrow.

I glance down, forgetting I'm in nothing but a little black thong and completely exposed.

"Shit! Shit! Shit!"

My hands dart in front of my junk even though he just got a full moon for God knows how long.

"You weren't this shy last night," Shane chuckles, his deep voice rough with sleep. Dark eyes roam my exposed skin as if he likes what he sees, and after that kiss, maybe he does.

Because straight boys don't make out with their best friends for no reason. *Right?*

"I obviously had a couple drinks, so I didn't care about being ninety-five percent naked in front of you like I do right now." I shuffle over to my dresser and grab a clean pair of basketball shorts, slipping them on before sitting back on the bed next to Shane.

"I see. And how do you feel about kissing me? Do you regret it?"

"What? No! Of course not." Panic starts to creep in when he continues to stare at me. "Why? Do you?"

Please say no. Please say no. Please say no.

"No."

Oh, thank God.

I hope the relief on my face isn't too obvious.

"It was nice."

Warmth blooms in my heart and in my cheeks, hope blossoming to life at the thought of kissing him again.

"A little confusing for me, but nice," Shane adds.

I know what it's like to be confused and question your sexuality. It's completely draining and isolating, and I don't want that for Shane. "I'm sorry," I whisper.

"Hey," he says, leaning forward in bed and cupping my cheek with his rough palm. "Do *not* apologize. I kissed *you*. Because I wanted to . . ."

My heartbeat whooshes in my ears, and I feel dizzy at his words.

How is this actually happening right now?

"Because I worry about you, Toby. You can't meet up with random guys."

Ohhh. I get it now.

"So, it was a pity kiss?" My voice cracks on the last word, and I glance away, fighting the tears threatening to spill over.

"Toby." I stare at the desk, chewing on my lip aggressively. "Toby. Look at me," he growls, and I can't ignore his deep voice calling my name any longer. Shane reaches out and releases my lip with his thumb, rubbing the tender flesh. "It was never about pity . . . I just . . . I can't *stand* the thought of another man putting his mouth on you. His hands . . ."

My world stops, and my mind goes blank.

"When I saw you in Tate's stories, the fear in my gut was visceral, and I had no choice but to leave work and come get you."

The reminder that Shane lost his job hits me like a ton of bricks, crushing any joy I was feeling at hearing him actually express his feelings. He hides his emotions and buries things deep down. Always has. "You lost your job because of me?"

"I didn't lose it, I quit." He folds his arms across his chest, unremorseful.

"What? Why did you quit?" Shane's on his own when it comes to money, and he's had a job ever since he was fourteen and legally able to.

"Because I left the kitchen during a shift again, and Raúl was gonna fire me. I can't have that. I should have quit a long time ago, Toby. You know I hate that asshole. Don't worry about it."

It still feels like it's my fault, but another thing he said rings like an alarm bell in my head. "You said *again* . . . When was the other time you left in the middle of a shift?" Shane hesitates to answer, and it feels a little weird. "Was it because of me again?" My brows crease, trying to think of when it could have been.

"When you had a coffee date across the street from The Sandbar," he admits, completely unashamed and unapologetic.

"Oh my God! You *are* a stalker!" I laugh, playfully slapping him on the bicep and letting my hand linger on his bare skin a little too long, maybe even giving it a squeeze.

"Not just *a* stalker. *Your* stalker," he corrects me with a shrug. "I have to keep you safe, Tobes. I always have, and I always will."

My heart melts at his words, completely understanding how all the damsels in distress feel in the historical romance novels I love. "Wait, so you sacrificed your job to protect me?"

That's kind of hot, even though I feel terrible about it.

"Yes," he says matter-of-factly, staring directly into my eyes and causing strange things to happen to my insides.

I swallow hard and lick my lips, wishing he'd make another move and kiss me again. His dark eyes dart down to my mouth and linger there.

"What're you gonna do?" I ask breathlessly, knowing he needs a job to pay for school.

Kiss me, Shane.
Kiss me.

He breaks the spell I was under and whips the covers back, getting out of bed. "To start, I'm gonna go make breakfast. Come down in thirty." Shane leaves me stewing in desire, and I flop back on the bed, staring up at the old ceiling fan with dust clinging to its edges.

I trace a finger over my lips, remembering the ghost of his kiss and dying for another.

It's basically my fault that Shane lost his job, so I made a phone call and got him an interview with the catering company my family has used a few times over the years. It pays a lot better than Raúl, so selfishly, I'm excited by the idea of him having more free time. And of course, less stress and more money.

But one thing about Shane is that he doesn't accept help very easily, so I have to go about this carefully and strategically, choosing my words wisely. "So, don't be mad, but—"

"That's not really how you should start a conversation, Tobes," Shane deadpans, continuing to work on his Econ homework at the kitchen island, while I attempt to study Music History and fail. My mind is preoccupied with how to tell him about the interview.

"Whoops. You're right," I chuckle, setting my highlighter down.

Guess that went a lot better in my head.

"But this is actually a really good thing. I promise!"

Shane looks skeptical, so I just blurt out the good news.

"I got you an interview with Coastal Cuisine, one of the best catering companies in town. It's pretty much a shoo-in because I've known Glenn for years, and he loves me.

They've catered a few of my parents' parties, and the food is amazing. You would fit right in."

Shane keeps his emotions close to his chest, so I can't tell what he's thinking. "Do your parents know? Were they involved?"

He doesn't want a handout from them, and I don't blame him one bit.

"No. Of course not. The owners of the company are a kind, older couple, and I know them personally. They don't even like my parents," I chuckle.

I can see the wheels turning, and I really hope he says yes.

He needs this.

He *deserves* this.

"Just let me help you for once, like you always help me," I plead, picking at the corner of my textbook.

"Okay. Thank you, Toby. *Really*. Just tell me when and where, and I'll be there." A small smile pulls at his lips, and my heart stutters at the beauty that is Shane Carmichael smiling and happy.

I need to see it more often.

CHAPTER TWELVE
SHANE

It's been over a week since I started my new catering job at Coastal Cuisine, and I think I like it here. Glenn and his wife have been extremely welcoming. I'm so grateful that Toby hooked me up with this opportunity, but I've had to work more hours than I normally would each day this week in order to get up to speed with my new responsibilities. That, paired with classes, means I haven't seen Toby all that much. To be honest, I feel a little guilty about it after our kiss. He's an overthinker, and the last thing I want is him spiraling into a panic attack.

It's Friday night, and I'm home late after a sweet sixteen party where I monitored the food tables and kept them stocked while also being harassed and hit on by over a dozen teenage girls. It wasn't ideal, but the tip sure as hell was.

When I step inside, I find my roommates sprawled on the couches in the living room with an action movie playing on the TV.

Toby looks up from his phone with a smile on his face. "How was your night?" he asks politely.

"Teenage girls," I reply, deadpan.

Jake hisses. "Yikes, man. I *know* they ate you alive. You're too pretty and too broody."

I turn unamused eyes toward him. "That suplex is calling your name," I warn.

Jake cackles, and Spencer tosses a throw pillow at his face. "Leave the poor man alone, he's clearly been through enough tonight."

I glance at Toby, whose attention is on his phone, thumbs flying across the screen.

Who the hell is he messaging?

I thought I got through to him.

"I'm taking a shower," I grunt, slipping off my work shoes by the front door. I make my way upstairs and go straight to the bathroom, locking myself inside.

The water feels incredible, loosening my overworked muscles and crowded mind. I can't stop thinking about Toby talking to random guys that treat him like shit. He's downstairs at this very moment, smiling at his phone and possibly arranging to meet up with someone. I can't let that happen. The urge to protect him burns like fire through my veins, making my blood boil at the thought of Toby getting hurt.

After thoroughly rinsing out the deep conditioning treatment that Daija got me for Christmas, I turn off the shower and wrap a towel around my waist. I slip out of the steamy bathroom and head to my room, quickly applying some lotion before throwing a pair of gray sweats and a white T-shirt on. Roughly scrubbing the towel over my head, I leave my hair messy and damp, jogging down the stairs to join my roommates.

They're right where I left them, Jake and Spencer staring at the TV like a couple of zombies, while Toby is still engrossed in his phone. I grit my teeth, walking over to the love seat and plopping down right next to him with my entire weight. Toby topples into me, dropping his phone to the ground. "*Shane!*" he cries, reaching for it.

The phone lands face up by my feet, so I lean down and snatch it up, catching a glimpse of the message thread before Toby rips it out of my hands.

"*Shane!*" he whisper-shouts. "Stop trying to look at my conversations. *God*, you are such a stalker!"

"Conversations, as in plural?" I ask cynically. "Are you talking to more than one guy?"

Toby huffs, folding his arms across his chest and refusing to answer the question.

That wasn't a no.

"*Why the hell are you back on Grindr?*" I hiss, glancing over at Jake, who's now stretched out on the couch snoring, and Spencer, who's fixing a sandwich in the kitchen.

I thought I got through to him after our kiss. I know I've been focused on learning my new job and proving myself to Glenn this week, but what the hell is this bullshit about a second date that I just saw?

None of those guys are good enough for him.

I need to show him what he deserves. Prove it to him.

The thought hits me full force, leaving me with no other option.

"I'm taking you out on a date," I declare, not caring what our roommates or anyone else will think.

"You . . . *what?*" Toby asks incredulously, uncrossing his arms and blinking slowly.

"I'm going to plan something special, take you out next weekend, and show you how a real man should treat you. Then you can delete that stupid app."

Toby's amber eyes flare with lust, flicking to my mouth.

We haven't kissed since the night I rescued him from the bar and that fuckboy Landon, but I can tell he wants to.

"Okay," he agrees, his smile slowly growing until his dimples pop out. "I'll go on a date with you."

What the fuck am I doing?

The last thing I would ever want to do is ruin this friendship. Toby's all I have. The best thing in my life.

The Crescent Bay Botanical Garden is about forty minutes away from campus and right on the ocean. Besides acres of beautiful plant life and an orchid observatory, they have a beer garden, nature trails, and a wildlife preserve. But most importantly, there's a butterfly house.

"I've been planning our date in my head all week," I admit, and Toby smiles over at me from the passenger seat of my pickup truck. We're still parked in the driveway, getting ready to start the short trip. "I have a clue for you."

Toby beams, sunlight flooding the truck and illuminating his golden irises. "What is it?"

"Close your eyes," I tell him, and he listens. I lean over and open the glove compartment, grabbing the purple origami butterfly I made last night and holding it in my palm. "Open your eyes," I whisper into his ear, eliciting a cute little shiver from him.

Toby smiles wide, picking it up to inspect it. "Hmmm. A butterfly. Are we going on a picnic?"

"Nope. Guess again," I reply with a small smile, feeling carefree and light. Placing my arm behind Toby's headrest, I twist in my seat and back out of the driveway slowly. The fact that he stares at me the whole time doesn't go unnoticed, and my smile only grows.

Toby clears his throat. "Um. A hike through wildflowers?"

A deep chuckle rolls out of me. "No."

"Gardening?"

"*What?* No," I laugh. "There will be no chores on this date."

"*Ooo!* I got it," he says confidently. "A nature museum."

"Close, but no cigar."

"What? *Ugh.* I give up," Toby says with a pout, sinking into his seat and staring out the window.

Keeping one hand on the wheel, I reach over to give his thigh a reassuring squeeze.

It just feels right.

"So are you really not going to tell me where we're going?" he tries again.

"Nope, but snacks are in the back and drinks are in the cooler," I inform him, glancing over to catch his dimples appear.

"Oh, sweet." Toby digs through the bags in the backseat. "Teriyaki jerky and gummy worms. My favorite road trip snacks."

"Grab me a Dr Pepper," I ask, happier than I've been in months.

The drive is easy, and soon enough, we're pulling into the parking lot of our destination. Toby's face lights up in recognition.

"Oh my God, we're going to see the butterflies!"

Before we visit the Butterfly Bungalow, we stop at the Orchid Observatory and walk through the humid greenhouse full of rock-wall waterfalls, climbing orchids, hanging moss, and a plethora of other exotic plant life.

It's beautiful here, and I know Toby agrees because he's taking photos of nearly everything.

"Are you ready to see the butterflies now?" I ask, throwing an arm around his shoulders and tugging him close. "I mean, they *are* still your favorite insect, right?" I tease, giving him a playful squeeze.

"Actually, yeah. They are, you asshole," he chuckles, fake elbowing me in the side and making me laugh.

I keep my arm around him as we walk down the path to the greenhouse where the butterflies live, observing the beautiful plants, flowers, and water features along the way.

"Hi! I'm Lettie. Welcome to the Butterfly Bungalow," a small woman with bright orange hair greets us. "Step in here, and I'll go over the rules." She smiles kindly, opening a curtain of plastic strips. "Okay, the rules are simple. Keep the curtains closed so no butterflies escape. Do not touch the butterflies. If they land on you, that's okay, of course. Stay on the path and watch your step. We have a lot of caterpillars as well, and we don't want any squished. There are nectar sticks in small bowls; be sure to grab one before you enter the bungalow. And most importantly, have a great time!"

"Ready?" I ask Toby, lifting my arm from around his shoulders and grabbing two sticks with small sponges on the end. I hand one to Toby, and we step into a tiny bustling world full of colorful butterflies, flowers, and cute little green caterpillars. We start slowly, watching our step as we begin walking the circular, looping pathway through the bungalow.

"Whoa," Toby says in awe. "This is so freaking cool."

I smile at the enthusiasm for science and bugs that he's had since he was a kid.

A butterfly suddenly lands on my stick, its tiny tongue sucking up the nectar.

Toby leans closer to get a better look. "That's called the proboscis. It's a coiled tube that unrolls to feed from flowers."

"Like a straw?" I ask.

Toby giggles, making the butterfly fly away. "Yeah, basically."

When the next butterfly lands on my stick, I call Toby over, slowly transferring it to his. I snap a couple photos for him and just stand there, watching the sheer joy on his face, and I realize I fucking love making him happy.

"This is a male monarch," Toby whispers, his golden eyes analyzing the butterfly closely.

"How the hell do you know it's male?" I ask, not really wanting to think about it, but Toby just laughs.

"It's actually really easy. They have two black dots on their hindwings. See there." He points to the bottom of the butterfly without getting too close, so I lean in, taking a better look at the little orange butterfly eating from Toby's nectar stick.

"Huh. Sure does," I murmur, impressed by his butterfly knowledge.

I take a few more photos of him before we get a selfie that we both upload to social media, tagging the location. Tate immediately comments how cute and happy we look, followed by Daija. I snort at Jake's comment, asking why he wasn't invited, and put my phone away, focusing on the date.

"Whenever you're ready, they have a beer garden that also has iced tea and lemonade," I tell him.

"Sounds perfect." Toby smiles back at me, his cheeks flushed from the sun and the heat. "But can we walk around the bungalow one more time?"

"Of course, Tobes."

I'm so glad he's having such a great time.

We make another loop, and I find myself watching Toby instead of looking at butterflies. Toby identifies even more, taking a photo to document them. We finish our second loop and thank Lettie before leaving.

Toby and I walk over to the Beer Garden for some shade and a cool drink. A small, wooden bar is shaded by trellises filled with different plant life, from climbing vines to bright, exotic flowers.

"This is so cute," Toby whispers as we make our way over, ordering two lemonades from the older lady behind the bar.

I buy the drinks, and Toby stuffs a ten into her tip jar. "Thank you, this place is so beautiful," he says politely before we head over to a large gazebo with picnic tables.

"I'm having a really great time, Shane," Toby says sweetly, before taking a sip of his ice-cold lemonade. "*Ahh.*" He smacks his lips. "So good."

He leans forward and slips the map from his back pocket, pointing at where we are. "We're here. And if we keep going down this trail, we'll hit the snapdragons and then the Rose Garden."

"Sounds good to me," I say, enjoying the shade and the cool breeze.

Toby takes his hand off the map for a second, and the wind picks it up, blowing it off the table and onto the ground. He turns around on the bench and bends over, his underwear peeking out of his jeans. It's not even a thong this time, just regular boxers, but I can't stop picturing him in that tiny black G-string and imagining what he would look like in something colorful and lacy.

What in the actual fuck?

I'm not sure what's happening to me. It's like ever since Toby came out to me, I've been questioning everything about my own sexuality. Because girls have always just been a means to an end for me, and the thought of another man putting his hands or lips on my best friend makes me want to destroy things. I push the life-altering thoughts away because now is not the time to figure it out.

We finish our drinks and start walking toward the snapdragons next, taking photos with the bright pink flowers before we end our date in the Rose Garden.

"Wow. It's stunning here," Toby says in awe, spinning around in a circle for a three-hundred-and-sixty-degree view. Towering rose bushes of all colors surround us, broken up by paved pathways and rows of arches looped and woven with even more roses.

The relaxing sound of flowing water from the many fountains, combined with bees buzzing, and the warmth of the sun, sends a shot of dopamine straight to my brain, happiness radiating from within me. I glance over at my best friend, and judging by the dopey smile on his face, it looks like he's experiencing the same thing. Stepping into his space, I stare down at his lips.

Fuck. I want to kiss him right now.

The thought comes out of nowhere, and I immediately shut it down, stepping back from Toby and the second kiss we were about to share.

What if it ruins our friendship?

Having Toby in my life is too important to me, and I'm not willing to mess it up. The disappointment in his eyes is clear as day, but these new desires are something I'm not quite ready to face.

"Ready to head home?" I ask, not missing the flicker of disappointment.

Maybe I'm already ruining our friendship without even realizing it.

CHAPTER THIRTEEN
TOBY

I wake up to the mouthwatering smell of bacon and something sweet. "Mmm," I moan to myself, rolling over and stretching my arms above my head while arching my back. The smell is so delicious, it's luring me out of bed before eight on a Sunday.

"Breakfast for the third morning in a row?" I ask with a yawn as I stroll into the kitchen.

"Now that I don't work so much, I have more time." Shane shrugs, and I wish I could hug him, but Jake and Spencer are sitting at the island, inhaling all the bacon.

"I'm not complaining. This is amazing," I say, grabbing a plate. "Save some bacon for me, assholes," I joke, taking my own handful before it's gone.

Shane is busy at the stove, adding more pancakes to the platter. He grabs a pair of tongs and serves two piping hot, round flapjacks to Spencer's plate. The next two are for me, and they're shaped like hearts.

"Aww. How sweet," I say, trying to laugh it off and fight the blush threatening to take over. It's a simple gesture, but it shows that he cares, and I don't take that for granted.

Jake's next, and Shane slaps two oddly shaped pancakes onto his plate, and I have to do a double-take at what I see.

"What the—" Jake's brow's scrunch together, and he tilts his head slightly.

I press my hand to my mouth, holding my plate with the other.

"Eat a dick," Shane taunts good naturedly.

"*Ahahaha!*" Spencer howls with laughter, nearly falling off of his barstool.

"Alright. Alright. You got me, you got me," Jake concedes with a grin. "But Ima still eat these. Should I start with the balls or the tip?"

"Oh my lord above," I murmur under my breath, scurrying off to the dining room table while Jake eats his phallus-shaped pancakes in private.

"So, what do you want to do today?" I ask Shane with a big smile, cutting into the fluffiest and cutest pancakes ever. I'm so happy the catering job is working out well and allowing him more free time to enjoy life.

"I already made plans," Shane says casually, taking another bite without looking up.

My smile drops, and a sharp pang jabs my heart. I guess the kiss was too much, and the butterfly date wasn't as epic as I thought.

Shane must see the spiraling despair on my face because he quickly corrects himself. "For both of us."

Oh, thank God.

"Another date?" I ask hopefully, my stomach fluttering with excitement and anticipation.

What did I do to deserve these surprises?

I guess the more accurate question is, what did I do to deserve Shane? Because he is the best man I have ever met, and he doesn't need to take me on a date to prove it. I've known for ten years. Shane is my person, and I hope that never changes.

"You didn't think I'd stop after one date, did you?"

A small smile tugs at my lips, and I shrug. I didn't place any expectations on whatever is going on here; I just keep reminding myself that Shane is straight.

"So where are we going?" I ask, finishing off my last piece of bacon. "Will you tell me this time?"

Shane nods. "Yeah. We have to pack accordingly, so I kinda have to. We're going to Driftwood Beach."

"No freaking way!" I shout in excitement. I've heard it's like another world out there, and I've always wanted to go.

"Yup. That's why I'm up so early. I wanna get there during low tide. It's the best time of day."

He's so thoughtful and so prepared. I fucking love being his passenger princess.

A narrow, sandy path cuts through the salt marsh, leading us from the parking lot to the ocean. It's close to a mile walk, but as soon as the palmettos thin out and we step onto the beach, my jaw drops in awe.

It was worth it.

"*Whoa.* It's like an ancient tree burial ground. This is so cool."

I feel like Simba when he finds the elephant graveyard, or like I just stepped onto an alien planet. It's otherworldly here, and I can't believe I've never seen this place before.

Weathered trees and broken driftwood for as far as the eye can see, their twisted, gnarly-looking carcasses littering the sand for miles. The wood is smooth and gray, polished by the sea and exposed by years of erosion.

It's heavily protected here, so we can't take anything home from the beach, even the shells. It's against the law and comes with a hefty fine, but man, is this an incredible place to visit.

"Would you look at the size of 'em," Shane murmurs, just as mesmerized as I am. He ghosts a hand over a large tree lying on its side like it was ripped straight from the ground and flung across the ocean. Some are buried deep in the sand and barely poking out.

"A sand dollar! Shane, look!" I shout with pure excitement, pointing down to the white disc-shaped creature that's been dead for God knows how long.

The seashells are so beautiful here, and it hurts my collector heart not to be able to take any home with me. One of my favorite things to do growing up on the beach in Crescent Bay was shelling in my own backyard.

As we explore the beach, comfortable and enjoying our date, I slip into a fond memory from the past.

"Hey, wanna collect seashells?" I ask with a big, excited smile. It's one of my favorite things about living right on the beach, and I've never had someone to go with me before. Sometimes it's not very fun being an only child, but now I have a best friend.

Shane shrugs like he doesn't really care either way, continuing to stare lifelessly at the TV in my bedroom.

"Do you not like the sand or something?" I ask hesitantly, or maybe he's afraid of the water.

"I've only been to the beach once, so I don't really know."

"But you've lived here longer than me. How have you only been once?" My brows crease, and I tilt my head in confusion, trying to understand how that could be possible.

"My mom works at the flower shop all the time and stays

with her boyfriend a lot. I don't really get to do anything but watch TV."

Sadness tugs on my heart, imagining him home alone all the time. I know exactly how that feels. "My parents are always working, too, but now we have each other," I tell him with a smile. "We can make our own fun. Come on." I grab his hand and attempt to pull him up from the couch. It doesn't really work since he's so much bigger than me, but Shane stands up, nonetheless. "Roll up your jeans and take off your socks. We're going to the beach."

Shane came over for dinner and met my parents a couple weeks ago, and now my mom said I can have him over whenever I want on the weekend. I'm pretty sure she's just happy I have someone to keep me busy so she doesn't have to, but that's okay because I feel the same. And I definitely didn't tell her Shane was held back a year, or she probably wouldn't be so welcoming. In fact, I know she wouldn't. My parents expect nothing short of straight A's, so they wouldn't understand someone else's struggles.

"Let's go explore!" I shout, grabbing Shane's hand again and tugging him across the porch and down the small boardwalk to the private beach in my backyard.

A sense of excitement fills me when I step onto the soft, fluffy sand that's nice and warm beneath my bare feet. I feel a sense of peace out here with nature that I can't really explain.

We find a dried sand dollar and a couple really cool intact whelks. I spread a towel down, sitting on it with Shane, and looking at our collection, when a flock of birds lands nearby.

"Look, pigeons!" I say excitedly, getting up slowly and tiptoeing over to them.

"Shhh. Walk very slowly or you'll scare them," I whisper to Shane, reaching into my pocket and pulling out a handful of birdseed I poured in there before we left the house.

I toss some on the ground, attracting the birds to me. I hold my hand out, keeping it still while they slowly peck their way over, eating right out of my hand until it's all gone.

Looking up at Shane, I block the sun with my hand. "What?"

"I've never met anyone as nice as you. Even to pigeons."

"Pigeons are really smart, actually. Humans domesticated them thousands of years ago, using them for communication until the telephone was invented. Then they were cast back into nature with no survival skills of their own. People give them a bad rap, but they're just trying to adapt to their environment and live, just like the rest of us."

"How do you know all that?"

I shrug. "I didn't have any friends until I met you, and I like to learn. Want to feed them?"

Shane squats down next to me, and I pour some birdseed into his hand, giggling when he looks a little squeamish as a pigeon gently pecks at his hand. I dump the rest of the seed on the sand for them and stand up. "Come on. Let's find some more shells. We can make friendship necklaces."

We lose track of time exploring the beach, and my stomach growls loud enough to be heard over the waves, alerting us both to the fact that it's already lunchtime.

"Guess I'm hungry again," I laugh, pressing a hand to my belly.

"Good thing I packed a picnic."

"Oh my God, no way. You did?!" That literally sounds so perfect right now.

"Yup."

We start the mile-long trek back to the parking lot, and

by the time we get there, I'm fucking famished, but I keep the urge to complain at bay.

Shane opens the tailgate and lays out a thick blanket before grabbing the cooler from the backseat. "We have chicken salad sandwiches, kiwi-pineapple fruit salad, and chips. Nothing fancy."

"It's absolutely perfect, Shane. This whole date has been. *Thank you.*"

Luckily, we're in the shade, so we get comfortable in the bed of the truck and dig into our food, completely drained by the sun and the sea.

"*Mmm,*" I hum, devouring half my sandwich in just a few bites. "So good," I murmur with my mouth full, washing it down with a swig of orange soda.

When I glance over at Shane, he quickly looks away, and I practically preen like a horny peacock. I don't say anything, of course, enjoying the feeling of power it gives me. I try the tangy fruit salad next, and close my eyes at the cool, refreshing flavors.

I could eat Shane's food for the rest of my life.

After we finish eating, we lounge in the back and rest our bellies. I'm so content and comfortable that I nearly drift off.

"Ready to hit the road?" Shane suddenly asks, hopping off the back of the truck and holding his arms out, offering me a hand.

I take the help and wrap my arms around his neck, sliding down his bare chest. Our sweat mingles, and my skin tingles where it touches his. My poor heart is beating so fast you'd think I was running for my life instead of being held in the arms of a beautifully strong man. Shane pauses for a second before he sets me down, staring deep into my eyes, then flicking his gaze down to my lips. The rest of the world melts away at this moment, and it's just the two of us.

Kiss me!

I shout the words at him in my head, too insecure to voice them out loud.

Indecision flickers in his dark eyes before he sets me on my feet and turns away instead. With a deep sigh, I steel my resolve and try not to let the lost moment ruin our date.

Persistence and patience are key here.

Today has been one of the best days I've had in a really long time, and there's something completely magical about being here with Shane.

I think I'm falling for my best friend more than I thought was ever possible.

CHAPTER FOURTEEN
TOBY

Our date to Driftwood Beach was just as amazing as the butterfly house, but Shane still hasn't kissed me. Not since that very first time, and it has me overthinking *everything*.

Another week of school passes, distracting me from the confusion that is my dating life, but now it's Friday night, and I'm back to contemplating my entire existence. Shane has a catering gig, so instead of pacing my bedroom alone, I'm hanging out with Tate and Daija at their apartment and having a much-needed sleepover.

"Strawberry margaritas are ready!" Daija calls from the kitchen. "Come and get 'em!"

Tate pauses the TV, and we jump up from the couch where we were just zoned out, re-watching *Bridgerton*.

"We need to bake cookies later. Before we get too drunk," Daija says, sipping her drink and humming. "Yum."

I take a tentative sip, but the sweet, strawberry flavor easily hides how much tequila she most likely put in these.

"Girl, these are so fucking good," Tate says, taking

another large gulp before we carry our drinks back to the living room.

"If either of you spills on my couches, you're getting a spanking," Daija says, brown eyes sparkling. "And not the fun kind." She tucks her long legs underneath her, pulling the turquoise throw blanket off the back of the couch and draping it across her lap.

"Don't threaten me with a good time, babe. You know I like that sort of thing."

Daija laughs, picking up the remote and throwing it at him. "Let's watch a movie, you freak. I've seen this episode three times."

"I already scrolled for thirty minutes before I gave up and put *Bridgerton* back on," Tate whines.

Daija sighs. "Fine, whatever. That way we can chat. Toby needs to update us on his love life."

Tate presses play on the episode we were just watching, turning down the volume and facing me enthusiastically. "Well, go on." He sips his margarita. "How was your latest date? To the beach, right?"

"Yeah. To Driftwood Beach. It was really cool. Beautiful actually. I just . . ."

"You just what, babe?" Daija encourages.

"I just wish it was for real. I wish he really liked me, and I wish he would *kiss* me. Something in the back of my brain keeps insisting this is all for pity."

Self-doubt is a bitch.

I didn't tell them that we actually did kiss before any of these dates started. It would feel like a betrayal to Shane. But they do know he's taking me out in order to show me how a man should treat me, and they also know I've been secretly pining after him for years. It's all just a mess. A confusing, gay mess.

"He likes you, silly! These dates may be PG-rated, but the man is practically in looove," Tate teases. "Listen, I can recognize a straight boy falling into a *gay for you* situationship when I see it." He picks up his phone from the end table, his painted thumbs flying across the keyboard.

"What?" I laugh.

"Oh, yes. That's totally what's happening here," Daija agrees. "He's so possessive."

"Those aren't just friendly, bro outings, they're full-on romantic dates without the kissing or fucking. I've seen this before, honey," Tate says confidently. "Let me give you the rundown. He's most likely going round and round in his head, winding the string tighter and tighter until one day . . . it all just goes *boom!*" Tate shouts the last word with an exaggerated hand explosion, making Daija and me both jump and nearly spill our drinks.

"Huh? What goes boom?" I'm so confused right now.

"His straight card, of course! And you, my dearest Toby boy, need to be prepared for that day." A few more taps on his phone before he sets it back down. "*There.* You have a special delivery coming."

"What?" I feel like a broken record, but I wish he'd just spit it out and stop talking in riddles. "What do you mean I need to be prepared, and what the heck did you just order?" I ask suspiciously, certain he didn't buy me the new strings I've been wanting.

"Call me when you get your package, and then we'll talk. If you still need your questions answered." Tate giggles, glancing at Daija with a sly, knowing grin.

"*You guys!* This isn't fair, just freaking tell me!" I whine, making them laugh even louder.

"Okay, okay," Tate gives in. "But don't freak out." He

grabs his phone again, smiling mischievously before handing it over.

I gaze down at the screen, a large, flesh-colored dildo, complete with veins and a pink tip, staring back at me.

"It's not as big as it looks in the picture!" Tate insists. "It's actually considered introductory size. Promise!"

"Yeah, you should see the size of Tate's dildo," Daija teases.

"And I'm proud of it!" Tate fluffs his curls. "It's taken me years to work up to it."

I swallow hard, completely intimidated by the idea of putting something up my butt.

Tate bursts out laughing, his blond curls bouncing around his face. "Don't look so scared, babe! It has ten different vibration modes, so you can start slow. I know you're gonna like it. You just have to get used to it. Think of this as another tryout for Team Dick."

Tate sets his drink down, standing up with a carefree smile like he didn't just order a massive, vibrating dildo that I'm supposed to practice with. "Face mask time?"

"*Yeah!*" Daija jumps up from the couch, running to the kitchen. "And cookies!"

"Tobes, it's your turn to pick something," Tate says, smiling down at me.

"And *Bridgerton*," I mumble reluctantly, completely embarrassed by his lack of a filter, even though I know he only has my best interests at heart.

Guess it's time to find out what butt play feels like.

I can't stop thinking about the X-rated package that's coming in the mail while I lie here on Tate and Daija's couch trying to fall asleep. It's past midnight, but my mind is dizzy with fantasies, and the two margaritas I drank sure aren't helping.

What will the dildo feel like?

Will I like it?

Can I even take it?

Soft, fuzzy images of Shane float into my thoughts. His kind, patient eyes provide comfort and reassurance, telling me not to doubt myself. Insisting I can do it.

I drift further into the fantasy, the edges of reality starting to blur when Shane kisses me. My fingers ghost over my lips as if to check whether this is real, and despite the fact that it's not, I can't stop what's playing out in my head even if I wanted to.

"Let me help you," Fantasy Shane urges, the dildo appearing in his hands in the blink of an eye, followed by an extra-large bottle of lube. "Let me make you feel good."

"Yes. Please, Shane. I want you to," I moan, and I'm so lost in the fantasy that I can only pray that I said the words in my head and not out loud.

His tall frame stalks toward me, the haze of dreamworld surrounding him and slightly morphing his features. He looks hungry and determined and ready to make me beg.

A sudden buzzing sound startles me, shattering the perfect facade I built so beautifully in my mind. I grab my phone from the coffee table, squinting at the way-too-bright screen. It's a text from Shane.

> Hope you had a good night.

Chewing on my bottom lip, I debate whether it's too late to text him back or not.

Fuck it. I'm too drunk to care. Besides, he texted me first.

> I did, but I missed you the whole time.

The text bubbles appear then disappear a couple times before he sends his response.

> Missed you too.

> Hope I didn't wake you.

> You didn't. Can't sleep.

I blush at what was actually going through my mind instead of sleeping, and now I feel a little guilty about my inappropriate fantasies involving my best friend.

> Everything okay? Want me to come get you?

Butterflies swarm my stomach, and I practically melt into the couch with his thoughtfulness. I'm on the verge of saying yes, but I decide not to be so dramatic.

> All good here. Just a restless brain, but thanks for the offer. See you tomorrow.

> Night.

I close my eyes, finally drifting off to sleep with a silly little smile on my face. If my fantasy were to ever come true, I think I'd simply pass away.

CHAPTER FIFTEEN
SHANE

What the hell am I doing?

Sure, taking Toby out on all these bro dates has been a lot of fun, but I've been delaying the inevitable reality of him eventually finding a boyfriend and dating someone for real.

Because it can't be me. *Right?* I'm not gay. I've never looked at a dude and thought, *I want to fuck him*. I've never even been curious enough to watch gay porn. But Toby is different. Toby is . . . my whole entire world. And he always has been.

Being with him just feels right.

Despite the fact that he's a guy.

A knock on my bedroom door startles me from my confusing thoughts. "Ready for the fair?" Toby asks through the door. "Daija and Tate just got there."

"Yeah. I'll be down in a second," I call back, spraying cologne on each pulse point. I grab my phone and wallet, hustling downstairs to meet Toby in the foyer.

Tonight isn't really a date since we're meeting up with our friends, but I can't deny that it still has date vibes. His golden curls are styled perfectly, and the tight white T-shirt hugs him nicely. His slim body is on display, showing off an incredible physique I've never appreciated enough. Baggy jeans with holes in the knees and white Vans complete his look, and there's no denying the attention he'll draw tonight.

By the time I'm done perusing him, and we make eye contact, Toby is grinning from ear to ear like the cat that got the canary.

"*What?*" I grumble. "You look nice."

"Thank you. So do you," Toby says sweetly, returning the compliment while eyeing my black T-shirt and dark jeans.

I grunt my acknowledgement, locking up the house and guiding Toby to my truck with a hand on the small of his back. I help him up, and then we're off to the fairgrounds just fifteen minutes outside of campus.

When we arrive, Toby texts Daija, and I text Jake to meet us at the bumper cars.

"This is going to be so fun!" Toby exclaims, practically skipping with joy. "After bumper cars, I need a deep-fried Snickers."

My stomach turns at the thought of such a monstrosity, and Toby laughs.

"Come on! Bumper cars are this way." He grabs my hand and tugs before reality hits him, and he drops my hand quickly, glancing around. Everything in me wants to hold hands with him, but this place feels too public, so I hesitate.

"*Ahh!* You're here!" Daija squeals, running over to hug Toby and me, breaking up the awkwardness.

Jake and Spencer walk over right after. "Aww, where's

my hug?" Jake asks Daija with a pout, holding both arms out.

"Jakey, no. You have to earn that, babe." She taps his chest with her long nails, strutting away to the bumper cars.

Jake clasps his heart where Daija touched him, sighing loudly. "Fuck, bro. I think I'm in love. She's a goddess."

"Oh, shut up," Spencer laughs, shaking his head and walking away.

"Come on!" Tate hollers from his spot in line next to Daija. "Let's go!"

"Y'all better watch out. I'm ready to do some damage," Jake snickers before jogging off to get in line with the rest of them.

"You're sitting with me," I say matter-of-factly, staring down into my reflection in his sunglasses. "I don't trust that idiot."

"Aww. Is my bodyguard here today?" he teases, looping his arm through mine and walking us over to our friends.

"Damn straight," I tell him.

I slam the giant hammer down like Thor, making the light fly up and hit the top, declaring me the winner of a giant-sized plushie.

"Pick anything you want," the carnival guy says with a bored look, completely unimpressed by my skills.

I watch as Toby's gaze scans the wall of stuffed animals, landing on one at the very top. "That one." He points, and the man sighs with annoyance, grabbing the pole propped up in the corner and struggling to unhook it for a good three minutes. He's broken a sweat by the time he hands it over, and I kind of feel bad for the guy, but at least Toby's happy. In fact, he's beaming.

A weird sense of pride rolls through me, even though it's just a stuffed animal. "What is it?" I ask, unable to make out what the creature is besides being kinda cute.

"It's a rainbow unicorn-sloth, Shane. Three-toed, to be precise," Toby says as if I should have known, cuddling the weird looking thing to his chest.

"If you say so," I mumble as we stroll through the fairgrounds, just the two of us. Jake and Spencer ran off to chase a group of girls from CBU, and Tate and Daija went for funnel cake.

"*Shit*," Toby suddenly curses, holding the sloth higher up so that it blocks his face.

"What's wrong?" I ask, my eyes scanning the crowd for any potential threats, and finding one when they land on that prick from the movie theater.

Even though Toby's hiding his face, the asshole still recognizes me, his eyes lighting up with malice instead of fear. "If it isn't the stalker and the virgin," he taunts, and in less than five seconds, he's pressed to the closest brick wall with my forearm across his throat.

"What's your name?" I growl.

"T-Tristan," he gasps, barely able to speak.

"I thought I told you to run if you ever saw me again?"

Tristan's mouth opens and closes like a fish, desperate for air and unable to form any words.

"But you decided it was a better idea to talk shit? Hmm?"

"*Shane!* Don't!" Toby cries out, running over. "Put him down!"

I release the prick, and he falls to the ground like a

pathetic sack of shit, coughing and sputtering to catch his breath before he hops up and takes off running. "You crazy motherfucker!" he shouts once he's a safe enough distance away.

A startled laugh bursts from Toby's lips before he presses a hand to his mouth, his body shaking with mirth.

"Told you your bodyguard's always around," I say cockily, glancing over at the food stall closest to us. *Corn dogs and cheese fries.* "Come on, forget that loser and get in line with me." I tug Toby over to the queue, and we stand there patiently, like I didn't just choke out someone in front of a small crowd of people. It must be a common occurrence around here because no one bats an eye. The line moves quickly since it's just hot dogs, and soon enough, I'm ordering food to feed five people. "Can you grab the drinks?" I ask, lifting the heavy tray.

"Yeah. Got it," he replies, grabbing the two large sodas from the cashier's grasp.

"Let's find a table." Toby follows me to an empty picnic table with a view of the Ferris wheel. We sit down, covering everything in ketchup and cheese sauce before devouring our messy food in silence.

When the last cheese fry is gone, Toby finally speaks. "Shane, you can't go around beating people up like that. No matter how satisfying it is."

"I didn't beat him up, I gave him his second warning. If it happens a third time, *then* I'll beat him up," I explain evenly.

"*Shaaane!*" he whines again. "I don't want you to get in trouble because of me. Please don't."

"Toby, chill out. I'm not in trouble. That guy is a complete asshole, and I won't let him disrespect us. *Ever.*"

"You're right. He's horrible. *Ugh*," Toby says with a shiver. "Let's just forget about it and go find Tate and Daija." He hugs the sloth to his chest for comfort, burying his face into the soft fur and closing his eyes for a second, likely trying to settle his anxiety over what just happened.

I wish I could wrap my arms around him and hold him tight.

"Funnel cakes are this way." I hitch a thumb to the left, and we walk side by side without a word spoken.

Nothing but the overpowering smell of fried food fills the air while the afternoon sun blazes down on us, making me break out in a sweat. The ocean breeze is the only thing stopping it from being unbearable. There's a mix of people here today. Some families, some couples, and a lot of students from both CBU and the local high school. Our slow stroll across the fairgrounds helps me digest the massive amount of greasy food we just ate for lunch.

"Wanna go for a ride?" Toby asks, nodding toward the temporary death trap that's set up right next to the funnel cake stand.

I don't trust carnival rides, and especially not a fucking roller coaster.

"Coaster time, bitches!" Jake suddenly shouts out of nowhere, rushing up behind us and jumping on my back like he's getting a fucking piggyback ride.

"Get off me." I shrug him off and punch him in the arm.

"*Ouch!*" He chuckles, rubbing the spot. "Turn that frown upside down, and get in line with us," Jake teases. "Me and Spence call dibs on the front row."

"It'll be fun. Come on, Shane," Toby encourages, smiling up at me.

"Fine," I grunt, not too thrilled about it, but unwilling to spoil the fun.

"Yo, Tate! Daija!" Spencer hollers at our friends sitting at a nearby picnic table and motions them over to us with both hands.

"If I barf up my funnel cake, one of you boys is buying me a new one," Tate says, reluctantly getting in line with the rest of us.

"Gross," Toby chuckles, climbing up and perching on the metal railing while I lean against it. His knees poke through the giant holes in his jeans, and his leg hairs shine in the sunlight, catching my eye. I glance away quickly before I'm caught staring.

"Looks like just a few more rides, and then it'll be our turn," Spencer informs us, standing on his tippy toes to look over everyone's heads. "Let people skip if you have to, so we can all be on the same coaster."

We all nod, and soon enough, it's our turn to climb aboard, with Spencer and Jake in the front, followed by Tate and Daija, and then Toby and me in the back. There are a couple more carts behind us, but it's a much smaller roller coaster than at an amusement park.

"Ready?" Toby asks with a big smile.

I grunt, tugging on his lap belt one more time because I don't trust the fucking teenagers running this thing. *It's sketchy as hell.* Facing forward, I rest my head back against the seat and close my eyes as we roll out of the covered loading area. We swing around the corner and immediately start our ascent for the big drop, which is the main feature.

"*Woohoo!* Yeah, baby! You can see the ocean up here, look!" Jake shouts, his arm sticking out of the ride and pointing at the horizon.

"Whoa," Toby murmurs in awe, and I barely hear him over the *thunk thunk thunk* of the chain on the tracks.

"Okay, everyone! Arms up!" Jake yells as we crest the

peak, and all my friends, including Toby, put their arms straight up like they have all the faith in the world that this thing was set up correctly in the middle of a parking lot.

"*Toby!*" I growl, but it's too late, and we're racing down the steep drop, my stomach floating up my throat like we're in zero gravity. Toby pops off his seat an inch, and in a lightning-fast move, I reach over, grabbing onto his thigh and keeping him pressed down. The wind whooshes in my ears, helping to drown out everyone's screams.

How can anyone call this fun?

After a few more sharp turns, we pull back into the loading area, coming to an abrupt stop and nearly causing me whiplash.

"*Oh my God.* I almost flew outta my seat!" Toby shouts, laughing hysterically.

"I know. Happens when you ride a shitty carnival coaster and don't hold on," I deadpan.

"Oh, boo hoo, Mr. Grumpy Pants," Tate teases, unbuckling his seatbelt and climbing out of the cart once the useless metal bar lifts. "Let's go look at the photo. Twenty bucks says Shane isn't smiling. Any takers?"

The rest of us climb out of the carts in silence, and I'm not even offended. I probably wasn't smiling.

"Crickets," Jake says like a smartass, making Daija giggle. He beams with pride, like he just accomplished a lifelong goal to make her laugh. "No one is dumb enough to throw away twenty dollars in this economy, because there ain't no way that man is smiling."

"Yeah. Yeah," I grumble, and everyone laughs.

We round the corner and stop at a small photo kiosk tucked between two palm trees. There's an old computer monitor on the counter, cycling through the most recent groups of people. When it lands on our photo, everyone bursts out laughing, and I just snort, shaking my head at how ridiculous the six of us look.

Toby is wide-eyed and full of excited terror, nearly slipping out of his seat. I'm stone-cold serious, reaching over to hold him down by a leg. Tate and Daija are relatively normal looking, with their arms up and big, wide smiles. Then there's Spencer and Jake, flipping off the camera with their tongues out like a couple of dogs catching flies on the highway.

"*Oh my God*. It's too fucking funny, I can't!" Tate cries, tears leaking from his eyes.

"It's like a bad album cover," Spencer chuckles.

"No, it's fucking perfect," Jake corrects. "I'll take one," he says to the kid behind the counter. "This is getting framed and going on our mantel, boys."

"Make that two, please," Tate adds. "Daija and I need a copy for our place."

"Do we really, babe?" Daija raises her eyebrow.

"You know you wanna see this handsome face in your living room every day," Jake jokes, holding up his copy and flapping it in the air.

Daija snorts and rolls her eyes, but no one misses her little half-smile. "I'll be right back. I'm going to the ladies' room."

"Coming with you, honey," Tate calls out, following after her.

Jake turns to us once they're gone. "I'm growing on her. *I know it*."

Spencer and I glance at each other and shake our heads while Toby giggles next to me.

She's completely out of his league.

"*What?*" Jake says defensively. "What was that look for? You don't think she likes me?"

Spencer holds his hands up in surrender. "Bro, I'm not getting involved in that one."

"Me neither," Toby adds.

Jake looks at me next. "Shane? Got something to say?"

"Nah, bro. Just don't do anything stupid," I warn.

"Why the hell are you gonna jinx me like that?!" Jake throws his arms up in the air, letting them flop back down in exasperation.

Jake doesn't need a jinx to do anything stupid. It's pretty much his default. A done deal.

"We're back!" Tate suddenly shouts, appearing out of nowhere. "Who wants frozen lemonade? Daija and I are gonna get some. It's by the Ferris wheel."

"I'm still stuffed," Toby says, "but we'll follow you over there." He looks at me with doe eyes brimming with anticipation. "Can we ride the Ferris wheel?"

When I don't answer right away, he resorts to begging. "Come on, Shane. *Please.* It'll be really fun."

"*Fine*," I grumble, unable to say no to him.

Toby beams from ear to ear, and all six of us head over to the other side of the fairgrounds. Our friends split off and get in line for frozen lemonade, while Toby and I keep going to the Ferris wheel line. We don't have to wait long, getting a spot in the next round.

"Whoa," Toby laughs as he steps into the wobbly bucket, holding his arms out to steady himself. I grab his elbow, making sure he doesn't fall.

I climb in after him, and the ride attendant closes the metal lap bar and locks it. There are no seat belts, and it feels a little sketchy, especially after the roller coaster incident.

We're one of the last pairs to get on, so the ride immediately starts rotating. The bucket gently rocks as we go around, and it's sort of relaxing.

"*Wow*. It's beautiful up here," Toby says in awe when we get to the very top. "Thanks for taking me on such amazing dates. I know this isn't technically a date, just a group thing, but it's special to me. *Memorable*. You're an incredible guy, and my problem was never realizing what I deserved, but finding it. No one can compare to you, Shane." Toby's face flushes, like he didn't mean to say all of that, and he looks straight ahead again.

My heart soars, doubling the pace and making me feel like I'm flying up here.

"Say something," he whispers, squeezing his eyes shut. "*Anything*."

He looks so fucking cute right now that I smile, pressing my lips to his and completely catching him off guard.

Toby pulls back, sucking in a sharp breath of air. "*Shane?* W-what are you doing?"

"I thought it was obvious. Kissing you," I reply with a crooked grin.

"But everyone can see us." He sounds shocked and hopeful, too.

Darting forward, I kiss him again. "Don't care," I mumble against his lips. "Let 'em." I tilt my head and deepen it, swallowing his moan and drinking him in.

I'm not much of a kisser. In fact, I can't remember the last time I kissed someone outside of sex or even during it. But with Toby, I like it. It just feels right.

"*Shane,*" Toby whines my name. "We better stop."

I pull back, panting and out of breath.

I don't want to stop.

I want more.

That reality hits me out of nowhere, spiking my arousal.

"I'm ready to go home," I growl, staring at his kiss-swollen lips. "I'm not done with you yet."

"*Oh God.*" Toby's voice trembles with lust and anticipation.

I chuckle, making sure I help him out of the bucket when it's our turn to hop out.

His knees nearly buckle with the first step on solid ground, and I snort. Shaky legs, and I haven't even touched him yet.

We walk back to our friends at the picnic table, and they cheer for us like we're state football champions returning home with the trophy.

"Yeah. Yeah. Eat it up," I say with a small smile.

"*Ahhh!*" Daija squeals, grabbing onto Tate's arm and shaking it frantically. "It finally happened!"

"Our baby boy is growing up so fast!" Tate jokes.

"That'll be twenty bucks," Jake tells Spencer, holding his hand out.

"What the hell?" My brows furrow.

"We had a bet on whether you two would kiss or not, and I just lost," Spencer elaborates.

"You fuckers," I laugh, shoving them both.

I can practically feel the heat radiating from Toby, so I wrap an arm around his shoulders, trying to absorb some of the embarrassment. I'm glad our roommates are so cool about it, but I've had enough jokes for the day. "It's been fun. But we're outta here," I inform our friends.

Toby and I say our goodbyes and head toward the parking lot. I grab Toby's hand, threading my fingers through his. He looks down at our entwined hands, then up at me with a crooked little smile. I give him a reassuring squeeze, and we walk the rest of the way to my truck in comfortable silence.

"Can . . . can we pick up where we left off when we get home?" Toby hesitantly asks once we're on the highway.

I reach over and squeeze his thigh. "I was counting on it."

CHAPTER SIXTEEN
SHANE

We come home to an empty house, slipping our shoes off by the front door. I'm so fucking glad that Jake and Spencer stayed back at the fair, because I'm ready to kiss Toby with no one watching and no one home.

"Should we—"

I cut Toby off, pressing my mouth to his soft, plump lips. He leans into me, whimpering and looping his arms around my neck. I run my hands down his back, over the swell of his ass, and grab the backs of his thighs, kneading them through his jeans. Toby gets the idea, jumping up as I lift him and wrapping his legs around my waist.

Something hard presses into me, catching me off guard, but my body instantly reacts. My cock starts to chub up, and I'm not even mad about it. I walk very carefully up the stairs with Toby clinging to me like a baby spider monkey. We crash through my bedroom door and tumble onto the bed.

Toby lands on top of me, straddling me with a sexy little smirk on his lips. I grab two handfuls of ass, squeezing and kneading and trying not to picture him in that tiny black thong. Or better yet, something red and lacey.

Fuuuck.

I've got it bad for him. Game over. I give in completely. It's not even about protecting him anymore or showing him how he should be treated.

I fucking want him.

Toby leans down and kisses me, grinding his erection against my abs while his tongue slips into my mouth, tangling with mine.

I squeeze his ass cheeks again, pressing him harder into my stomach while his hips rock against me. "Fuck, Tobes. I love your ass," I groan into his mouth. "It's perfect."

I want to bite it and lick it and try everything possible with it.

The sexed-up thoughts fill my brain out of nowhere, and it's so unfamiliar yet so exhilarating. I've never lusted after anyone this hard. Toby trails feather-soft kisses across my jaw and down my neck, nipping the delicate skin and sending goosebumps sprawling across my body.

How does that feel so good?

He pulls my T-shirt to the side, stretching it out and biting the sensitive spot where my neck meets my shoulder. My body automatically jerks, and a shiver runs down my spine, making my cock throb painfully inside my pants.

Toby lifts his head, pupils completely blown. "Is this okay?"

I nod, my chest heaving and nostrils flaring. "You can do whatever you want. No one's watching, and no one's judging. It's just you and me, Tobes." I slip my hand into his curls and pull his mouth down to mine, angling his head just right and sealing my words with a kiss.

He starts grinding against me again, but faster this

time, shamelessly seeking more friction. I deepen the kiss, grabbing a handful of hair and tugging lightly.

I'm so fucking hard for him, I feel like I could explode.

I bend my knees and grip his hips, thrusting against his ass while my cock presses into the seam of my jeans. I don't give a fuck if I end up with a zipper imprint, I can't stop moving with him.

Toby whimpers, pulling back ever-so-slightly and moaning into my mouth. "I . . . I think I'm gonna come."

Red-hot desire shoots through me, my heart rate spiking and adrenaline surging.

I've never wanted something so badly in all my life.

My cock aches for him.

"Come for me, butterfly," I whisper, encouraging him to let go.

Toby immediately cries out, stilling against me as his cock pulses inside his jeans. "*Oh my God, Shane!*"

Hearing him moan and groan and call my name has my whole body twitching as I come without so much as a gust of air on my dick.

"Holy fucking shit," Toby pants. "I just came in my underwear." His already flushed face turns crimson.

There's absolutely no reason for him to feel embarrassed. "That was the hottest thing I've ever fucking seen. I came too," I admit, reaching down to adjust my pants and grimacing at the sticky mess.

Toby sucks in a sharp breath of air, his eyes widening in surprise. "*You did?*"

I nod, and Toby rolls off with a laugh. He flops to the bed next to me, his arms resting above his head. We both stare up at the ceiling, lying there in shock with sticky, cum-filled boxers.

What the fuck did we just do?

I thought it might be awkward hanging out around our roommates after we kissed, but I'm glad I was wrong. Jake and Spencer came home later that afternoon, and I offered to make everyone dinner if they were up for steaks, baked potatoes, and salad. After we all pitch in and help clean up, we decide to spend our night at home watching a movie.

"Oh man, I'm so full," Jake whines, holding his stomach and plopping down on the couch. "That was delicious, bro. Thanks."

I grunt, stretching out on the love seat with my legs hanging off and holding my arms out for Toby to come lie on me. He glances over at Jake and Spencer sprawled out on the couch, then back at me hesitantly. I know he's unsure how far to take things in front of our friends, but he can just follow my lead.

Nodding in reassurance, I reach out and grab his hand, tugging him down. Toby lies on top of me, settling between my slightly spread thighs. With his hands on my chest, he leans forward and kisses me in front of our friends. I tilt my head, kissing him back, and making sure I keep my hands on his back instead of wandering down to his ass where I want them to be.

"*Shit.* Maybe I'm gay, too, 'cause that's kinda hot," Jake says, instantly making us pull apart.

"Maybe the whole house is gay, 'cause I concur," Spencer adds.

I grab the pillow from behind my head and throw it at him. "Not gay," I grunt.

Jake snorts in disbelief, and I narrow my eyes at him before helping Toby off of me and sitting up straight. "I'm not gay," I repeat, and I can practically feel Toby shrink in on himself. *I need to fix that.* "I . . . I think I'm bi. I'm still attracted to girls, but the only person I like is Toby. And he's a guy."

That felt really weird to say out loud. But also good.

"*Yeah?*" Toby whispers, his amber eyes sparkling with concern. He reaches over and rubs my thigh reassuringly.

"Yeah," I confirm.

"That's awesome, dude," Spencer says with a smile I know he means.

"In all seriousness, bro. You really do seem happier ever since y'all have started going on your bro dates."

"Mhm," Spencer hums, agreeing with Jake's observation.

"Thanks, guys," I mumble, uncomfortable with all of the attention. I wrap an arm around Toby's shoulder, pulling him into me and hugging him tight. "I think we need a real date now," I whisper into his ear, nipping at it while Spencer puts on one of his favorite superhero movies.

Toby shivers in my arms, so I grab the soft throw from the back of the couch and lie down with Toby in front of me. I drape the blanket over us, hiding my wandering hands as they explore his body before landing on his perfect ass. I lean forward, nuzzling my nose into his curls and breathing deeply.

"Are you smelling me?" he whispers, trying to keep his voice low so our friends don't hear.

"Mhm," I hum into his ear, breathing him in again.

"Why?"

"'Cause you smell good. Like honeysuckle and sunshine. *Like home.*"

"Shane," he whimpers. "You can't just say stuff like that. *I want you.*"

"*Shh.* Just watch the movie," I tell him, wrapping an arm around his torso and settling my hand over his heart.

"No jerking off under that blanket!" Jake suddenly shouts like a jackass.

"Oh, fuck off," I grumble, and Toby just chuckles. "You think that's funny?" I murmur, going in for a tickle.

"Don't you dare!" he warns, and I make my move, tickling his sides and under his armpits. "*Ahh! No!*" he cries, laughing hysterically and tipping over sideways. He thumps to the ground like a sack of potatoes and rattles the coffee table.

"*Shit!*" I curse, slipping to the floor next to him. "You okay?" I ask, cradling his face between my palms.

"*Ouch,*" he laughs. "My butt."

"Alright now. You guys need to take your weird foreplay to the bedroom," Jake teases, making Spencer burst out laughing. "I think we need to set some ground rules around here. First one. No handies in the living room, bro." He fake gags, adding insult to injury. "If I ever sit in splooge, I'm gonna crash out."

"Dude, shut up," I tell him, helping Toby up off the ground. "Kinda sound like a prick."

"I was kidding, Shane! Geez! Chill out."

"You chill out," I repeat, staring him down. My dark hair hangs in front of my eyes, giving me some protection, but if he's got shit to say about me in my own house, then we're going to have a problem.

"Don't be like that." He looks hurt, but I don't care right now.

"Alright, enough," Spencer says, intervening. "Jake, maybe take your humor down a notch when it comes to other people's relationships, yeah? Shane, maybe take a breather?"

I narrow my eyes, but he's not wrong. "Come on, Toby. Let's go upstairs. I've got some studying to do anyway."

"Yeah. Same," Toby agrees, and we walk to his room in silence.

"Forget about him," I say once we're behind closed doors. "He's always a dick. It's one of his main personality traits."

Toby nods in agreement, unzipping his backpack and getting out a thick Music History textbook. He drops it on his desk with a loud thunk.

"I know where I'm taking you on our first *real* date," I say, changing the subject and hoping to make him smile.

"Really? Where?" His dimples pop out, and I lean down, kissing each one.

"Not telling," I say with a grin, "But prepare to be wooed."

CHAPTER SEVENTEEN
SHANE

School and work actually fly by when I have something to look forward to each day. Someone special to come home to. Another week passes, and it's already Saturday again. The day of our first real date. Unlike Raúl, Glenn was happy to give me the night off and even hooked me up with a restaurant reservation.

"Rise and shine, sleepy head," I whisper to a sleeping Toby. "Breakfast is ready." I kiss the hollow beneath his ear, making him shiver.

"*Mmm.*" He smiles with his eyes still closed. "Spoon me first?"

Always desperate for a cuddle.

"Can't. Hashbrowns will burn. Come on." I slap his ass through the comforter, unable to resist the rounded bubble beneath the blanket.

I'm obsessed.

Toby yelps, finally opening his eyes. "Leave my ass alone," he faux-pouts before wiggling it under the covers.

"I'll never leave your ass alone. I haven't even gotten

started with it yet," I growl, leaving him gaping behind me while I head downstairs to the kitchen.

I've been thinking about it a lot lately. Toby's ass, that is. And by a lot, I mean multiple times a day, every day. It's even featured in my dreams. I watched some gay porn clips so I could get an idea of what it's like, and the thought of doing that to Toby got me so fucking hot, I jerked off into a sock like I'm still living in my mother's house. I want to try *everything* with him. I'm embracing my newfound sexuality, and I'm embracing it with Toby.

After breakfast, we split off and do our own thing. Toby heads to the music department to practice, and I head into the catering kitchen to fill ten dozen cannoli. I guess there's some sort of Italian family reunion happening tonight, and we were booked for the desserts. As soon as I finish the cannoli and portion out the tiramisu, Glenn said I'm free to take off.

No one's here to distract me, so I finish in half the time I expected and grab a small cake box, placing an extra serving of tiramisu and two cannoli inside. This will make the perfect shareable dessert after our date tonight.

I rush home, hiding the dessert in the back of the fridge behind a big bag of salad so Jake doesn't eat it while we're gone. After he was a dick the other night, I'm just looking for a reason to punch him in the face.

Taking the stairs two at a time, I hurry upstairs to get ready for our date. I've never tried this hard or even cared when it came to dating girls. But with Toby, everything needs to be perfect. I won't settle for anything less.

Huge oak trees draped in Spanish moss fill the park, casting dark shadows over everything, even though the sun hasn't set. The fog is thick and heavy, settling along the ground after this afternoon's rain showers and hovering there like a meddlesome ghost watching the living.

"Okay, this is kinda creepy. Where exactly are we going, Shane?" Toby wonders out loud.

A large, brown horse comes trotting down the road, pulling a carriage steered by an old man with a curly white mustache and a top hat.

"Is that for us?" Toby asks in awe when it comes to a stop in front of us.

"*Toot! Toot!* All aboard the Crescent Bay Express!" the old man bellows, chuckling as he climbs down to open the tiny carriage door.

"Hi, I'm Toby, and this is Shane," Toby says for both of us. I hold his hand as he steps up into the carriage and takes the far seat.

"Good afternoon. The name's Cormac, and it's a pleasure to meet ya. This beautiful boy here is Chestnut," he says, patting the horse's hindquarters.

I give Cormac a respectful nod, stepping up and taking my spot next to Toby on the plush bench seat.

He shuts the door, locking us in before he takes his seat up front behind the reins. "Are we ready?!" Cormac hollers, and Toby once again answers for both of us.

"*Yeah!*"

"Off we go!" He shakes the reins and makes Chestnut start off at a slow trot through Crescent Bay's historic park.

"This is so cool," Toby says over the rattling of the wheels and clomping of hooves on the uneven cobblestones. A few small children stop and stare, pointing in wonder at the giant horse and carriage. "I wish I had candy to throw out, I feel like we're at a parade," Toby laughs.

Making a full loop around the park, Cormac drops us off right where he picked us up. I slip the old man a nice tip, and then we head toward downtown, where all the shops and restaurants are.

It's romantic here, walking around the cobblestone streets together, hand in hand and completely unbothered. No one's watching, no one's looking, and no one cares. We can be ourselves. *Whoever that may be.*

We come to a gate with a quaint outside patio draped in string lights and mostly hidden by tall hedges and flowing green vines.

"*Whoa.* This is magical," Toby whispers in awe, staring up at the giant, wrought-iron gate with an elaborate golden *E* in the center.

The Esquire is a stunning, seven-story-tall, historic hotel with a Michelin Star restaurant on the first floor. They're usually booked out for three weeks, but my boss, Glenn, has the hookup, and he was especially happy to call in a favor when I told him I was taking Toby.

"This is such an amazing surprise. How'd you even get us a table so fast?" Toby asks.

"Let's just say, I know the right people," I reply with a wink, making him blush.

After our delicious dinner, we go for a walk next to the waterway, enjoying the scenery before the sun sets. As we're strolling down the sidewalk holding hands, the familiar sound of violin strings fills the air, beckoning us over.

When the person playing comes into view, Toby's eyes light up in excitement. He tugs me toward the music, crossing the street carefully. "Oh my God, this is so cool!" Toby whisper-shouts. His long, lithe fingers dance in the air like he's playing his own invisible strings.

The street performer finishes his set and takes a bow. Toby claps excessively, dropping a twenty into his open case. "That was amazing! Your technique is so smooth and clean. I'm Toby, and this is Shane. What's your name?"

"Thank you, Toby. My name is Jules. You look like you know a thing or two about playing violin, care to join me?" Jules nods to a second violin case sitting on the sidewalk.

Toby looks at me, and I just shrug. It's up to him. I don't know violin etiquette.

"You sure you don't mind if I use it?" he asks.

"Nope. Here's an alcohol wipe for the chin rest." Jules winks, getting back into position. "Any requests from the love birds?"

Toby smiles at me, then leans over, whispering into Jules's ear and making him grin.

"I'll follow your lead, young man."

Toby nods, getting into position.

Slow, seductive notes harmonize with each other, and it takes me a moment to recognize the song as "Pony" by Genuine.

They draw a crowd, and before I know it, people start tossing in fives and tens.

Toby really gets into it, dancing around like he does out on the dock when no one's watching. The crowd cheers, wanting more, but Toby hands the violin back to Jules.

"Thank you. I had a blast."

"No, thank you, son. You made this old man's day in

more ways than one," he chuckles, picking up his violin case and laughing at all the money inside.

"You deserve it, Jules. Have a wonderful day."

As soon as we walk away, Toby explodes with creative energy.

"That was so much fun! I could—"

"No," I answer his question before he even asks it.

"Huh?" His nose scrunches up in confusion, and it's so cute that I boop it.

"You're not playing violin on the street for money. Don't even get any ideas about it," I warn him before he wastes any time.

Toby gets a mischievous look in his eyes. "Why not? I bet I could make a lot of money. *Like tons,*" he teases, trying to egg me on.

"Because you're too pretty, and I don't wanna have to fight every guy that looks at you wrong."

Toby giggles, "But you're my bodyguard. It's your job."

"Exactly. That's why I can't go to jail. Who'd be around to catch you when you trip and fall?"

"Ha. Ha. Very funny," Toby deadpans with a hint of a smile. "I've actually had a pretty good *safe streak* recently." Just as Toby says it, the toe of his shoe gets caught on an uneven cobblestone, and he lurches forward.

My arm whips out lightning fast, grabbing hold of his bicep and stopping him from face-planting into two-hundred-year-old stones.

We're not having any skinned knees tonight.

Nothing is ruining our first date.

Toby quickly rights himself, brushing the invisible dirt off the front of his shirt. "You completely freaking jinxed me, Shane!" he whines, glancing around to see if anyone saw that and turning beet red when he makes eye contact with a pretty girl across the street. "*Oh God*. How embarrassing," he mumbles, ducking his head in shame. "Let's go."

I chuckle, looping Toby's arm through mine and escorting him the rest of the way back to the truck. My phone vibrates in my pocket on the walk back, but I wait until we're buckled in to check it.

It's my mom.

I haven't heard from her in a couple months. She usually only reaches out when she's going through a breakup or needs money. Wonder which one I'll get today?

> Hey Shaney. I hate to ask, but can you send me some money? Buck and I broke up last night, and he took off with all my cash.

Sighing loudly, I pinch the bridge of my nose. Looks like I got both this time.

> You okay? He didn't hurt you?

My mom doesn't have the best track record with picking guys, including my father and her latest boyfriend, Buck.

> I'm fine, honey. Don't worry.

I take a deep breath.

> You didn't answer the question.

> It's just a small sprain, Shaney. I'm the one who tripped and fell. Can you send me some money or not? Electric's due.

With an over-the-top sigh, I open my bank app, sending her a hundred bucks for now. I glance over at Toby, seeing the concern written all over his face.

"Is everything okay?" he asks.

"No. I need to make a pit stop at my mom's place on the way home."

CHAPTER EIGHTEEN
TOBY

I'm worried about Shane. He bottles up negative emotions like a shaken soda can ready to pop. He was never taught to express his feelings in a healthy manner, suppressing them for years on end. *Just like me.*

We pull into the driveway behind a pickup truck older than Shane's. He grips the steering wheel, squeezing tightly. "You've got to be kidding . . ."

"What?" I ask, slightly alarmed. "What's wrong?"

"That motherfucker is seriously here right now?"

"Who?" I sound like a parrot, but Shane isn't telling me anything.

"Buck. My mom's ex-boyfriend and soon-to-be dead man."

"Shane, stop. Don't say that."

Dark, fathomless eyes turn to me, shining with long-repressed pain and anger. "Stay here."

"What?!" I shout at such a ludicrous request. "No way, Shane. I'm not letting you do something stupid, not after we just had an amazing date. I *refuse* to let it end like this."

"I won't do anything stupid. Just gonna talk to him," he

tries to reason, but I know him better than that. For being so calm and mellow, Shane has been in a few fights over the years.

"Then I'll come with you," I retort stubbornly. "Since you're just going to talk."

"*Toby,*" Shane growls under his breath.

"Oh, come on. I haven't seen your mom in forever. I wanna check on her, too," I insist. "Let me have your back like you always have mine."

Shane stares at me for a moment, contemplating his next move before he darts forward, kissing me unexpectedly and resting his forehead against mine. "Stay next to me," he whispers.

I peck his lips one last time before we hop out of the truck and walk up to the tiny, unkempt house that Shane grew up in. Dead bushes line the front porch, and the grass is mostly dirt and sand. The roof is missing half its shingles, and the front shutters are hanging on by a couple of nails. It almost looks like it came out of a horror movie, and that's what it feels like when Buck answers the door with an evil, smug grin on his face.

"You need to call before ya just stop by like this, boy," he sneers. "Go away."

Shane sticks his foot in the doorway, stopping it from shutting. "You don't live here, Buck. Now move out of my way. Where's my mom?" Shane pushes his way inside the house, and I follow, practically glued to his back and nearly tripping over his heels.

"She's taking a nap," Buck says, acting shifty and blocking the bedroom door.

"Move, creep," Shane growls.

We push past him and barge into Shane's mom's

bedroom, where she's resting in bed with her ankle propped up on a pillow.

"We just had a disagreement, is all," Buck says defensively, folding his arms across his chest and resting them on top of his beer belly.

"Shaney? What are you doing here?" his mom asks groggily.

"Checking on you, Mom. What the hell is going on? What's *he* doing here?"

"Show some respect, boy," Buck retorts, and the sound of his slimy voice makes my skin crawl.

Shane will never respect the asshole who purposely burned his entire origami collection last winter when they ran out of firewood, claiming he thought it was a box of trash. I helped Shane grab the rest of his shit after that, not leaving a single thing behind. Luckily, our house on campus has an attic, so he can store all of his belongings.

"Don't speak to me like that," Shane growls, practically vibrating next to me. I grab his wrist for a second, stopping him from stepping up to Buck. I refuse to let this amazing date end with violence. He looks down at me for a second, saying a million things to me without even moving his mouth.

"Buck's right, honey. It was just a little disagreement, and I really did trip down the front steps. They're uneven as hell."

"What was the disagreement about?" Shane asks, pinning his dark eyes on her. "The money he stole from you?"

"*What?!*" Buck shouts. "That was *my* money, and I decided I wanted it back. Your mama just quit her job at the flower shop on a whim. We had plans to move in together and split the bills, but my disability only covers so much, and I had something to say about it." He turns to Shane's mom like he's ready to resume their argument. "I'm not movin' in here just to pay all the damn bills myself, Ruby."

"Mom, this true? You quit?" Shane sounds tired and, quite honestly, a little fed up.

"I lost my passion for flowers, honey. I need to paint! I need to be free!"

"You need to pay your bills," Shane reasons.

"That's why I'm going to sell my paintings, Shaney!" Ms. Ruby laughs as if it's the obvious solution.

The urge to reach for his hand is strong, so I step closer to him instead, offering my silent support. I know this is hard. He has a complicated relationship with his mother, but when it comes down to it, he loves her and only wants the best for her.

"You should call Diane and ask for your job back, Mom."

She scoffs, looking off to the side. "Of course you don't believe in me. Neither of you do."

"Just until you sell your first painting," I interject, smiling politely. "Hi, Ms. Ruby," I say with a little wave when she glances over and finally notices me. She has long, dark hair and deep brown eyes, just like Shane.

"Tobias! My goodness! Come give me a hug!"

I hesitantly make my way over and give her a gentle hug, all too aware of Buck's eyes on me.

"My oh my, look at you. Aren't you just the cutest?" Ms. Ruby gushes over me.

I blush, unable to control it, and steer the conversation back to her art. "Do you have any paintings on display? I'd love to see some of your work."

"That one over there." She points to an abstract palm

tree with bright splotches of color that's actually really cool. "And the bouquet of flowers above the TV."

"Wow. Those are really beautiful, Ms. Ruby. Very impressive." And that's the honest truth. She's a wonderful artist.

She beams at the compliment. "Thank you, honey. You really think so?"

"Absolutely. I'm sure you'll sell something quickly, but it never hurts to have two revenue sources," I add.

"I suppose that might be a good idea," Ms. Ruby ponders.

"So you take advice from some baby-faced kid, but not me?" Buck throws his arms up in the air. "Unbelievable!"

"Oh, stop, Buck. I'm not even sure I can work right now since I've hurt my ankle. I can't stand up all day."

"They're obligated to make arrangements for you, like a stool behind the counter so you can sit and still be a cashier," I inform her.

"Really?"

"Yes, ma'am," I reply politely with a small smile.

"Okay, well, I guess I'll do that. But I'm gonna take a few days off first. I think I've earned it."

"I don't know how you did it, kid, but I suppose I owe you my thanks," Buck says to me, thumping me on the back and making me stumble forward a couple steps. "She's one stubborn woman."

Ms. Ruby rolls her eyes at the comment, but the way she looks at that greasy slob turns my stomach.

"You don't owe him shit," Shane sneers, making Buck grin like he actually enjoys these exchanges. "And don't *ever* put your hands on him again." I grab onto Shane's thick arm, stopping a fight once again.

I will not allow this asshole to sour our first real date.

"Yeah, yeah," Buck huffs unperturbed, shooing us away with his hand.

Shane nearly shows his teeth before softening his face only slightly for his mother. "I'm outta here, Mom," he grumbles, clearly not wanting to stay a second longer. "Take care of yourself." He grabs my wrist and tugs me toward the exit.

"Bye, honey! Don't be a stranger! Text me!" she hollers across the house as if there wasn't almost just a brawl between her boyfriend and her son.

"Thanks for helping to diffuse that situation," Shane murmurs once we get back into his truck. "That actually went a lot worse in my head."

"Me too," I admit. "But that's why we make a good team. You have to let me help you, too. We can be there for each other."

Shane nods, recognizing that we're in this together and reaching over to give the back of my neck a squeeze. I close my eyes and sigh, melting into his touch and ready to get the hell out of here.

"I know the mood's kind of ruined after that, but I have dessert in the fridge for us," Shane says once we get home and change into our pajamas.

"Nothing's ruined," I assure him. "I'm always up for dessert."

Shane gets a cute little box out of the fridge, setting it on the counter and opening the lid. I peer inside, finding a delicious-looking piece of tiramisu and two cannoli.

"This looks amazing, Shane. Did you make them?"

Shane nods, picking up a cannoli and holding it out for me.

I lean forward and take a bite, opening my mouth wide to fit the pastry inside. I bite down into the crispy, flaky cannoli, and hum at the flavor of the cream cheese filling with mini chocolate chips.

"*Oh my fucking God.* They're delicious. I need these at my wedding one day," I joke.

Shane stares down at me, his dark eyes pinning me to the spot.

"What? Do I have some filling on my face?" My tongue darts out, licking at the corner of my mouth. "Did I get it?"

Shane sticks his index finger into his own cannoli and swipes it across my lips. "You missed a spot," he murmurs, leaning in to press his mouth to mine, licking and kissing my lips until the cream is gone.

"You taste so sweet, butterfly," Shane whispers, and I'm an absolute fucking goner, melting into the floor like a puddle of goo.

I want him so badly, I can't take it anymore.

"Let me taste you." I kneel down on the hard kitchen floor, peering up at him with desire and yearning. "*Please,*" I beg, gripping both of his thighs through his pants and squeezing. I'm desperate to feel the weight of his cock on my tongue. Desperate to taste him.

I need his cock in my mouth, now.

"You don't have to say anything. Just let me blow you."

Shane's hands move toward his belt buckle as if in slow motion. I tear my gaze away from his intense stare and watch in awe as he unzips his pants and tugs them down along with his boxers.

His thick cock springs free, already hard and dripping.
Holy shit.

It's beautiful.

And huge.

My jaw drops twice, and I sit back on my heels, admiring it. "Of course it's extra large. I mean, why wouldn't it be? That would only make sense, given your overall size. Maybe I should have worked my way up. Started smaller, ya know?"

"Butterfly," Shane growls, and I nearly kick my feet and giggle at the sweet nickname I've completely fallen in love with.

I reach out and wrap my hand around his shaft. He's warm and soft yet rock hard. My own dick throbs in my pants uncomfortably. I'm so turned on right now, I might faint. I give his dick a tentative squeeze, and he lets out a long, low groan.

"*Fuuuck*. Toby. Jerk me," he begs, and I obey, hesitantly stroking his shaft. "Yes, just like that," he encourages, knowing this is the first time I've ever done this. "You're doing so good," he moans. "*So fucking good.*"

The praise goes straight to my dick, and I want to impress him further, so I lean forward and swipe my tongue along his slit, collecting the glistening beads of precum. Shane sucks in a sharp breath of air as his salty flavor bursts across my tongue.

"*Tobes . . .*" His breathy plea spurs me on, so I take his entire cockhead into my mouth and suck, teasing the sensitive underside with my tongue. Shane weaves his fingers into my curls, grabbing hold and guiding me. I use one hand to grip the base of his cock and stroke him while I suck. Shane grunts and twitches, tightening his grip on my hair like he's fighting his control.

I release his cock with a pop, continuing to stroke him. "Just let go, Shane. I got you," I whisper as I peer into dark, vulnerable eyes. "I promise. I got you. *Always.* Trust me and let go."

Without another word, I focus on his dick again and start sucking and stroking him in time with his small, gentle thrusts.

Not even a minute later, Shane's movements stutter. "Gonna come," he murmurs, warning me moments before.

Instead of pulling off and letting him finish in my hand, I press my face further into his groin, inhaling his musky, clean scent. Shane's cockhead fills the back of my throat, triggering his release *and* mine. His dick pulses in my mouth and I suck harder, draining every last drop before his softening cock slips out of my mouth.

"*Fucking hell, butterfly,*" Shane pants in pure amazement, staring down at me in awe.

I smile up at him with warm cheeks, feeling proud, sticky, and also satisfied after I came in my pants.

Again.

CHAPTER NINETEEN
TOBY

Ever since the blow job last weekend, Shane has been more touchy-feely than usual. When we're around the house, he doesn't care if Jake or Spencer sees when he gives me a quick kiss in the hallway. But between Shane's job and my extra practice sessions for the end-of-the-year symphony and concerto, we haven't had time to hang out or hook up since.

My phone suddenly buzzes in my early morning English Lit class, pulling me from my thoughts. I sneak it out and check my texts under the desk. This class has a hundred students in it, and I'm sitting at the top, so the professor can't see me.

> I can't stop thinking about your mouth.

The simple yet hot-as-fuck text has my face turning bright red as if the entire class can read his message. My heart starts to beat faster, and my dick chubs up.

Shit.

I take a deep, calming breath and will the boner away.

> I can't stop thinking about your dick.

I hit send before I can second-guess myself, chewing on my lip nervously while I wait for Shane's response.

> Meet me by the fountain in the quad at noon.

> I'll be there.

I put my phone away and attempt to focus on the professor's lecture. But it's hard because all I can think about is what else I want to do with Shane's cock.

My next class crawls by just as slowly, but it's finally noon and time to meet up with Shane.

I'm sitting on the edge of the iconic pineapple fountain, surrounded by flowers and palm trees, waiting for Shane to get here. A refreshing breeze surrounds me, but the sun's too bright, so I dig my sunglasses out of my bag and slip them on.

A penny suddenly flies past my head, plopping into the water next to me. I glance up, shielding the sun with my hand.

"Hey," I say, getting up from the edge and just standing there in front of him.

"Hey," he replies, sweeping his hair out of his eyes with a shake of his head.

"What was that?" I ask, hiking a thumb over my shoulder at the penny in the fountain.

"Just making a wish I hope will come true."

"Oh yeah?" I murmur as he steps into my space, staring down at me intensely.

He reaches out, tracing the curve of my face.

"Shane," I breathe. "Everyone on campus is going to know about us by tomorrow if you do this."

"Don't care," he mumbles, cupping my cheek and staring into my eyes. Or more accurately, into my soul. "I can't make it through the day without kissing you."

My knees feel unsteady as a wave of euphoria washes over me. Shane wraps an arm around my waist, tugging me to him and kissing me *hard*. Like he's staking a claim for all to see. His touch is hot and possessive, and I *crave* it. Desire flares to life inside of me, urging me to take this home, but I can't. I have to get to class. We both do.

Besides it feeling like a movie-worthy moment, nothing earth-shattering happens when Shane kisses me publicly. No one catcalls, no one whistles, no one cares. Everyone is just going about their daily routines, minding their business, and unconcerned with mine.

It feels good. It feels freeing.

Shane breaks away from the kiss, pressing his forehead against mine and breathing heavily. "I gotta get to class. Will you wait up for me tonight? I should be home at ten."

"Yeah," I breathe out. "I'm looking forward to it."

Shane growls low, nipping at my bottom lip one last time before he turns and storms down the pathway like he has to physically force himself away from me.

I feel the same way, and I can't freaking wait to have alone time tonight.

"Toby! One more time, from the top!" my orchestra teacher, Professor Goldblum, shouts at me, moving his baton in a downbeat followed by a quick rebound upward to starting position.

I sigh, adjusting my chin and neck before starting my solo performance—my concerto. For the fifth time this afternoon.

Don't get me wrong, I'm excited for the end-of-the-year symphony and especially my concerto, but right now, I'm ready to get the hell out of here and get ready for tonight with Shane.

Distracted by my thoughts, I miss a note, my violin screeching unpleasantly. Heat rushes to my cheeks as Professor Goldblum stops the whole class.

"Again, from the top!" he shouts. "Tobias, please try to stay in tune, considering you *are* the centerpiece for this part of the symphony, hmm?"

Luke snickers next to me, enjoying my humiliation. "Yeah, *first chair*," he sneers, like he doesn't think I deserve it.

Asshole.

His opinion doesn't matter and won't change anything.

I get through the rest of class without any hiccups, but as we're leaving, Luke decides to corner me outside the classroom. "Quit daydreaming about your boyfriend and focus on the performance, Toby. If you fuck up, you ruin the whole show."

"I . . ." I'm stunned by his words.

"I saw you in the quad with Shane Carmichael."

"He's not my boyfriend." I don't know why that's the only thing that comes out of my mouth, the words tasting sour and untrue.

"Whatever," he snorts. "I don't care about any drama you have with your *boyfriend*, just don't let it fuck up the symphony, or I'll have no other choice but to go to Professor Goldblum and request that second chair takeover as the principal."

Of course. Because *he's* the second chair.

This prick has been gunning for my first chair position since I beat him out for it at the beginning of the semester.

"There is no drama, and my personal life has nothing to do with my music," I snap, pushing past him with my shoulder and getting the hell out of here.

Luke sticks his foot out, and suddenly I'm airborne, landing with a loud thud on the hard, linoleum floor. My violin case goes flying, sliding across the floor and crashing into someone's feet. I follow the familiar-looking sneakers up a long pair of jean-covered legs, followed by a tight black T-shirt, until I meet a pair of furious yet concerned eyes. I glance over my shoulder, and the fear on Luke's face is real when he sees who it is.

Shane.

My best friend and supposed *boyfriend*.

Professor Goldblum comes rushing out of the classroom and thankfully snatches Luke up before Shane can rush over there and get his hands on him. "What in tarnation is going on out here?" His bushy gray eyebrows bunch together as he peers around, assessing the situation.

Shane picks up my violin, then kneels down and helps me sit up. I rub my sore wrist, hissing at the raw skin. I glare at Luke, completely shocked that he would take things this far. "What the hell, Luke?" I demand, not giving two craps about cussing in front of our teacher. My wrist hurts.

"It was an accident," he replies with zero remorse in his cold blue eyes. He brushes perfectly styled blond hair off his forehead, completely unbothered by what just happened.

"That's it. You're going to the dean, young man," Professor Goldblum barks at Luke, shaking his head in disappointment. "And you," he says to me. "You're going to the nurse." His kind yet stern eyes dart to Shane. "I gather you can help him get there, young man?"

Shane nods. "Of course."

"Nurse Miller will give you a note for your next class if you need one."

"Thank you, sir," I say genuinely, allowing Shane to wrap his arm around me.

Luke just snorts, rolling his eyes and further ruining his reputation and his spot in the orchestra. I wouldn't be surprised if he loses the second chair position over this. He certainly doesn't deserve it. Luke isn't a team player and never has been.

"Let's go, Luke. Dean Williams can deal with you and your attitude."

"I already said it was an accident," he whines uselessly. "It's not my fault Toby is so clumsy."

Shane practically growls at Luke while Professor Goldblum leads him down the hallway in the opposite direction, scolding him the whole way.

"Are you okay?" Shane whispers, focusing his entire attention on my wrist and the red, raw skin.

"Yeah. Think so. It's just a little sore and stings from the floor burn." I rotate my wrist in a circle, thankfully not feeling any sharp pain.

"Let's get you to the nurse anyway. Can't take any risks with your playing hand."

I melt into Shane's side, allowing his strength and compassion to hold me up. He is the pillar in my life and always has been.

And I'm going to reward him for it later.

CHAPTER TWENTY
SHANE

Later that night, when I get off shift, I hop in the shower before sneaking into Toby's room and crawling into bed behind him.

"*Mmm,*" he moans, half-asleep. "Tried to stay up for you. Couldn't make it."

"I know, I'm sorry. I'm a little late," I whisper, glancing at the clock and seeing that it's after eleven. "Just roll over and let me take care of you." I shimmy down the bed, getting into position.

I've been thinking about this a lot lately, and I'm finally ready.

Toby rolls over, staring down his body at me. The room is dim, only the lamp in the corner is on, but I can see him clear as day. His chest is bare, and a pair of silky basketball shorts rests low on his hips.

I slip my fingers into the waistband of his shorts, pausing for a moment. "Can I?"

His sultry eyes appear catlike in the soft, golden glow of the room, drawing me in and hypnotizing me. He nods slowly, unable to break the spell while I slowly pull his shorts and underwear down. Toby's cock springs free, already hard and ready. It's long and slender, with a slight curve and a dusky pink tip. His belly hollows out when my hands travel up his ribs and over his pecs, brushing his nipples and teasing him.

"Your body is so sexy," I murmur, feeling a sense of rightness like never before when I wrap my hand around his warm, velvety cock.

Toby hisses at the contact, my own cock pulsing with need.

I squeeze a little harder, stroking him faster, and he grips the sheets on either side of him. Toby grunts and twitches quietly, his abs contracting. "*Oh God.* Shane," he whines, closing his eyes and tipping his head back.

I take the opportunity to lick his shaft from root to tip, causing him to cry out and grab hold of my hair. Toby bends his knees, rocking into my face as I suck him down. He keeps my head pressed between his legs like a man possessed.

Fuck this is hot.

I pop off his cock, gasping for air before I dip my head further south and lick along the seam of his sac.

Toby moans and groans, squirming too much. I reach up and press a palm to his belly, stilling him. My tongue dances south, firmly pressing against his taint and making him cry out.

"*Shane!* I'm gonna come!"

Before he does, I quickly swallow his cockhead once again, desperately wanting to taste him. Toby moans loudly while he unloads inside my mouth, and I can only hope our roommates didn't come home during this, because we never turned the music on. I swallow every last drop, wiping the corner of my mouth before plopping onto the bed next to him.

"That was fucking incredible. Let me return the favor," Toby says with a dopey smile and half-lidded eyes.

He looks sleepy, and we both have class early in the morning. "Don't worry about it, Tobes. You need to get some rest."

"You can jerk off on me," he offers with a yawn and a stretch, his naked, lean body on full display.

My cock pulses in my sweatpants. "*Yeah?*"

"Yeah. Come wherever you want," he offers breathlessly, bending his arms and threading his fingers behind his head.

I climb to my knees, slipping my sweats and boxers down far enough to pull my cock out. I start to stroke myself slowly, wanting to enjoy the sexy sight in front of me. "Your body is perfect," I murmur, picking up the pace as his cock starts to thicken once again. I watch it grow before my eyes, and he makes it twitch on purpose, smirking at me with a single dimple. "Gonna paint you with my cum," I grunt, dipping my fingers into my slit and smearing the precum around my sensitive head.

"Fuck. Do it," Toby whimpers, reaching down to stroke himself. "I need to come again."

Lust shoots through my body, my dirty mind picturing something I saw during my *research*. "Wanna try something?" I ask somewhat hesitantly. This will take things a step further than we've gone so far.

"*Yes,*" he breathes out. "I'll try anything with you, Shane. *Anything.*"

I slip my sweatpants all the way off and pull my T-shirt over my head, dropping them to the floor. Standing before

Toby completely naked, I feel a little vulnerable and a hell of a lot turned on. Crawling on top of him, I settle between his open thighs and our cocks brush, making both of us gasp.

"*Oh my God,*" he cries when I slot our cocks together and grip them in my hand, rubbing and stroking them as we start to move against each other. "Not gonna last long," Toby pants. "Feels too good."

"Me neither," I confess, continuing to stroke us together as one. The feel of his soft, warm skin against mine is indescribable. I lean down and kiss his lips, sweeping my tongue into his mouth while he moans. Toby wraps his legs around my waist, digging his heels into my ass as we both grind into my fist.

Is this what it would feel like to fuck him?

Chest to chest. Skin to skin.

God, I want that.

I want to own him.

The primal thoughts hit me out of nowhere, and I combust, my cock erupting against Toby's and triggering his release. He cries out and bites down on the sensitive spot where my neck meets my shoulder, likely leaving a mark. Our cum mixes together in my hand, creating a sticky mess that has my cock staying at half-mast.

I climb off of him, careful not to drip on the sheets. I grab my T-shirt from the floor and wipe up quickly. "Be right back," I murmur, slipping my loose sweats on and rushing down the hall for a warm, wet washcloth. I return to the bedroom and clean him up as he drifts off to sleep. Brushing the curls off his forehead, I give him a tender kiss before crawling into bed behind him and pulling him to my chest. It doesn't take long to fall asleep with the reassuring comfort of Toby wrapped in my arms.

CHAPTER TWENTY-ONE
TOBY

I stare at the flesh-colored, silicone dildo in my hands, Tate's wise words echoing in my head.

Be ready for him.

Shane's and my relationship has been steadily progressing, and I don't want to get to the point where I'm not prepared for the next step.

Penetration.

Tate said I need to practice, so that's what I'm going to do.

Shane's at work until ten tonight, and I finally mustered up the courage to open the package from Tate that arrived weeks ago. He said I could call him if I had questions, but it's pretty obvious what I'm supposed to do with this, given the large bottle of lube he sent with it.

As I'm stroking the dildo, feeling the weight of it in my hands and contemplating whether I can take it or not, the door to my bedroom suddenly swings open.

Shane stands frozen in the doorway, his dark eyes wide and unblinking.

"Y-you're home early," I stammer, fumbling with the dildo before successfully hiding it behind my back.

"I am." Shane is so tense that I think he might be shocked back into being straight until he finally speaks. "Have you ever used that thing before?"

The question is curious with a hint of concern, but no judgement in sight. He's as calm as ever.

"Um. No. I just opened it." I point to the cardboard box on the ground by my feet. "It was a gift . . ."

Shane growls under his breath, narrowing his eyes and stalking toward me.

"From Tate!" I add quickly before he gets the wrong idea and thinks it's from someone else.

"How do you use that alone without hurting yourself?" The concern on his face is both hot and mortifying, and for some reason, the slight embarrassment makes me even hornier.

"Do you really want the details?" I ask, not sure he's ready for the logistics of gay sex. Not that I've had any experience either.

Shane nods, lust gleaming in his dark stare and melting my last remaining defenses.

"Lots of lube and stretching first," I inform him. Heat radiating from my entire body.

"Stretching?" he asks, the open curiosity in his question makes my cock thicken in my shorts, and I know he can see it.

"Y-yeah. With my fingers."

I can see the moment it clicks for him. That I'm talking about stretching my hole with my fingers. His gaze turns feral, his nostrils flaring like a predator ready to ravish his prey. *And that prey is me.*

"Show me," he demands.

"W-what?"

He can't possibly mean what I think he means.

"I want to see. Want to watch."

Fire erupts in my cheeks, but I need to clarify. "You . . . you want to watch me finger myself?"

Shane nods, his dark eyes swirling with a carnal sort of hunger. He sits in the desk chair, wheeling it over to get a front row view of the action.

"I-I've never done this before," I admit.

Shane places a hand on top of my shaky one, steadying me. "Neither have I, Tobes. It's okay. Just do what feels right. Forget I'm even watching," he whispers encouragingly, opening the bottle of lube and setting it on the nightstand.

"How should I do it?" I ask vulnerably, knowing he's going to be watching the first time I ever try this.

Shane thinks for a moment. "Lie on your back and bend your knees up toward your chest."

I strip down and do as instructed, completely exposing myself to Shane in a way I never have before. It's thrilling and hot and a little scary, too.

He rubs my shin reassuringly. "You're doing great. You look so fucking sexy like this," he murmurs, making me gasp when he squeezes lube over my hole, dribbling the cool liquid down my crease. "Touch yourself, baby. I wanna see you stretch that hole."

I whimper at his dirty talk, hesitantly reaching between my legs and gently circling my opening. I tense up, unfamiliar with the sensation.

"Just relax," Shane encourages, squirting more lube on my wandering fingers.

I press against my hole, and a single finger slips in

easily. Grunting at the odd intrusion, I probably make a really unattractive face.

"So hot," Shane whispers breathlessly, and the pure reverence in his voice is the only thing spurring me on.

I start to move my finger, slowly pushing it further before pulling back and adding a second. Hissing at the stretch, I reach down and give my cock a tug, adding pleasure to the full and somewhat uncomfortable feeling in my ass. But as my body relaxes and loosens up, I start to enjoy it more and more.

"Another, baby. This toy is a lot bigger than your fingers. I wanna see you stretch yourself."

I add a third finger, practically howling as I stretch my body to its limits and push through the slight sting of pain.

"Holy fucking shit," Shane murmurs in awe as I slowly push three fingers all the way inside my ass until only my thumb and pinky are sticking out. I pause, tipping my head back while I stroke my cock faster until my thighs shake, and I can barely hold them up.

Shane stands up, pushing my legs even farther back and holding them for me. The new angle causes me to hit some sort of magical button inside my ass, and I cry out, painting my stomach and chest with my cum.

I very carefully slip my fingers out, whimpering at the loss of fullness.

Shane keeps my legs pushed back, and I can feel his eyes glued to my body. "Fuck, butterfly. Your hole is stretched so beautifully and still pulsing. Let me do the next part?"

"*Please*," I pant, my chest heaving and my cock already excited again. The mere thought of Shane fucking me with my new dildo has my brain misfiring and incapable of words.

My secret fantasy is about to come true.

He grabs the dildo and drizzles lube all over it, then squirts more on my open hole. The cool liquid feels nice against my sensitive flesh. "Ready?" he asks, and I nod, locking eyes with him as he presses the large, blunt head of the toy to my opening. "Breathe in," he says, and I listen, taking a big lungful of oxygen. "Now out." As soon as the air begins to leave my lungs, Shane pushes the dildo into me. "Bear down," he encourages, and the toy pushes past the tight ring of muscle. The oddest noise leaves my throat, like when you try to scream after expelling all the air in your lungs.

Shane pauses for a moment, allowing me to catch my breath before he continues the intrusion. He keeps going until my new toy is fully inside me, filling me up and stretching me to the max. "You okay? Doesn't hurt?"

I shake my head frantically. "So full," I moan.

He traces a finger around my rim, tickling the sensitive flesh. "I wish you could see how fucking sexy you are. All stretched out and loose for me."

Oh God.

I wish I could see it too.

I'm not going to last.

Shane starts moving the toy, pushing and pulling it inside my ass.

"Shane," I whine, unsure what I'm even asking for as he continues to peg my prostate with the soft, silicone toy.

He reaches over, not breaking his rhythm, and grabs something from the nightstand. The toy in my ass suddenly comes to life, vibrating intensely and tickling my new favorite spot.

"*Unghhh!*" I cry out, my voice shaking as he cycles through the different modes. I forgot it had a remote control and a million settings. I need to thank Tate later because I'm hanging on by a thread, and I never want this sensation to end.

I can't even imagine how good it would feel if Shane actually fucked me.

The mere thought of my best friend pulling out the toy and fucking me has a flood of precum oozing out of my slit and dripping onto my abdomen.

"Gonna come," I grunt, my body shaking with the force of Shane fucking me with the vibrating toy.

"Do it," he demands, leaning down and swallowing my cockhead.

The high-pitched squeal that leaves my throat would normally embarrass me, but I'm too far gone to care. The dual sensation of my ass being filled and my cock being sucked has me instantly exploding. Shane sucks me through my orgasm until the final wave rocks me.

"*Holy fucking shit,*" I murmur, wincing when Shane turns off the toy and slowly slips it out.

That was intense and incredible and ten times better than the fantasy in my head.

I've never come that hard in my life, and I can feel my hole pulsing with aftershocks. I'm definitely going to be sore tomorrow, but I don't even care. *I want to remember this feeling forever.*

"What about you?" I ask, glancing down at the large tent in his pants.

"I'll be fine," he lies, pressing the heel of his palm into his hard-on and grimacing.

"No, you won't," I laugh, rolling my eyes. "You . . . you could jerk off on me again if you want?" I offer. "I really like that."

"*Where?*" he growls, his voice deep and rough with lust.

"Anywhere you want," I reply with a husky tone that sounds nothing like me.

I guess I'm a horny, needy little slut when it comes to Shane.

I watch as his pupils dilate, his intense brown eyes turning solid black like a man possessed. *"Anywhere?"* he asks just to be sure, and I nod slowly, chewing on my lower lip as my dick starts to thicken for a third freaking time.

Shane tugs his pajama pants down, his hard cock springing free and slapping his lower abdomen obscenely. He starts to stroke himself, staring at me intently while I continue to lean back with my knees bent and my feet flat on the bed. He grips my shin and pushes my knees back, exposing me once again. I gasp when he presses his tip against my opening and starts to jerk off. With each bump and jab of his cock against my tender flesh, I get more and more desperate for him to fuck me.

"Fuck me, Shane," I beg. "Please, just stick it in and fill me up. My hole is ready." I pull my knees back even more, practically folding myself in half and completely submitting to him.

"Not tonight," he pants. His jaw clenches as he grits his teeth, attempting to hold himself back from fucking me, while I continually beg for it. The veins in his neck protrude, and the tip of his cock just barely presses into me. My outer muscles squeeze the life out of his crown as he teeters on the edge without penetrating me. Shane continues to beat his dick until his thighs tense up and he stiffens, shooting load after load directly into my open hole. Most of it drips out, but not all of it. I marvel at the feel of it.

"You like it when I come inside you?" Shane murmurs, scooping up his cum and pushing some back in with two fingers.

I whimper, feeling like I just finished a marathon, and I

need to crash. "Yeah," I breathe out, a pile of boneless flesh. "*A lot.*"

"Good. 'Cause next time I won't hold back. I'm going to fuck you so good, Toby."

I swallow thickly, already desperate and excited for next time.

CHAPTER TWENTY-TWO
SHANE

After everything we've done, I feel closer to Toby and even more possessive of him. I've never felt this way about a girl, but with Toby, I have an obsessive need to always know where he is and what he's up to. And unfortunately for me, tonight he wants to go to another frat party on campus.

Guess that means I'm going, too.

"Sure you don't wanna stay in and mess around?" I ask, hoping to coax him into staying home and avoiding another house full of loaded frat boys. I'm sitting on his bed in a simple pair of black jeans and a matching T-shirt, while Toby is standing in front of his closet, trying to decide what to wear tonight.

Toby giggles, his face turning a tempting shade of pink. "I just want to go for a little while. All of our friends will be there, and you know how much I hate FOMO." He walks over and straddles me on the end of the bed. "But I'll take a rain check on messing around," he murmurs. "We don't even have to stay that long."

I dart forward, capturing his lips with mine while I slip

my hands under his shirt and run them up his bare back, squeezing and massaging.

"*Mmm,*" he moans into the kiss as I thrust my hips upward, poking him in the ass with my hard-on. "Quit trying to have your way with me, Shane. I know what you're trying to do."

Gripping his shoulders, I give him a good squeeze and press him down harder onto my lap. "You're the one who's on top of me," I point out, continuing to dry hump him.

"Fuck, Shane," Toby breathes, resting his forehead against mine for a moment and enjoying the ride before he reluctantly climbs off my lap and goes back to the closet. "I just wanna go for a little bit, okay?" He grabs a loose tank top that nearly shows his nipples and a small pair of Bermuda shorts that I already know hug his ass so fucking nicely. I watch with interest as a flash of purple and a pair of socks get added to the pile before he hurries toward the door. "I'll be right back. I'm gonna change in the bathroom and freshen up."

I raise a single eyebrow at him in question.

Freshen up?

Or jerk off?

Toby blushes, adjusting the tent in his pants. "I know exactly what you're thinking! But I promise I'm not doing *that.*"

I smirk at him all cute and flustered, a deep chuckle rolling through me.

"Oh, be quiet, you!" Toby whines, but I can see his dimples. "Besides, I'm saving it all for later," he whispers huskily. I growl and practically lunge for him as he darts out of the door, laughing all the way down the hall to the bathroom.

He's definitely going to get it later.

The party is in full swing by the time we pull up to the scene and park a few houses down. Frat Row is littered with cars, lifted trucks, and drunk college students all over the block. With zero discretion taken to hide all of the illegal activities happening right now, some rich asshole *has* to be paying off campus security because somehow, Frat Row parties *never* get busted.

"Toby!" Daija shouts excitedly, rushing over to him with a big smile and an even bigger hug.

And of course, Tate is right behind her, wrapping his arms around both of them. "So, how was the thing I got you?" Tate asks way too loudly, glancing over at me, then back to Toby. "Did you enjoy it? Practice with it? Think you're ready for the *real* thing?" He waggles his eyebrows and laughs, already drunk and being way too obvious.

"Oh, stop it, Tate!" Daija scolds. "Don't make our baby boy uncomfortable. Rein it in."

"I'm just checking on him, honey. No one even knows what I'm talking about. *Chill.*" Tate makes eye contact with me, giving me a cheeky little wink that I narrow my eyes at.

I appreciate him helping Toby come into his own, but it's none of his damn business when and how he used it.

I lean down and whisper into Toby's ear. "Let's go get a drink."

We slip away from Daija and Tate and head toward the kitchen. I spot an unopened bottle of rum and grab two red Solo cups. I pour a generous amount into one, and less than a shot into the other since I'm driving. Popping open two cans of Coke, I fill the cups, adding a little ice before mixing it all together with a plastic straw.

"Careful," I warn, handing the extremely full and extremely strong drink over to Toby. "Pace yourself because I'm not pouring you a drink from an open bottle tonight."

I don't trust these frat parties, and I have a weird feeling about this one.

Toby's face scrunches up when he tastes the drink. "*Oh, yuck,*" he coughs. "That's disgusting, Shane."

I chuckle. *Perfect.* This way, he has to sip it slowly.

"*Yo, yo, yo!*" a familiar, obnoxious voice shouts behind me.

I set my drink down and spin around quickly, stopping the asshat from jumping on my back. Jake daps me up instead, making himself a drink with the rum I just opened.

"What's up, Jake? Where's Spencer?" I ask, leaning against the counter behind me while Toby attempts to take another sip of his rum and Coke without cringing.

"I dunno. Chasing ass. *You know?* Like how you used to before—"

"Before what?" I interrupt, stepping up to Jake.

What's he trying to say?

"Before you were *gay,*" he tries to explain, but only makes it worse, like a drunken fool.

I grit my teeth, completely annoyed by him right now. "I'm bi," I say, correcting him.

And it's really none of his business to comment on.

"Jake. Just shut up," Toby blurts out, equally as irritated as me.

Jake just laughs it off, holding his hands up in surrender. "I didn't mean anything by it. *Honestly.* You guys know I'm a dumbass."

"And a loudmouth," I add.

"That too," he admits. "Look, I'm sorry, okay? I love you

both. I'm just drunk. You know I don't care if you're straight, gay, bi, or whatever."

"How can we be mad at that?" Toby asks with a laugh, staring up at me.

"Not mad," I agree, giving Jake a pass this time. "But going forward, don't comment on my sexuality out loud at a party, bro."

"Gotcha," Jake replies with a salute. "Thanks, guys. I'm gonna go find Spence. Catch ya later." He gives us drunken finger guns and disappears into the living room.

Shaking my head in exasperation, I sigh and focus on the only reason I'm here, staring at him while I sip my drink. His matching hair and eyes shimmer like long-lost treasure as he dances under the overhead kitchen light.

Toby tries more of his drink and doesn't make a face this time. "Think I'm getting used to it," he says, smiling up at me with glassy eyes and warm cheeks. "Can hardly taste the rum now."

"Take it slow," I whisper huskily, running the back of my finger along his cheekbone.

"Dance party!" someone hollers from the living room, and Tate and Daija come rushing into the kitchen to surround Toby.

"Time to shake it, baby boy!" Daija encourages Toby as they sandwich him in between them and whisk him away to the makeshift dance floor in the living room.

I grab both of our drinks and follow after them like the personal security that I am.

Toby grinds and dances against me while I feed him sips of alcohol like I would grapes to a Greek god. My dick likes it, too, and I think I'm ready to go home soon.

After half an hour of dancing and drinking with our friends, Toby finishes off his drink, and I slip away for two seconds to toss our empty cups in the trash. When I get back, Toby, Tate, and Daija are surrounded by three creeps, as if they were waiting for their chance to pounce.

What the fuck is going on?

This isn't a club.

As I get closer, I recognize two of them from Stick Shift. The assholes who were trying to get Toby and Tate drunk. *Landon*, I think. Don't remember the other one. I come up behind Toby, slowly letting my presence be known so I don't startle him.

Leaning down, I whisper into his ear. "You okay?" I ask while giving Landon the evil eye.

"Aww. How sweet. Is your big, bad, bestie protecting you again?" Landon sneers. "Pathetic. Just like you were that night, accepting free drinks from everyone."

Toby shrinks in on himself in my arms, and I fucking hate it. *It feels wrong.* Toby is a bright, shining flame, and I am the circle of stones protecting the fire. No one will *ever* dim his light and make him feel small.

"I'm his boyfriend now," I declare without a second thought, maneuvering Toby safely behind me, where Tate and Daija are currently standing. "You're the one who's pathetic. A desperate creep trying to get innocent people drunk."

Landon scoffs, rolling his eyes as if it's not true. "This slutty twink was about two drinks away from letting me and my bro fuck him. Needy little—"

My fist swings, stopping his mouth from spewing any more disgusting lies.

Landon stumbles back in shock, covering his mouth with wide, bulging eyes. "You hit me," he mumbles in disbelief. He drops his hands, baring his blood-stained teeth. "*Motherfucker!*" he bellows like a war cry before charging me.

His grimy little friend doesn't have time to stop him like he did at the bar, so the creep gets a swing in. I dodge the first punch, but before I can recover, the second one clips me in the chin. A sharp burst of pain splinters through my jaw, shaking my teeth. I see red, tackling Landon to the ground and trying to put him in a chokehold. He rolls us instead and hits me right in the fucking eye.

Sonofabitch.

"*Stop!*" Toby shouts, but I can't look away from my opponent for even a second, or I could lose.

I dodge the next blow, crossing my forearms in front of my face and taking the hit there. Grunting at the impact, I thrust my arms forward as hard as I can, knocking him backward off of me.

Landon's friend from the bar takes the opportunity to grab his unhinged friend and hold him back.

I quickly climb to my feet, raising my fists, ready for him to charge again.

"You're a complete fucking psychopath!" Tate yells at Landon, speaking the truth, but not helping the situation in the slightest.

"Shhh," Daija murmurs, attempting to shush him because his words are only rubbing salt into Landon's wounded ego and making him even more rabid.

"Shut your fucking mouth," he growls out, struggling to get free from his friend's grip.

Toby runs his hands and his eyes over my face. "*Oh my God.* I'm so sorry."

"Not your fault," I grunt. "The asshole had it coming, and I was willing to take a couple hits for it."

"Shane . . ." he says breathlessly, but I brush it off because it was honestly nothing.

I would die for Toby.

Spencer and Jake suddenly rush down the stairs and run over to us. A bit too late, to be honest.

"*Shit.* You okay?" Spencer asks with concern, inquisitive eyes roaming my face.

"Yeah," I grunt. "Fine." But I can already feel my eye swelling up.

"*Ouch, bro,*" Jake hisses. "Sorry we weren't here. Where is the fucker?" he snarls, scouring the room before finding a still-fuming Landon being held back by his friend. "Who are these losers?" Jake laughs mockingly.

"The rabid one is Landon, and the guy with dark hair who's holding him back is Alex. Who I'm never speaking to again," Tate says, wrinkling his upper lip in disgust. "*Alex, don't text me anymore! It's over!*" Tate shouts across the room.

"*What?!* Seriously?" he yells back, looking heartbroken. "Come on, Tate! What did I do?!"

"You're friends with that fucker! *Major red flag!* Now delete my number, Alex!"

Spencer wraps an arm around Tate, pulling him into his side for comfort. "Fuck that loser, you hear me?"

"Yeah. You don't need him, babe," Daija adds.

"Tate, don't be like that, please!" Alex hollers, looking devastated, before his pain turns to anger, and he shakes Landon roughly. "I'm gonna let go now. Just chill the fuck out, okay? This is all your fault."

"I'm cool, man. Just let go of me," Landon sneers.

"Can we get out of here?" I ask no one in particular, grimacing when I touch my sore cheekbone. I really don't want to fight again.

"Go home, guys. We got your back," Spencer whispers with his arm still around Tate.

"We'll get these two home safely," Jake says, offering his elbow to Daija. "I already called an Uber."

She slips her arm through his, and they bring up the rear as we all leave this fucking place. Our friends wait out front for their rideshare, while Toby and I head to my truck.

I swear I will never go to another frat party as long as I live.

CHAPTER TWENTY-THREE
SHANE

We get home from the party and kick our shoes off by the front door. My face throbs, and my eye is swelling up from the fight with Landon, but I'm not one to whine, so I don't say anything.

"We need to get ice on that," Toby urges, his brows creased with worry. "It'll help stop the swelling."

I follow him to the kitchen on autopilot, my mind spinning with replays of tonight. He gets out a soft ice pack and fills it with ice from the refrigerator door. I lean against the kitchen counter and fold my arms across my chest, staring at the grout lines in the tile while everything goes out of focus.

"Put this on your eye, Shane. He hit you really hard," Toby hiccups, and I glance up from the floor at the distressed sound, narrowing my eyes on his quivering lip and watery stare.

"*Butterfly,*" I murmur, taking two large steps forward and wrapping him in my arms. "I'm okay, I promise. He barely got me." That might be a half-truth, but he doesn't need to know that my teeth ache, and my eye socket is throbbing from Landon's punches. Because I'd take a thousand more for him. "Thanks for the ice, it'll help," I add, pressing the soft fabric to my eye and relishing the cold. I take a deep breath and close my other eye, trying to shake off tonight. Landon's disrespect makes me want to protect Toby from the world and make him mine. Officially.

"I hate that tonight ended like that," he sniffles. "I just wanted us to have fun. You were right, we should have just stayed in."

"*Hey*. Listen. I'm fine. Don't be so hard on yourself," I murmur gently, lifting his chin with my forefinger. "None of this is your fault. Absolutely none of it," I reiterate, giving him a soft peck on the lips.

"Okay. Thanks, Shane." Toby smiles weakly and grabs two water bottles from the fridge before leading me toward the stairs. "Let's get you to bed," he says over his shoulder, and I can't help but stare at his perfect ass taking step after step all the way up. I follow him into my bedroom, where he pulls back the covers and motions for me to get in.

I slip out of my jeans and T-shirt, sliding into the cool sheets in nothing but my boxer briefs. I got a small glimpse of the underwear Toby grabbed before he went to the bathroom to change, and I'm dying to see him in it. "Gonna join me?" I ask

"Yes. But put that back on your eye," Toby insists, so I listen to my nurse, sighing when the cold relieves some of the ache. He slips the loose tank top over his head and then shimmies out of his tight Bermuda shorts. My breath hitches when he's standing before me in nothing but a silky purple thong. "My feet are cold," he says innocently, turning around to look in my sock drawer.

I grit my teeth and curse the sharp pain that radiates through my aching jaw.

Fuck, his ass is amazing, and I can't wait to get my hands on it again.

"Get over here," I growl, and Toby just giggles, knowing exactly what he's doing when he bends over to slip my socks on.

Toby spins around with his dimples on full display, standing there in a purple thong and my tall white crew socks. I drink him in, taking a mental picture that I will cherish forever. He laughs shyly, running a hand through his thick, messy curls.

My dick is rock-fucking-hard for him.

"Come here, butterfly," I demand, pulling the covers back and thrusting my hips upward to show him just how hard my cock is.

Toby bites his lip, the blush I love so much settling into his cheeks. I glance down and nearly come at the sight of his erection stretching and straining against the tiny dick pouch in his underwear.

I've never seen something so fucking alluring in all my life.

Slowly making his way over, Toby slips into the sheets, facing me.

"Hi," he says innocently, hiking a leg over my thigh and rubbing our cocks together.

"Mmm. Hi," I moan, grabbing a handful of his plump ass and pressing us harder together. I capture his lips, kissing him deeply while we grind against each other.

Toby suddenly pulls back. "We need to be careful, Shane. I don't want to hurt you," he says softly, chewing on his lower lip. "You're injured."

I chuckle at how thoughtful he is. "I'm fine. You won't," I tell him. "Your kisses only make me feel better."

"But you still need to ice it," he insists, setting the pack on my bruised eye once again. "Right away." Toby kisses me while he holds it there, raking his other hand through my long, unruly hair.

I grab his waist and haul him on top of me, slightly grimacing at the pain in my shoulder from when I tackled that asshole.

"What's wrong?" Toby asks observantly, his eyes searching my bare torso, but finding nothing. "What hurts?"

"I'm fine. Just a little sore from the fight."

"Where?" he questions further, running his hand over my bare chest and brushing against my nipples.

"Shoulders," I murmur, staring at him through half-lidded eyes.

"Let me draw you a bath, then. It'll help your sore muscles," he offers. We have a separate tub that nobody but Toby uses, so I know it's always clean.

"Okay," I agree, staring at his ass while he climbs out of bed, imagining burying my face between his cheeks while warm water splashes around us. I lick my lips, allowing my eyes to slowly roam his body until I get to his smiling, blushing face. "Only if you take it with me."

"These are my favorite bath salts," Toby says, sprinkling a handful of something that smells like vanilla cupcakes into the water. "It's all natural and scented with essential oils, so it's really good for your skin." He mixes it around with his hand, allowing it to dissolve into the hot water.

Once the tub is nearly full, Toby turns it off. Steam hovers in the air, fogging up the mirrors. Beads of moisture cling to my skin before I even get near the water. I drop my boxer briefs and climb into the old porcelain tub, sinking down into hot, soothing water. "*Mmm,*" I hum, feeling better as my tense and bruised muscles instantly relax.

"I was right, huh?" Toby teases, "A bath always helps."

I peek my good eye open. "Then join me," I murmur, and we lock gazes as Toby slowly steps out of his thong, leaving the tiny pile of fabric on the bathroom floor.

His cock is hard and desperate for release, the tip a pretty dusky pink. I lick my lips, wanting to taste *all* of him.

Toby steps into the tub while I hold one of his hands, helping him settle between my legs with his back to my chest. He gets comfortable, and I know he can feel my erection digging into his back.

Toby sighs, leaning his head against my chest. "The water feels amazing, and so does your cock."

I chuckle, wrapping an arm around him and tracing small circles on his belly. "A bath is nice with you in my arms," I admit, letting my sore muscles soak.

"Mhm," Toby agrees, and we both close our eyes, relaxing into one another and allowing the silky water and fragrant steam to dissolve our stress.

Toby suddenly jolts in my arms as if on the verge of sleep, moaning when I press my cock against his back, reminding him where he's at. I start drawing circles on his stomach again, continuing lower this time, enjoying the feel of his smooth skin as my hand wraps around his cock. "This okay?" I murmur into his ear, nibbling on the lobe.

"Y-yes. More," he encourages, arching his back for me. I kiss his neck, sucking on the tender flesh. I'm sure I'm leaving marks, but I don't care right now. *He's mine.*

I let go of his cock, making him whine until I slip my finger underneath his balls and circle his hole. Toby whimpers, bending his knees and exposing himself further.

"You like that, don't you?" I whisper into his ear. "When I touch you here?" I press my finger firmly against his hole without penetrating him.

"Y-yes," he stutters again. "Shane, please."

"Please, what?" I tease, licking into his ear and making him whimper.

"*Please, just finger me,*" he nearly cries.

"Not here, and not without lube," I reply, continuing to dance my finger around his rim before I stroke his cock once again. "I want you to be comfortable when I fuck you for the first time," I whisper, my lips moving against his ear.

"*Oh my God,*" Toby sobs. "Shane. I need you." He abruptly stands, water sloshing everywhere.

I instinctively grab his arm so he doesn't slip and fall. The last thing we need tonight is another injury. Toby carefully steps out of the tub and onto the towel laid out on the ground. He turns the shower on, testing the water temperature. "Let's rinse off and take this to bed, then," he says, blushing at his own eagerness.

My cock pulses with desire. I've never had a partner so desperate and needy before. It makes my dick harder than I thought was even possible.

Especially because it's Toby who wants me.

"Wanna try something?" I murmur, staring hungrily at Toby's towel-wrapped body, fresh from the shower.

"Yeah?" he asks with a curious, little half-smile.

I slowly step forward like I'm afraid I'll spook him.

Releasing Toby's towel, I let it drop to the floor and step back to admire his glistening, toned body fully lotioned up. He shaves *everything*. As I just confirmed in the shower.

"So fucking sexy. Do you think you can get on your hands and knees for me?" I whisper gently.

Toby licks his lips and swallows thickly, nodding slowly before crawling onto the bed and looking over his shoulder at me.

"Good boy," I encourage, running a hand along his spine and pressing down between his shoulder blades so he arches his back, exposing his hole to my starving eyes. "Mmm. So beautiful," I praise, running a finger between his cheeks and circling his hole the same way I did in the bath.

"Shane," he breathes out like a prayer, hanging his head with desire. His wet curls drip water onto my sheets, and his body glistens with moisture.

I can't take it any longer, I'm just as desperate as he is, so I spread him open and swipe my tongue up his crease, starting with his balls.

"*Ungh! Fuck!*" Toby cries out, panting and spreading his legs further apart to give me more access.

I focus on his hole, circling my tongue before I stiffen it and prod at his entrance until my tongue wiggles its way in, and I start to fuck him with it. The moans and cries that pour from Toby's mouth sound inhuman. *Animalistic.* I keep him spread with one hand, continuing to rim him within an inch of his life while I reach around to stroke his cock with my other hand.

"Oh God. Shane. *Oh God.* Please. I need you to fuck me. *Please, fuck me,*" Toby begs as his thighs begin to shake. I stand up and grab the lube from the bedside table, popping the cap and pouring some on my finger as well as Toby's hole.

He hisses when the cool liquid drips down his crease, moaning when I start to rub it in and press a finger inside him. "Mmm. Shane," he groans, dropping his head and sticking his ass up even further.

I fuck him with one finger before pulling out and pushing another into him. "You like that?" I ask, continuing to fuck him with two fingers.

Just as he's about to speak, I push my fingers all the way in, twisting and curling them until I find his spot. Toby's words come out in a garbled cry, and he starts to bounce his ass on my hand.

"That's it, baby," I encourage. "Make yourself feel good. Think you can take three?"

Toby nods frantically, continuing to move fast until I slow him down by grabbing his hip and slipping my fingers out.

He whimpers at the loss. "*Shh, baby.* I got you." I press three fingers against his hole, meeting resistance. "You can do it, just relax your muscles and bear down like with the toy." Toby takes a deep breath, and I push forward, three of my thick digits sinking into him and stretching him open. I press his upper back down, making him lift his ass even higher. I spread my fingers, stretching him further and making his breathing pick up.

What a fucking view.

"Shane. I'm so full," he nearly sobs, but he hasn't felt anything yet compared to my dick.

"Are you ready for me to fuck you, butterfly?" I gently slip my fingers out before he can even answer, and Toby collapses to the bed as if my hand was the only thing holding him up.

"Yes. Please, Shane. Fuck me. *Please.*"

I push one of Toby's knees up so that it's bent as high as

it can go. "Now arch your back and pop your ass out for me, baby."

Toby does as instructed, and I crawl between his open legs, grabbing both hips. I admire his pulsing, stretched hole. Ready and waiting for me. Gripping the base of my thoroughly lubed-up cock, I give it a few pumps before pressing against his hole.

I pause for a second. This may be redundant after the other night, but I respect him and ask, nonetheless. "Do you want me to use a condom? I'm negative, but it's your decision."

"No. I trust you. *Always*. I want to feel you inside me, with nothing between us, and I want you to fill me with your seed."

Holy fucking shit.

I growl like an actual dog, baring my teeth and all.

Slowly pressing forward, I meet resistance, even though he's nice and open.

Toby whimpers at the pressure, clenching up and pulling away. "I can't do it," he whines. "It's too big."

"*Shhh*. Yes, you can." I hover over him and kiss his neck, rubbing a hand down his thigh and ass, massaging him. "Just relax, Tobes. Take a deep breath and remember to bear down when you feel me pushing against you." I reach around, stroking his cock and getting him hard again.

"Okay. I'm ready" Toby whispers, wiggling his ass against me.

I try again, continuing to push past the first ring of muscle, making Toby cry out as I pop inside. I pause, glancing down and staring in awe at my cock disappearing inside of his ass.

I almost can't believe it.

"*Oh God! Shane!*" Toby shouts, and I remain frozen, allowing his body to get used to me before I continue.

"You're doing so good. *So fucking good*," I murmur, rubbing a hand down his spine, admiring the sexy arch of his back.

After a few deep breaths, he's finally ready. "Keep going," he breathes out, and I push my hips forward, gliding the rest of the way into him until I bottom out.

The wail that comes out of him sends goosebumps shivering down my spine and almost makes me blow my load.

Holy shit. He's so fucking tight.

"You alright?" I ask, completely out of breath, even though I haven't started fucking him yet.

Toby remains silent for a moment, his cheek pressed to the mattress and his eyes pinched closed.

"Talk to me," I urge, starting to get a little worried. "You okay, baby?"

"I-I've never felt so full," he whimpers. "I want you to stay inside me forever."

Toby contracts his inner muscles around my cock and I grunt, squeezing his hips even harder.

"Fuck me, Shane," he finally says.

I stare at the place where we're connected, my dick completely disappearing inside him. I pull back gently and press forward once again, my eyes rolling into the back of my head.

So fucking tight.

Continuing the gentle pace, I kiss his neck and nibble on his ear, leisurely fucking him. Nothing too hard and nothing too rough.

"More," Toby whispers.

"More what?" I ask, continuing to be gentle and slow. "Tell me. I need to hear you say it."

"*Harder*. I may be clumsy, but I'm not made of glass. Fuck me harder, Shane!"

I do as he says and pull back quickly, surging forward fast and hard. Toby spreads his legs further, and I grab hold of his hips, pistoning in and out of him as fast as I can. I fuck him *hard*, spearing into him before slowing down and grinding my pelvis into his sensitive rim. Reaching around, I grab hold of his cock and stroke him in time with my thrusts.

"I'm gonna come, Shane. I'm gonna come," Toby chants over and over until his muscles constrict around my cock, triggering my own orgasm. We both cry out at the same time, Toby's high-pitched wails mixing with my low grunts and moans.

I've never come so hard in all my life.

Not even close.

My dick starts to soften, and I carefully slip out of Toby's ass, making him wince. "You okay?" I ask. Toby doesn't speak, only nods into the pillow while he lies motionless in his own release. "My turn to take care of you," I murmur, and Toby just hums with his eyes closed. "Don't move."

Grabbing a towel, I quickly wipe myself off before wrapping it around my waist and rushing to the bathroom to clean up and relieve myself. I return with a couple of warm washcloths for Toby, finding him exactly where I left him.

I get a clean pair of boxers from my dresser drawer and slip them on before climbing back in bed. "You awake?" I whisper, gently rubbing his back.

"Mhm," Toby responds with a sleepy smile, and his eyes still closed.

"Gonna clean you up," I warn him, spreading his cheeks and making him jump. "Shh. I just need to make sure everything's okay and get you cleaned up."

Toby relaxes and allows me to inspect him. He's a little red and puffy, but I'm sure that's to be expected. I use the second washcloth to wipe his spent cock and get as much off the sheets as I can manage.

"Let's move to your bed. Gonna stick the sheets in the wash," I tell him after we lie there spooning for a little while. "Think I heard Spence and Jake come home, so make sure you get dressed," I warn him, and he groans.

"We need more privacy," Toby complains, and I couldn't agree more.

Toby slips on one of my oversized T-shirts, wearing it like a nightgown. I throw on some basketball shorts and a T-shirt of my own. Toby sneaks off to his room while I take my bed apart, lugging the sheets downstairs to the laundry room.

Luckily, I make it back to Toby's room without an encounter with our roommates. I'm not in the mood to rehash what happened tonight. I'm currently in my own world with Toby, and I never want to leave it.

"Hey," I murmur as I step into his bedroom with a crooked smile.

"Hey," Toby replies, a warm blush filling his cheeks, and I find it so endearing after what we just did in my bed.

"Ready to cuddle?" I ask, undressing down to my underwear.

"Yeah. But take those off, too," Toby says with two mischievous dimples I can't say no to.

I step out of my boxer briefs, my dick getting hard once again. He pulls the covers back, revealing his own naked body and half-hard cock. I climb in, wrapping him up in my embrace.

"I like feeling small in your arms," Toby admits quietly, further sinking into me. "I like feeling safe."

I squeeze him tighter, every atom in my body feeling the universe push us closer together until I can't deny it any longer. Can't deny *us*.

Like a thief in the night, my world is forever changed. It's in this very moment that reality hits me.

I love him, and in a way, I think I always have.

"Can I tell you something?" I whisper vulnerably.

"Of course," Toby replies, his brows creased and face tense as he sits up and waits for me to speak.

I push myself up, too, and lean against the headboard, giving him a half-smile. I hold my palm out, and Toby places his hand in mine, scooting closer.

"It's taken me a while to admit this to myself, but I think a part of me has always known it . . . I'm in love with you."

"*What?*" Toby gasps, his eyes instantly welling up with tears. "You . . ."

"I'm in love with you, Tobias Livingston. You don't have to say it back. I just needed you to know." It feels like a weight I didn't know I was carrying has been lifted from my shoulders.

"Of course I have to say it back," he chuckles, the laugh turning into a sob. "I love you, too, Shane. *So freaking much.* I've loved you since high school and probably before. You have no idea."

"*Butterfly,*" I whisper, memorizing his delicate features and glistening gaze in this movie-perfect moment. Leaning forward, I kiss him softly, wrapping my arms around him and squeezing him tightly to my chest. "You're my best friend, my lover, and the key to my happiness. I want you to be my boyfriend, Toby. Will you?" I ask, peering down into mesmerizing golden eyes.

"Yes, Shane. That would make me the happiest person in the world."

I lean down and seal my lips to my boyfriend's.

He's mine now. And I will do everything in my power to keep him happy and safe.

CHAPTER TWENTY-FOUR
TOBY

"Tonight is going to be so much fun!" I practically squeal, so excited that Shane agreed to cook for the dinner party that I'm planning for our friends. Every single one of them has been there for us in one way or another, and I'm excited to tell them that we're officially dating now.

As in, we're actually boyfriends.

Shane and me.

I still have to pinch myself when I think about it sometimes.

He's cooking a three-course meal to celebrate, and tonight he's featuring his favorite dishes from Coastal Cuisine. Spencer and Jake are upstairs getting ready, and Tate and Daija should be here any minute.

The doorbell suddenly rings, and I hop up from the island, where I was sitting and keeping Shane company. I offered to help, but he said he didn't trust me with how sharp his knives are. *"They're here!"* I announce to everyone and no one, scampering off to the front door and greeting two of my best friends with hugs and cheek kisses.

I usher them into the kitchen, where Shane is stirring the seafood risotto he's cooking for his main dish. He gives them both a silent nod, heading over to the wine rack. "I have red and white. Whichever you prefer. They both pair well with dinner."

Tate and Daija look at each other and giggle, absolutely delighted by the white glove service. "We'll take the chef's recommendation," Tate says with a wink and a big, flirty smile.

Shane doesn't even flinch at the flirting, robotically pouring two glasses of red wine and handing them over. "If you all want to take a seat in the living room, I can bring out the appetizers when they're ready," Shane offers before going back to shucking a bowl of oysters covered in ice.

We follow the chef's instructions, and I give him a quick kiss when everyone's out of the kitchen. "Thank you for doing this," I whisper before heading to the living room to entertain our guests.

Shortly after, Jake and Spencer come stampeding down the stairs in a wave of hair gel and cologne.

"'Sup, everybody," Jake says, plopping down right next to Daija. "How are we doing on this fine evening?"

"Hey, Toby," Spencer says sweetly. "Thanks for putting this together. I'm looking forward to dinner."

"You're welcome." I beam. "Thanks for showing up."

"Wouldn't miss it." Spencer takes the open spot next to Tate on the love seat, and I don't miss the way Tate's bright blue eyes eat him up.

"How are you, Tate?" Spencer asks kindly, clearly still worried about him after the encounter with Alex.

"I guess I'm okay," Tate says with a shrug and a half-smile.

"You sure?" Spencer presses, placing his palm on Tate's

bare thigh and staring him directly in the eyes. "It's okay if you're not."

Is something going on between them?

My eyes dart over to Daija, but she's too busy being chatted up by Jake to notice what's happening over here with Tate and Spencer.

"Yeah," Tate breathes out, twirling a lock of hair around his finger. "Thank you for checking on me, though."

"Good," Spencer says with a satisfied nod. "Of course."

Tate clears his throat awkwardly, which is something that doesn't happen often. He's never flustered by guys and never shy. I mean, we're talking about the boy who wears sequin booty shorts and a leather harness on the regular.

"So, what's the big news tonight, honey?" Tate asks, switching the focus to me. "Are you pregnant?"

My friends chuckle, and I can feel the blood rush to my cheeks. I know my face is bright red right now.

Ugh. Damnit, Tate.

Luckily, Shane saves me from having to respond. He's carrying a multi-level oyster tower filled with ice, lemon slices, and tons of raw oysters.

"*Ooo,*" everyone murmurs in unison, making way for Shane to set it on the coffee table that I decorated with a beach theme earlier. I even added some cute little origami crabs, fish, and seahorses that Shane made for me.

"I present to you, hand-shucked oysters with fresh lemon and shallots."

"Oh my God. This looks absolutely amazing, Shane," I compliment him, and everyone else follows. "Thank you."

Shane nods, passing out small white plates. Everyone loads their plates with oysters, being well-acquainted with how to eat them, living in Crescent Bay.

"You know what they say about oysters?" Jake says,

waggling his eyebrows at Daija before messily slurping one down.

"No. What do they say, Jake?" she deadpans, clearly messing with him while she sips her wine.

"Oh, um. You know?" he says awkwardly, wiggling his eyebrows *again* before looking to Spencer for help.

"Do I?" she asks innocently, tipping her head back and sucking another one down.

"They're an aphrodisiac," Jake whispers out the side of his mouth.

"Well then, I guess we're all going to be horny now because of Shane," Tate blurts out, making everyone burst out laughing.

Shane shakes his head in exasperation, but I don't miss the little smile tugging at his lips. He eats a few more oysters before standing up and excusing himself. "Please continue to enjoy yourselves, I'm off to plate up the main course. You can head to the dining room when you're done." Shane's professional chef voice gets me just as hot as his chef coat and apron do. Add in the aphrodisiacs, and I'm ready to jump his bones later.

Jake sucks back the last oyster before we make our way to the dining room that I also decorated. Sheer white fabric flows down the center of the table like an ocean wave. Beautiful seashells dot the fabric as well as sand dollars and a few starfish. A small lighthouse-shaped lantern glows in the center, creating a relaxing ambiance.

"*Baby boy*," Daija gasps. "This is absolutely gorgeous. You did so well!"

"Thank you," I say shyly, taking a seat across from her.

"You really did. You could think about pursuing design," Tate insists, making me beam with pride.

I really enjoy planning parties and decorating, but I love playing violin even more.

We're all laughing and chatting about upcoming finals when Shane confidently strolls in with a steaming plate in each hand. Low hums fill the room, everyone's mouths likely filling with saliva.

"I present to you, seafood risotto with locally caught lobster, crab, and shrimp." Shane sets a plate down in front of me and Daija first. I breathe in the delicious smell and smile up at him. "Thank you."

Daija and I both wait for him to go back two more times and serve the rest of the plates before we begin to eat. Shane takes his seat next to me, holding up his glass of water for a toast. I do the same, and our friends follow.

"To good friends, good food, and the best partner I could ever ask for," Shane says, leaning down to press a kiss to my lips, completely catching me and everyone else off guard.

"I'm sorry. Did you just say *partner*?!" Tate shouts, the first one to speak. "*As in boyfriend?!*"

"Yes," Shane replies evenly, rubbing my lower back with his opposite hand.

Tate squeals loudly, nearly tumbling backward out of his seat.

"Hell yeah! *Cheers!*" Jake shouts, clanging his glass against Shane's and then mine.

Spencer follows, and then they're all cheering us on.

"That's why I planned this dinner tonight. I wanted to announce it to you guys—our best friends—and celebrate together. I love Shane, and I wanted to share that with the people that mean the most to me," I say, attempting to hold back the tears.

I'm just so happy right now.

"Aww, babe!" Daija shouts, jumping out of her seat and rushing around the table to hug me. "I love you so much, and I'm so happy for you. Shane is an amazing man, and you finally found what you deserve." She wraps her arms around me and squeezes, before whispering in Shane's ear. "Take care of my baby boy," she warns. "Or Tate and I will come for you in your sleep," she threatens, and I smile at her cute little snarl.

"Got it," Shane confirms with a nod and a small smile.

"Good," she says, holding her head high and returning to her seat across from us and blowing me a kiss.

"Well, now that that's settled," I giggle. "Everyone dig in!"

Shane's risotto is perfectly cooked and deliciously creamy, filled with fresh seafood he picked up from the pier himself. The tender lumps of buttery lobster are my favorite thing about it.

"Mmm. That was amazing," I say to Shane, rubbing my full belly. The entire table agrees fervently, nearly licking their bowls clean.

"Thanks, guys. I'll go grab dessert." Shane rises from his seat and disappears into the kitchen with a stack of empty bowls.

I'm so full, but I always have room for Shane's banana pudding.

It's my absolute favorite dessert.

"So, does this count as our first date?" Jake asks Daija with hearts in his eyes.

"Did you pay? Or cook?" she asks with a raised brow, swirling her wine around her glass and peering at him out of the corner of her eye.

"Uh, no?" Jake replies with a question, looking confused as if he's unsure of the right answer.

"Then no, this doesn't count as our first date, Jakey-poo."

"Are you saying I have a chance, though?" Jake's face lights up like I've never seen before.

Daija shrugs noncommittally, pushing her braids off her shoulder and taking a sip of wine. Jake clasps his hands together and looks up at the ceiling, mouthing *thank you, Jesus*.

"You need to watch your boy before he ends up heartbroken," I hear Tate whisper to Spencer, and I can't help but listen in.

"Jake's a big boy; he can handle himself," Spencer chuckles.

"And what about you?" Tate asks, lowering his voice.

"What about me?"

"Are you a big boy?" Tate's question is so breathy, I almost don't hear it.

Rolling my lips inward, I press them together to stop from laughing. I don't know why Tate has always had a thing for straight guys, but Daija confirmed he's been like this since high school.

What I'm *not* expecting is Spencer's husky response. "I can show you later and let you be the judge."

"Challenge accepted," Tate murmurs, sucking on his lower lip.

"Dessert is served," Shane announces, and I quickly shut my gaping mouth before my friends notice my eavesdropping.

But seriously though, what the fuck is going on? Does this old house have some sort of magical powers to turn straight boys gay?

CHAPTER TWENTY-FIVE
TOBY

Things are going great.

Shane and I are officially boyfriends. The dinner party with our friends went better than expected, and when we hold hands on campus, no one cares. Even though I know I need to tell my parents before they find out on their own, I just haven't been able to face them yet. College is a lot to handle, and I don't need their added stress.

Besides, I've been so busy with my classes and practicing violin that I've hardly even seen my boyfriend. Finals are coming up, and it's been pretty all-consuming for both of us, especially with Shane's work schedule added in.

Even though we live in the same house, I miss him, so I asked him to take the weekend off. I decided to plan a getaway for us. We deserve a break from how hard we've been studying, and Shane deserves a break from work. After all of the fun dates he's planned for us, now it's my turn.

"You gonna tell me where we're going?" Shane asks while I lie on my stomach, half on him and half between his legs. We're relaxing in bed after he just got off work, watching some old comedy.

"*Nope,*" I reply, popping the *p*.

"Then how am I gonna drive us there?" He boops my nose with a smirk.

"Oh, um . . ." I didn't think about that. "I can put the address into your phone," I propose, really wanting to surprise him the way he has for me.

"I'd feel more comfortable knowing where I'm going."

Guess he doesn't appreciate a good surprise the way I do.

"Fiiine. We're going to the mountains in Tennessee. It's about four and a half hours away, so not too bad. I rented a cabin and booked us an appointment at the local spa."

Shane wraps his arms around me, the best he can in this position, kissing the top of my head. "You didn't have to do that, Tobes."

"We deserve this trip, and we deserve to relax. Just three more days, and we can leave after classes on Friday."

I can't wait to unplug from the world and spend some quality time alone with Shane.

We're about an hour into the trip, and I am so excited and slightly impatient to get there and see the cabin in person. I hope it's as amazing as it looks online. Shane's driving my Audi since it has all the modern features that his truck doesn't have, making it safer and more comfortable for long trips.

I lean my seat back, fold my arms behind my head, and stretch out my legs. "Ahh," I sigh contentedly. "I love not driving."

Shane snorts. "I love you for not driving, too."

"*Hey,*" I whine, giving him the side-eye. "That pole came out of nowhere. It wasn't my fault," I laugh, referring to my parking lot faux pas from last year that I can finally laugh about instead of cry. Even though the damage was minimal, my parents weren't happy, to say the least, and it only further drove the wedge in our relationship.

Not wanting to think about my parents for another second on this trip, I grab the bag of trail mix from the console between us and stuff a handful into my mouth. I check the map, making sure we don't miss our next exit.

"So, I got you something," Shane suddenly says.

"You and your surprises," I tease. "Always trying to one-up me."

"You're the one whisking me away for a weekend getaway," Shane says matter-of-factly.

"Touché. So, what did you get me?"

"You'll see tonight." Shane reaches over and gives my thigh a squeeze, allowing his hand to roam up to my crotch.

Blood instantly rushes to my cock, and I get hard in his hand, thrusting into it. "*Shit,*" I curse, knowing we have another three hours on the road, and I'm about to be left hanging.

I'm too easy.

Shane chuckles, fondling me through my shorts one last time before returning his hand to the wheel. "It'll be worth the wait. Trust me."

"I'm gonna take a nap," I grumble, folding my arms across my chest and closing my eyes. "*Don't miss our exit.*" I might be pouting, but he just left me horny and curious. *Ugh.*

Shane laughs again, and it's loud and carefree with a

little roughness around the edges. It's magnetic and just for me. It's officially my new favorite sound.

The cabin is everything I hoped it'd be and more. The back deck is nearly as big as the inside, with a hot tub, sauna, and a complete outdoor kitchen area that Shane got excited about. He ordered groceries as soon as we unloaded the car, insisting on cooking us dinner instead of going out, and I sure as hell won't say no.

I'm currently lounging in the hot tub while Shane cooks our dinner on the large gas grill. My stomach growls at the delicious, chargrilled smells wafting my way while the soothing sounds of bubbling water and birds chirping fill my ears. It's beautiful here, nestled in a lush green forest with picturesque mountains.

"I needed this," I say with a sigh, leaning my head back and smiling into the warm heat of the sun. There's something so rejuvenating about being in the mountains.

"Me too," Shane agrees. "Thanks for planning this. It's nice here."

I crack one eye open, creeping on my boyfriend while he flips homemade kabobs without a shirt on. His skin glistens with a slight sheen of sweat, making his muscles look even sexier.

God, my boyfriend's hot.

How did I get so lucky?

When Shane closes the lid to let our dinner finish cooking, I try to convince him to get in the hot tub with me, so I can do more than just ogle him. "You should join me. Play Marco Polo with our dicks."

"As tempting as that sounds, the kabobs have to come

off the grill in ten minutes, and I'm *definitely* gonna need more than ten minutes in there with you playing Marco Polo. Rain check?" Shane asks, strolling over to give me a quick peck on the lips.

"Okay," I faux-pout. "But only 'cause I'm hungry and that tops horny."

"I'll show you who tops who," Shane growls with another kiss on the lips, making me giggle. "Be right back." He disappears inside, returning with a stack of plates and silverware in one hand and a bowl of rice in the other. Making one more trip, Shane comes back with a delicious-smelling sauce and a plate of warm pita bread.

"Oh my God. That looks amazing. Are the kabobs ready yet?" I ask like an impatient child waiting for their parents to finish cooking dinner. Honestly, he's lucky I slept most of the drive here, or I probably would have asked the dreaded, *are we there yet?*

Shane just chuckles, grabbing a plate and a pair of tongs before making his way over to the grill. "Just about. Go ahead and dry off."

Overeager and a little impatient, I leap out of the hot tub, missing the top step completely and slipping on the edge with my wet feet. "*Fuck!*" I shout, but before I make painful contact with the deck, Shane's strong arms wrap around me, and I face-plant into his hard, bare chest. My heart is racing. That could have been bad. That could have ruined the whole weekend before it even started.

"I'm no psychic, but I saw that coming," Shane murmurs into my ear before setting me back on my feet. "Gotta be more careful with yourself. You're too important."

I blush at his words, staring into dark, intense eyes.

Shane steps away with his arms held out in front of

him, like I might fall again. "You gonna be okay? We don't need any injuries." He tosses me a towel, and I catch it with an eye roll, wrapping it around my waist.

"Ha. Ha. That was just a freak mishap. Won't happen again." I don't even look his way, scurrying to the sliding glass door and down the short hallway to one of two bedrooms in the cabin. I quickly pat myself down, slip off the wet trunks, and put on dry clothes. It's nothing special, just a pair of black athletic shorts and a loose white tank top. But I don't miss the way Shane's eyes travel the length of my body when I step out while he's setting the table.

"Wow," I say, in awe at all the food. "Everything looks delicious. Thank you, Shane."

The table is fit for a king, and I know I am beyond lucky to get to eat his cooking on the regular. I take a seat across from him, while he serves me a little bit of everything from the kabobs. Tender chicken and perfectly seasoned veggies like onions, bell peppers, and mushrooms fill my plate. Next up is a scoop of sticky white rice and a dollop of tzatziki sauce. I help myself to three pieces of pita bread and lean back to admire this incredible plate of food and the amazing chef who prepared it.

I hold my glass of water up. "To friendship, love, and enjoying our lives together."

"And to my incredible boyfriend for planning this trip," Shane adds, clinking his glass with mine. "I love you."

"Love you too," I whisper, trying not to get choked up.

"Dig in," Shane encourages, picking up his knife and fork.

I stab some veggies and place them on a pita with a spoonful of tzatziki sauce on top. *"Mmm,"* I moan, rich flavors bursting across my tongue. "This is so good, Shane."

He nods in acknowledgement, busy making a mini chicken pita.

We eat in comfortable silence, enjoying the fresh air, each other's company, and most definitely the food.

After dinner, I wander to the bedroom with sleepy eyes until I spot a perfectly wrapped gift sitting on top of the bed. "Ahh. My surprise," I murmur.

Shane wraps his arms around me, resting his chin on top of my head. "Did you forget?"

I nod, shimmying the lid off the gift box, plucking the sheets of tissue paper out, and tossing them in the air like it's my birthday. When I realize what's filling the box, my stomach hollows out and arousal burns low in my belly.

Shane got me lingerie.

A lot of lingerie.

"Is this a present for me or you?" I giggle, holding up a tiny piece of lace fabric. It's a red thong with matching garters and thigh-high stockings. The next one is a black mesh one piece that definitely goes up my ass.

"*Both of us*," Shane growls, his eyes zeroing in on me and not the lingerie, as if he's dying to see me in it.

The next piece I hold up is a silky purple thong and matching crop top cami. I love it.

"Did Tate help you?" I ask, thoroughly impressed with his choices.

Shane just shrugs with a coy little smirk on his lips, keeping his secrets close to his chest as always. "Couldn't decide what I wanted to see you in, so I bought it all."

Oh my God. My heart.

"Thank you," I murmur, feeling so loved and cherished by him. "I love everything. *Seriously*. I'm gonna try this one on." I grab a shiny silver set, completely distracted by his intense stare and that lock of dark hair hanging in front of his eyes. I'm not even sure what I grabbed, but I rush to the bathroom to find out.

I shut the door and lean against it, closing my eyes and taking a deep breath. Once I slow the heartbeat whooshing in my ears, I look down at the metallic silver scraps in my hands. Holding up the pieces, I realize it's a crop top and cheeky boy shorts. One side of my lips pulls up.

I really like this one.

As soon as I slip into the sexy, metallic lingerie, I feel so confident. Strutting down the hallway like a supermodel, I do a little twirl when I get back to the bedroom so Shane can see how hot my ass looks in these booty shorts.

Shane's eyes widen in shock for a brief second before darkening with lust. "*Butterfly* . . ." he growls out the nickname I love so much, giving me full-body goosebumps. "Come here," he says softly, holding his hand out for me while he leans against the headboard.

I place my fingers in his, and he pulls me onto his lap so that I'm straddling him.

"Hi," I squeak when he grabs my ass with both hands.

"Hi," he murmurs back. "You look so fucking hot right now, baby."

I grind my hardening cock against his erection, desperate for more friction. "I wanna feel you against me," I breathe into his mouth before pulling back and helping him tug his boxers down.

Shane's hard cock springs free almost comically, slapping against his lower abdomen and making an obscene sound that sends a jolt of electricity straight to my dick.

He grabs his length, giving it a few pumps before we start moving against each other and kissing. I'm still in the lingerie, and there's something so sexy about being restrained by the fabric while Shane's hardness rubs against me. "I . . . I want you to come on my underwear. I wanna see it. Jerk yourself off on me," I plead, loving it when he comes on me.

Shane rolls me over, kneeling between my open thighs. He hovers above me, slowly stroking his cock. "I'm gonna paint you with my cum, baby. Just the way you like it."

I whimper, my dick twitching in the tiny boy shorts. I'm so horny right now, desperately spreading my legs further as Shane picks up his pace.

"Gonna come," he grunts, and I watch in awe as his muscles tense up and he shoots load after load onto the silver fabric, painting it with ropes of cum.

"*Oh fuck,*" I cry, so turned on by the sight of his jizz on my underwear.

"Damn. You look so beautiful covered in me, butterfly."

"I need to come. *Please.* I need you." I reach for him, panting and desperate.

Shane's pupils fully dilate, making him look like some sort of sex demon as he yanks down my bottoms and leaves me with nothing but a crop top and a hard cock. "You look so pretty all dressed up for me," he says, running his hands up my body and under the top, pinching both of my nipples and making me arch my back.

"Mmm. Touch me more," I beg.

"Get on your hands and knees."

I'm so horny, I do as instructed right away and arch my back, looking over my shoulder at him while I expose my ass. A large hand rubs my cheeks, giving me a squeeze before following the contour of my spine all the way up to my neck. He rubs and massages the tense muscles there before returning to my ass and spreading me open for his viewing pleasure. I hang my head and close my eyes, enjoying the admiration and the anticipation of what he might do next.

"*So fucking sexy,*" he growls, his hot breath ghosting over my sensitive hole. I gasp when I feel something warm and wet along my crease. A loud moan pours from my throat as I sink into the incredible sensations. Shane's done this a couple of other times, but I swear he somehow gets better each time.

"Oh my God, Shane," I breathe out, shamelessly arching my back and quietly asking for more.

He licks me again, running his tongue along my taint and circling my hole. His thumbs apply pressure and spread me open just enough to allow the tip of his tongue to slip in. "*Ungh!*" I cry into the pillow, my thighs shaking while I near the edge.

As if he can sense it, Shane's tongue retreats, and he reaches around, squeezing the base of my cock and stopping the building orgasm. I whimper unintelligibly, my legs ready to give out.

"I'm not done with you yet. That was just the warm-up." Shane presses down on my upper back, making me stick my ass up in the air even more. "Ready for me to stretch you open?"

"Yesss," I hiss out as he circles my rim with his lubed-up finger. "*Please.* Fuck me, Shane."

Relaxed from his tongue, Shane easily slips a digit in. I groan at the wonderful fullness, rocking against his finger and wanting more.

"You like that, baby?" Shane asks, adding another finger and scissoring them but never hitting that spot deep inside that I love so much.

"Yes. More," I beg shamelessly.

Shane squirts more lube on me and pushes a third finger into my ass, stretching me wider. I whine at the slight burn, so Shane pauses, leaning over to pepper feather-soft kisses along my spine. "Relax, butterfly," he whispers into my ear, nipping and sucking at the sensitive flesh while he slowly begins to move his fingers until he fills me up. Shane curls them, hitting that spot deep inside me and forcing a loud, mangled cry from my throat.

"*Ungh!* Oh my fucking God. Shane!" I squeeze the pillow while I bury my face in it and scream.

Shane continues to milk my spot until I'm on the edge, and my body tenses up. He slips his fingers out, leaving me empty and wanting. My hole pulses with need. The need for Shane to fill it up.

"Please," I whine. "Fuck me, now."

Shane squirts more lube directly on my hole, stroking his cock to get ready. He presses his tip to my opening, teasing me with slow, relentless circles without applying any pressure.

"I need it," I beg, trying to push back against him.

Shane grips my hips and stills me. "Gonna fuck you so good, baby. There's no one within miles to hear your cries. Don't hold back." He presses his cockhead into me slowly, stretching me to the point that it's almost too much. I bear down and push against him until he slips past the tight ring of muscle and his head pops in.

I cry out, panting heavily at the intrusion.

"You okay?" he murmurs, holding his body still.

"Yeah. I'm good," I pant, a slight sheen of sweat forming on my face and body.

Shane's cock slowly fills me the rest of the way, and I let out the longest, loudest moan as if his dick physically pushes all of the air out of me. He stays still for a moment, letting me get used to his size. He feels so deep like this. I peer over my shoulder, meeting a pair of dark, lust-filled eyes. His bare chest is sweaty, and his hair is in complete disarray.

He looks fucking hot.

"Fuck me," I demand, ready for him to start moving.

Shane slowly pulls his dick out, and my eyes roll into the back of my head. I once again press my face into the pillow, surrendering to his slow, deep thrusts.

"*Mmm,*" I moan. "Faster."

Shane picks up the pace, never losing his rhythm. "Let me hear you."

I start to moan with every thrust, not holding back at all.

"Louder," he demands.

"Harder!" I taunt, even though he's fucking me faster and harder than I've ever experienced.

Shane curls around my back, holding himself up with one arm and wrapping the other around my chest while pounding into my ass. "Hard enough, butterfly?" he growls, curling his hips and grazing my prostate.

"*Ungh! Shane!*" I scream loud enough to wake the neighbors, if we had any out here.

"That's it, baby. Say my fucking name," Shane grunts, and I'm so turned on right now, I'm moments away from coming.

"*Shane*. I'm gonna come."

"Not yet," he demands, banding an arm across my torso and pulling me up so we're both on our knees. Shane slips a hand under my crop top and pinches one of my nipples, twisting and playing with the tight bud while he continues to plunge into my ass. "You're doing such a good job taking this cock," he grits out.

Shane finally grabs hold of my leaking cock and strokes me roughly, smearing my precum around the head while he continues to torture my nipples and fuck my ass.

It's overstimulating in the best ways possible.

"*Ungh. Yes. Yes,*" I chant, bouncing between his fist and the dick in my ass. I tip my head back, resting it on his shoulder, while I completely surrender my body to Shane.

"I got you, baby. I got you," he whispers into my ear, licking the lobe and continuing his praise.

I explode, my cock pulsing in Shane's hand while my ass contracts around his length. The moans that come out of my mouth are obscene, but I don't care because no one's here but us, and Shane loves it.

He grunts, pressing deep inside of my ass and holding himself there. His cock pulses and warmth shoots through me.

"*Oh my God,*" I cry. "Fill me up, Shane!"

He continues to unload inside me before his softening cock slips out, and we both flop to the bed, panting and exhausted. I can feel his cum dripping out of me, and I know I need to get up and take a shower, but I hardly have the energy.

I must have drifted off because Shane's suddenly kneeling in front of me with a couple of warm washcloths.

"Pull your knees back," he demands, and even though we just had sex, a blush still fills my cheeks. I do as he says, allowing Shane to clean me up. "You, uh . . ." Shane clears his throat awkwardly. "You probably need to use the restroom to get it all out."

"I like the way it feels to keep some of you inside me."

"*Yeah?*" he asks in amazement.

"Yeah."

"Then I'm getting you a plug," Shane informs me, and I can't deny the thrill that shoots down my spine.

I want it.

CHAPTER TWENTY-SIX
TOBY

I jolt awake to a loud boom that practically shakes the whole cabin, my eyes blinking into a black void. "What was that?" I whisper groggily, half-asleep and breathing heavily as if I just woke from a nightmare. A bright flash of light illuminates the entire bedroom in the blink of an eye, and my brain finally puts it all together. A thunderstorm. Another deep rumble makes the windows rattle.

"It's close," Shane murmurs. "Gonna check the weather app." He reaches out, trying to feel for his phone on the nightstand.

Another flash of lightning, followed by a loud crack, has me whimpering and sinking deeper under the covers. The heavy rain pounds against the roof, and the wind howls, whipping around the cabin like an angry banshee.

"Can't find my phone. Close your eyes one sec," Shane warns before I hear the click of the lamp switch, but sense no light behind my closed lids. "Shit. I think the power's out," he grunts.

"Really?" I roll over and attempt to turn on my own

bedside lamp with no luck. "Shit," I parrot. My heart rate spikes, and I lie back down, curling myself into Shane. "What are we gonna do?"

"I scoped out the shed in the back when we first got here, and I saw a small generator. It should be enough to run the fridge and maybe a light or two. Water still works, it'll just be cold. No harm in that. We'll be fine, Tobes. Promise." Shane gives me a big, reassuring squeeze, easing some of my worry but not all of it. "Go back to sleep. I got you."

Another loud boom gives me a scare, making me jerk in his arms. "I think Mother Nature has other plans because there's no way I can sleep through this," I admit. "Any idea when the storm's gonna end?" My anxiety won't allow me to relax, knowing we're surrounded by potential danger. "What if a tree falls? It would crush the entire cabin!"

"Stop worrying. It's passing over us right now," Shane reassures me. "This is the worst of it."

"How do you know?"

"My phone still works, and I also counted the seconds between the lightning and thunder. The storm is moving away from us. I promise, baby."

"But—"

"Shhh . . ." Shane interrupts, rubbing my back slowly and methodically, helping me relax further so that I can try to enjoy the soothing sounds of the thunderstorm as it finally starts to move away. He continues with the soft circles on my back, and I fall asleep easier than I thought I could, safely wrapped in the arms of the man I love.

I think I may actually like thunderstorms when they're with Shane.

The next morning, I wake up and find the bed empty. Shane's already up, so I crawl out of the sheets and quickly make the bed. It's hot and stuffy inside with no AC, so I grab a pair of comfy shorts and a tank top to throw on. It doesn't take me long to find Shane on the back porch, grilling our breakfast.

As soon as I open the sliding glass door and step outside, a refreshing breeze sweeps over me and cools my flushed skin. We'll have to open some windows today and get some air flow inside.

"That was crazy last night," I say. "Now it's all bright and sunny, as if the storm never happened."

"Don't be fooled. Scattered thunderstorms all day."

"I guess it's a good thing I booked a couple's massage and mud masks instead of a hike," I laugh, making Shane smile as he continues to cook breakfast.

"But we're still getting muddy," he deadpans.

"Hey! This is different. This is healthy mud."

"Healthy mud?" He looks over with a skeptical brow raised.

"Yes, you'll see," I reply matter-of-factly, changing the subject because he can't knock it until he tries it. "Any news on when the power will be restored?"

"By ten tonight, unfortunately. Lightning hit a transformer," Shane informs me. "But we've got food, water, a generator, and a grill." He looks over his shoulder at me. "And each other."

"It's not that bad, huh?" I murmur, and he just laughs, coming over for a morning hug.

Shane envelopes me in his arms, burying his face in my

messy mop of curls. He breathes deeply before kissing the top of my head. "Coffee's in the French press. I'm going to start the generator now that you're awake. The table's already set. I'll just be a minute. Then we'll eat."

"Thank you," I say with a blush, while he stares intently down at me. My belly swoops low, and my face heats even more, knowing I'm the center of Shane Carmichael's attention.

He leans down and kisses me sweetly before jogging down the wooden deck stairs to get to the generator.

I quickly make my coffee at the cute little coffee bar Shane set up, adding a splash of milk and stirring with one of the wooden sticks. There's also honey, cinnamon, and nutmeg, so I sprinkle a little in. I sit under the umbrella, sipping my delicious coffee and watching my sexy boyfriend exert himself.

He's wearing a black tank top and matching athletic shorts, and it looks like he didn't even comb his hair today. Just how I like it. He yanks the cord three times before the old generator kicks to life, a low rumble filling the air.

Blowing on my coffee, I grin into my mug, when he looks up with a smirk, catching me creeping on him. I quickly spin around in my seat as he makes his way over to the stairs.

"Enjoy the show, hmm?" he teases.

"As a matter of fact, I did. And I also enjoyed the coffee bar. You get an A plus, boyfriend," I giggle.

"Oh yeah? Wait until you try this frittata," Shane says, making his way over to the grill. "Bet I'll get extra credit." He checks the food, taking everything off the grill and plating it family style.

"I bet you will too," I laugh, my stomach growling loudly. "Need any help?" I offer, still sitting at the table.

"If you don't mind getting some drinks for us. Water's fine for me."

I nod, setting my coffee on the table and slipping back inside. I grab two bottles of water while Shane finishes up with the food.

"Spinach artichoke frittata with grilled tomatoes and feta crumbles on top," Shane announces, serving us each a large slice.

"*Mmm*. This looks amazing. Thank you."

We inhale our food, both of us going back for seconds.

When I'm done, I set my knife and fork down, leaning back in my seat and staring across the table at my boyfriend. "I am the luckiest guy in the world to be dating such a talented chef. Every single day, I'm amazed by you. I love you. So much."

Shane smiles, and it's so carefree and happy that I almost don't recognize him. He leans forward and reaches his long arm across the table, grabbing my hand. "I can say the same about you, Toby. You've opened my eyes to a world I didn't know existed. One full of love, acceptance, and kindness. Your soul is as beautiful as the music you create. And I'm honored to call you my boyfriend."

I squeeze his hand. "Thank you," I murmur, lost for words. Both of us want a better family dynamic than we had growing up, and I think maybe we've found that in each other.

Mountain Bliss Day Spa is right off the main road in town, so it's easy to get to and easy to park. I'm ready for a massage, and excited to see Shane's reaction to the mud.

We walk hand in hand to the front door, and Shane

opens it like a gentleman, allowing me to walk through first. I wait for him to follow, and we go up to the girl at the reception desk.

"Good afternoon. My name is Rylee," a pretty blonde girl says with a bright smile. "How can I help you today?"

"Hi. Tobias Livingston. Reservation for two."

"Okay. Yep. Right here. I have you down for a couples massage and full-body mud masks."

"That's us."

She smiles warmly and stands from her desk. "Right this way."

We quietly follow her down the dimly lit hallway as soft music plays mixed with nature sounds that create a soothing, dreamlike ambiance.

"Right in here," Rylee says. "This is Vanessa and Simon, your masseuses, and they're going to take great care of you."

"Thank you," we both murmur, introducing ourselves to Vanessa and Simon before slipping into our robes in the changing room.

"This is my first massage," Shane whispers to me before we head back to the room where our massage therapists are waiting.

"I know. But you deserve many more. Especially with how hard you work in the kitchen."

Shane leans down, pressing his lips to mine. "I love you."

"Love you too. Now let's go get the kinks worked out."

"I'll show you *kinks*," Shane growls, and I giggle, darting out of his grip and out of the changing room.

"Rub the mud on each other, let it harden, then rinse off and soak in the natural hot spring behind the building," Rylee informs us, taking us to the mudroom before she disappears back to the front desk, leaving us to our own dirty devices.

I scoop up a handful of cool mud and slap it against Shane's chest with a splat, spreading it down his abdomen and getting another handful for his arms.

"How does it feel?" I ask, slathering more cool, wet mud on his body.

"Cold and kinda slimy but also gritty," Shane admits with a shrug. "Not bad."

I chuckle. "Well, it's detoxifying and exfoliating. You should glow after. So I'm gonna put some on your face, too."

Shane stares me in the eyes while I carefully apply the mud mask to his face. "What?" I laugh. "Quit distracting me before I get it in your eye. Or your . . . Whoops." I grab the towel to wipe the mud from his lips, but before I can, he darts forward and kisses me. "*Yuck! Bleh!* Shane, I can taste it," I whine.

"You started it," he counters, and I laugh loudly, feeling like we're just two kids again without the worry of college, careers, and our sexuality. "My turn to do you," Shane says, and I swallow thickly, my mind instantly going to the gutter.

Shane carefully coats my body in the gritty, cold mud. We don't joke around anymore, the lust too high and the moment too sensual as his hands roam my body, squeezing and massaging while he cakes it on.

"So, we just let it sit now?" Shane asks, smearing the remainder of the mud around in his hands like lotion.

"Mhm. Until it starts to dry. Then we go outside, rinse off, and soak in the mineral spring."

Shane and I lie down on lounge chairs covered in dark towels and place fresh cucumber slices on our eyelids, starting the thirty-minute timer built into the wall.

By the time it goes off, I'm nearly asleep, but as soon as I notice how tight my skin feels covered in dried mud, I'm ready to go.

"I feel crusty," Shane mumbles, hardly moving his mouth. He stands up from the chair and holds his arms out in front of him like a mummy.

I giggle, feeling the mud around my mouth split and crack. "Come on, let's go rinse off."

The back deck is an intricate network of pathways and smaller decks, but it all surrounds one focal point. The hot springs.

"Wow," I murmur in awe. "It's so beautiful." Steam hovers above the surface of the naturally fed, geothermal hot spring, the crystal-clear water beckoning us in. There are a few other couples and a handful of individuals, but it's pretty secluded and private out here.

Shane and I walk over to the showers at the end of the deck, turning the water to hot and rinsing the majority of the mud off before we enter the springs.

We tiptoe across the smooth stone, carefully stepping into the hot spring hand in hand. We both hiss as the hot water envelopes our feet and then our calves while we slowly wade deeper into the natural pool.

"This is perfect," I murmur, slipping further into the steaming water.

"*Ahh*," Shane sighs. "Feels fucking amazing."

We soak in silence, allowing the minerals and heat from the earth itself to soothe our bodies and rejuvenate our souls. I grab Shane's hand under the water, squeezing tightly. I will never forget this experience or this trip.

We showered at the spa, knowing our power would most likely still be out when we got home. And we were right. Luckily, Shane found a container full of candles and a box of matches, and we lit enough of them to turn the once scary and dark room into a cozy, candlelit cabin.

"I'll be right back," I murmur, getting up from the couch without another word and carefully picking up a small candle. I disappear into the bedroom, digging through my gift box full of lingerie to pick out the lacy purple set.

I come strutting out of the dark hallway with a candle in hand and do a little twirl for good measure. I know Tate would be so proud right now.

"*Fuck, Tobes,*" Shane murmurs breathlessly. The flickering flames dance across his face and reflect in his dark eyes. "You're stunning."

"I want you," I whisper, setting the candle down and slowly strutting toward him.

His stare is intense, never taking his eyes off of me. I grab his hand, and he stands from the couch, silently following me to the bedroom. When I push him onto the bed, he falls back willingly, leaning on his elbows and staring up at me in adoration.

Feeling bold and confident in my purple lingerie, I crawl up Shane's big body and kiss all my favorite spots along the way. I straddle him, sitting on his lap while I stare into his seductive eyes. Without a single word spoken between us, I press my lips to his and kiss him deeply. Thoroughly. "I want you inside me," I pant into his open mouth. "No prep. No nothing. I fucking need you," I whimper impatiently.

Shane wraps his strong arms around me and flips us so that he's now on top. He pins my wrists above my head and settles between my spread thighs. Our cocks bump, and I'm so fucking ready that I wrap my legs around his waist and arch my back, wanting him to just impale me through the lacy fabric already.

"Slow down, Tobes," Shane urges. "You gotta be prepped."

"I want it to hurt a little," I plead.

"No," he says sternly. "Never."

He reaches down and tugs my lacy underwear off, along with his own. Then I hear the click of a cap, and suddenly my legs are being pushed back. Cold lube drips down my crease, and two fingers press against my opening. I jolt, realizing I can never just jump into sex if I can't even handle two fingers. Shane switches to one, and then I'm moaning loudly, writhing on the bed and spreading my legs further. After a minute, he adds a second digit, and this time, there's no trouble.

"More," I demand, and Shane squeezes in a third, making me feel oh so good. "Give me your cock," I pant desperately.

Shane growls, nearly showing his teeth as he quickly lubes up and presses into me, not stopping until he pops past the first ring of muscle.

"*Ahhh!*" I cry out, tipping my head back and exposing my neck.

Shane bites down, sucking hard and surely leaving a mark. But I don't care. I'm his now.

"Fuck me harder," I chant over and over.

Shane's sweat drips from his brow, landing on my face

and trickling into my mouth. I lick my lips, not giving two fucks when he's already had his cum all over every inch of me. He practically folds me in half, driving into my ass with a skilled precision and nailing my prostate.

I nearly scream, my balls drawing up and my dick exploding against my chest while Shane continues to fuck me. I lift my arms above my head and brace myself against the headboard, providing resistance to his plowing.

"*Mmf! Mmf!*" I grunt as he fucks me roughly. A few seconds later, Shane stills, grabbing hold of the headboard with both hands and grinding his cock into me as deep as he can possibly go. Shane spurts inside me, and I can feel the warmth in my channel. "Ohhh," I moan, reaching around and grabbing two handfuls of firm ass while he pumps into me. He leans down and messily kisses me, our sweat and saliva mixing.

I love being this close to Shane. I want him to stay inside me forever and never pull out.

As if he hears my embarrassing thoughts out loud, Shane settles his weight on top of me, staying inside as long as he can until his softening cock slips out on its own.

Shane finally rolls to the side, taking a deep breath. I unfold myself from the pretzel position I was being fucked in and finally stretch my legs. Shane's cum instantly oozes out of my hole, and I whimper, wishing I had a plug to keep it there.

"I'll get you a plug as soon as we're home. Don't worry," Shane says as if he read my mind again. I hum my approval, excited that he seems to like toys too. He pulls me into his chest, and we just lie here for a moment, sticky and satiated.

It's been so nice not having to worry about being interrupted or being too loud. "We should get our own place next year," I blurt out, unable to keep the thought inside my head. "We already live together," I reason when he doesn't say a word. "It's not like I'm asking you to move in with me. We'd just be moving out. Together."

Shane's mouth quirks up on one side.

"Are you laughing at me?" I scoff, crossing my arms with indignation, but I can't stop the smile from spreading.

"Never. I think it's a great idea." Shane wraps his arms around me, hugging me tightly.

I can't wait for this private weekend to be our new reality.

CHAPTER TWENTY-SEVEN
SHANE

"So, what did you think of our spa day? Specifically, the full-body mud masks?" Toby asks with a giggle as we lie in bed on our final morning at the cabin. We slept in and can't seem to get going. Toby's head is resting on my chest, his wild curls tickling my chin. I lean forward, inhaling the fresh, honeysuckle scent of his hair and releasing the breath slowly, like I just took a hit of the most addictive drug in the world.

"It was nice," I say evenly. "Kinda reminded me of that time I pushed Adam Collins in the mud."

"What?" Toby laughs breathily. "Random much?"

I shrug. "It just triggered that memory for me."

There's nothing more satisfying than seeing the school bully sitting in a puddle of mud.

Toby lifts his head, staring down at me with sleepy eyes and a small smile. "I was so paranoid that we were gonna get detention for a month, and my parents would ground me for the other eleven months of the year," Toby chuckles, and I rub his back, my fingertips gliding over his soft, smooth skin. "Actually, though," he says thoughtfully. "You never told me why you pushed him down."

"You really wanna know?" I ask just to be certain after all these years of keeping Adam's hateful words to myself.

"Yeah. Why not?" His brows crease in confusion.

"Because he's a dick, of course."

"Well, I think enough years have passed that I can handle it," he says resolutely.

"Okay then."

Toby rests his head back on my bare chest, and I squeeze him to me, slipping into the memory from sixth-grade PE class.

"I really don't get why you like hanging out with the little dweeb so much," Adam sneers, staring at Toby while he runs laps around the track.

I clench my fists so I don't punch him in the face. Mom would be so mad at me if I got suspended. "Shut up, Adam." I won't let him run his mouth about my friend.

"Look at him trying to keep up with everyone. It's pathetic," Adam laughs, pointing at Toby as he lags behind on the track.

Coach Blair split up the class and sent half of us to run laps around the track, and the other half to run soccer drills, which is where I'm at with the douche squad. Toby is smaller and younger than the rest of us, and I won't let Adam get away with bullying him.

"I said shut your mouth," I growl, stepping into Adam's personal space. "Say one more thing, I dare you."

"Tobias Livingston is a wimp," Adam says very slowly, sounding each syllable out disrespectfully with a stupid smirk on his face.

I snatch him up by the front of his Pokémon shirt, catching him off guard completely. His expression morphs comically, from cockiness to fear.

Toby finishes his lap and comes running over while I'm staring Adam down. "Shane! Stop!" he cries, but I don't listen, instead shoving Adam's chest and making him stumble backward. He trips over his own two feet, losing his balance and falling into a muddy spot on the side of the soccer field.

"Ahh!" he cries out as he falls, but I have no remorse for this bully.

"Oh my God! Mud butt!" His so-called friends laugh, pointing at Adam instead of helping him up.

The wet ground squelches underneath him as he attempts to stand, but he just slips and falls again. I glance over at Toby, and his hand is over his mouth, his eyes wide with shock.

"Don't talk about people anymore," I command, not wanting Toby to know that Adam was picking on him specifically. "In fact, don't even think about them."

Adam's face heats, but he nods, agreeing to stop his weird fixation on Toby. I turn my back on him, leaving him to crawl out of the mud in front of his friends. Toby and I head over to the rest of the class, distancing ourselves from the mess.

"Hey, Collins!" Coach yells, finally noticing Adam sitting on the ground, half covered in mud. "Now isn't the time to play in the dirt. Get your butt up and hit the locker room! Class is dismissed!"

"Why did you do that?" Toby asks suddenly, peering up at me with worried eyes that I want to protect. "You could have gotten in trouble."

"He needed to learn a lesson on how to treat people," I say with a shrug. "Worth the risk."

Toby's brows crease, but he doesn't ask me anything else. We make our way to the locker room and quickly change, leaving before the mud butt comes in to wash his shame away.

I hope everyone else on the field saw what happened to Adam, so they can spread the word.

Toby and I are not to be messed with.

"So, what you're saying is, you've been my bodyguard since we met? Before I even realized it," Toby says with a laugh when I finish telling my story.

"Damn straight." I give him a squeeze, wanting to stay in this bed forever. I don't want to leave this place. I really do love it here. The privacy, the intimacy, and the amazing views. I could easily stay another week. But unfortunately, the real world and finals are calling us home.

"But in all seriousness, I really do appreciate you protecting me then and now," Toby whispers, his warm breath tickling my bare skin.

"Always," I murmur.

For the rest of our fucking lives.

Toby climbs on top of me, straddling my hips as he stares down at me with half-lidded eyes. "Fuck me one last time before we leave. Please, Shane," he pleads desperately. "I love you."

I quickly flip us, pressing my hard-on into his erection. Only the thin fabric of our underwear separates us from a repeat of last night. "I'll give you anything you ask for, butterfly. I love you so much." Darting forward, I seal my lips to his, ready to show him.

CHAPTER TWENTY-EIGHT
SHANE

The overpowering aroma of disinfectant, rubbing alcohol, and fresh ink goes straight to my head and clings to my nostrils. As much as I love my tattoos, I can't say I love the process. "I want a realistic butterfly," I tell my tattoo artist. "But make it purple." The black leather chair squeaks as I get situated, resting my forearm on the large, cushioned armrest.

"You got it, boss. A purple butterfly coming right up," Travis says with a big, white smile. "Can I ask the meaning? If it's personal, it's no problem."

I pause for a second, weighing my options. I'm not hiding, and I'm not in the closet. I've known Travis for a couple of years now, as he's done most of my tattoos. "Yeah, man. It's for my boyfriend."

After getting home from such an amazing weekend getaway and deciding we want to move into our own place, I decided to do something big to show Toby just how much he means to me.

"Oh, really?" he asks, sounding a little surprised. "I didn't realize we were part of the same community. I'm bi."

"It's kinda new, but yeah. I'm bi too."

"Nice, bro. Well, if you ever wanna meet other people and connect, like on a friendship level, then you and your boyfriend should totally come out to Stick Shift sometime," Travis offers, and I just smile.

After my last experience there, I don't plan to ever go back.

"Thanks, I'll think about it."

"So, where are we putting this purple butterfly?" Travis asks, pulling his rubber gloves on with a snap and grabbing the bottle of rubbing alcohol.

"Right here," I say, pointing to the empty spot next to the lone wolf, because I'm no longer alone, and if I'm honest with myself, I haven't been since the day I met Toby in fifth grade.

"Good choice. I like it. Goes nicely next to the wolf—which, by the way, is *still* my absolute favorite piece I've ever done. Do you mind if I take photos and add the butterfly to my portfolio? I already know it's gonna be a banger."

"Yeah, no problem." It's just my arm, so I don't really care.

"Cool. Cool. I'm just going to shave the area real quick, clean it off, and apply the stencil. Then we'll get started."

"Sounds good," I murmur, slipping my earbuds in and clicking on the relaxing playlist I created to take my mind off the pain.

The buzz of the tattoo gun starts, and I close my eyes, focusing on the music instead of the tiny needle burning my skin. I think about Toby's dimpled smile and our stay at the cabin. I think about how much he means to me and how he's the only one who's consistently been there for me in my life. I think about his golden eyes lighting up when he sees the butterfly tattoo, and before I know it, Travis begins wiping off my arm like he's finished.

"Take a look before I seal it," he tells me, smiling at his own work.

I stand up and walk over to the mirror, twisting and turning my forearm, admiring my new artwork. "Fucking sick, dude. Absolutely perfect. Thank you," I tell him, handing over a generous and well-deserved tip.

Despite the dull ache in my forearm, the anticipation of what Toby will say is keeping me going, so I head to the jewelry store next. I'm searching for something pretty specific, and I'm hoping I'm lucky enough to find it.

By the fourth store, I'm ready to call it quits, but I finally find what I'm looking for, as if the universe itself guided me here. *A wolf pendant.* And not just any pendant, it's a bust, with the wolf howling at the moon. It's perfect, and it matches my tattoo. If I'm adding a butterfly to my body to represent Toby, then I want him to have a piece of me close to his heart as well. I just hope he appreciates the sentiment and doesn't freak out when he sees the tattoo.

When I get home, Toby's Audi is the only car in the driveway, so I know Spencer and Jake are both gone. My lip quirks, excited for an empty house to go along with this big of a surprise. Toby was right, we definitely need our own apartment next year.

As soon as I open the front door and walk in, the smooth sounds of Toby's violin come dancing down the stairwell and into my ears. *Good.* He's busy right now. Before I go see him, I quietly jog up the stairs and disappear into my bedroom, shutting the door behind me without a sound.

I tug a gray hoodie over my head, hiding the jewelry box in the oversized front pocket. Next, I rifle through my sock drawer, searching for something I stashed there earlier this week. My fingers wrap around the smooth silicone, and I slip it into my hoodie pocket, too, before I make my way to his bedroom.

"Hey," I murmur, knocking on the doorframe before I walk in. Toby's perched on the end of his bed with a music stand in front of him, adjusting the tuning pegs on the top of his violin. He's been practicing more than normal, getting ready for his end-of-the-year solo. It's a big deal, for him and for the orchestra, bringing in vital donations for the music department. I know he's stressed about it, so I hope I can help take his mind off it. Even if just for a night.

"Hey. I didn't even hear you come home. How was the mall?" Toby asks with a sweet and interested smile. He sets his violin and bow down, giving me his complete attention.

"Good," I say, reaching into my hoodie pocket and making sure I pull out the right gift at the right time. I hold the small blue box in the palm of my hand. "I got you something," I tell him.

"You did?" Toby's dimples pop out, and he takes the small box, opening the lid and gasping. He freezes, his eyes downcast and staring at the silver pendant intently.

"Do you like it?" I murmur, starting to get a little worried.

"*Oh my God.* No . . ."

My heart drops like a two-ton weight inside my chest.

"*I love it.*"

I take a deep breath, letting the relief wash over me. "I wanted you to always have a piece of me with you, like I now have of you."

Toby finally lifts his eyes from the pendant, tilting his head in confusion. "Did you get one too?"

I shake my head, carefully lifting up my sleeve and showing off my new purple butterfly tattoo.

Toby gasps when he sees my forearm, covering his mouth and staring at me with wide, unblinking eyes. "You got a tattoo for me?" he asks in utter disbelief.

I nod, grabbing his hand and stroking his knuckles with my thumb. "I did."

"It's a butterfly..."

"Yes. It represents the first time we met *and* our first date. A symbol of our love." I can't fully express how Toby's love makes me feel, but it makes my chest heavy in a way that feels good, like a warm, weighted blanket or a bowl full of my nonna's spaghetti. Our bond requires no effort, and it never has. We have the type of love that just is and always has been. *Always will be.* "You're my soulmate, Tobias Livingston. My beautiful, delicate butterfly, and I will protect you for the rest of our lives."

"*Shane,*" Toby cries out, practically launching himself at me and clinging to my body as I walk us backward to the bed. "I love you so much," he whispers into my ear while I lay him down, settling between his spread thighs and hovering above him while my forearms cage his head.

"I'm lucky to know you and honored to love you, butterfly." I peck his lips softly. Reverently.

"Make love to me," Toby whispers against my mouth. "Please, Shane. I need you inside me."

So needy, and I love it.

I take my hoodie off, careful not to bump my arm or spill the remaining contents of my pocket, setting the bundle of fabric on top of Toby's desk and slipping my T-shirt off next. I glance back at him and find him completely naked, propped up on his elbows and staring at me hungrily while he strokes himself. I unbutton my jeans next, never taking my eyes off of him as I drop my pants to the floor with a thud and step out of them. My cock tents the front of my boxer briefs, and Toby's eager eyes zero in on it.

"You like this, baby?" I tease, squeezing myself through the fabric.

"*Yes*. Hurry," Toby whimpers, completely impatient.

My thumbs slip into the waistband of my underwear, pulling them down slowly and making my cock spring free, slapping my abdomen obscenely.

Toby giggles, but his tinkling laughter dies out the moment I place a knee on the bed. He bites his lip, spreading his legs for me as I crawl up his body. I seal my lips to his, kissing him with my whole body and soul, our tongues tangling and energy colliding.

"Show me how much you love me," Toby pants into my mouth, so I reach over and grab the lube from his nightstand drawer.

"Pull your knees back," I instruct, pushing them toward his chest and revealing his cute little hole. Toby hooks his hands behind his knees, keeping himself exposed for me.

"Prep me fast," Toby begs with shimmering eyes. "I need to feel you."

I'm desperate to be close to him just as badly, so I quickly prep him with two, then three fingers.

"I'm ready, Shane. Please. I'm ready," Toby pants, pulling his knees back even further. "Make love to me."

I quickly lube up my cock and press the tip to his glistening hole. Holding the base steady, I push forward until my crown slips in, and Toby cries out.

"*Keep going!*" he shouts with his eyes squeezed shut.

"That's it, baby. You're doing so good. Just a little more," I say through clenched teeth while I push my hips forward torturously slow until I bottom out. Toby groans wantonly, and I brush the sweaty curls off his forehead, leaning down to kiss him there. "I love you," I whisper, pulling my hips back slowly and making Toby's eyes roll into the back of his head. "I love you so fucking *much*." I punctuate my last word with a long, deep thrust.

"*Oh God, Shane.* I love you. I love you. I love you," Toby chants, throwing his head back while I gradually pick up my pace.

I tilt my hips, continuing to plow into him faster and harder, forgetting we're no longer in a cabin in the woods but back in our shared house on campus, instead.

"*Mmf! Ungh!*" Toby cries out as the sound of skin slapping against skin fills the room. He lifts his arms above his head, bracing himself against the headboard. "Come inside me, Shane. I wanna feel it."

His filthy words do me in, and my rhythm stutters, my cock unloading inside of his ass, triggering his release all over both of us.

Toby lies limp on the bed with his eyes closed and arms above his head.

"Time for your third surprise of the night," I whisper as I carefully pull out and immediately press the tapered end of the butt plug to his hole, easily slipping it in and sealing my seed inside of him.

Fuck, that's sexy.

Toby grunts, looking down at his body with half-lidded eyes.

"You look so sexy with a plug stuffed in that tight, little hole," I murmur, rubbing and massaging his taint.

"A plug?" Toby asks on a moan, halfway to another orgasm. "You got me a plug?"

"The same kind you've been asking for, only a little . . . fancier. You're stuffed full and so fucking hot."

"*I am?*" The incredulous tone to his voice does something funny to my stomach.

I chuckle. "Yeah, baby. Full of my cum."

"I wanna see," Toby says curiously. He gets a spark of energy and crawls to his hands and knees, groaning when the toy moves inside of him.

"Impossible," I chuckle. There's no way he can experience the view that I'm appreciating right now. I caress the smooth globe of his ass, running my finger around the base of the plug before I tap on it and make him grunt.

"Take a picture," Toby pants. "I wanna see." He wiggles his ass at me, and I have the tempting urge to spank it.

"*Butterfly,*" I growl. "I'm not taking a photo of your sexy ass with a purple plug shoved in it. That's just for me."

"It's purple?" he asks, completely distracted and not getting the point.

"Yeah. There's actually a butterfly on the base."

"Now I *really* need to see. Please?"

"Fine," I grunt, grabbing my phone and aiming it at Toby. *I can't believe I'm doing this.* He arches his back, sticking his ass out and looking over his shoulder at the camera.

Jesus Christ.

I quickly snap a photo and show it to him, wanting to delete it before someone gains access to my phone in the next thirty seconds and steals this sexy-as-fuck nude of my boyfriend.

"Wow. I look hot," he says in disbelief.

"Of course you do," I grumble.

"You can save the photo if you want," he offers. "You know. For later."

I delete it instead, even going to my recently deleted album and clearing that, too.

Toby chuckles. "Well, if you're just gonna erase all the evidence, then we might as well have some more fun."

"No," I grumble, not wanting the camera to see what's mine, nor do I want the photos uploaded to the cloud by accident or something.

"Pretty please? I wanna see a close-up."

"Absolutely not."

Toby laughs and then groans when I grab the base and tug on it. "Oh. *Wow.* That feels different."

"You like it? Think you'd like it to vibrate?" I murmur, continuing to tease him with it. I saw a plug with a remote-control app on the same website I got this one from.

"Oh God, yes."

I smirk, knowing exactly what I'm getting him next.

CHAPTER TWENTY-NINE
TOBY

My mother texted me for the first time in weeks. She unfortunately wants me to come home for dinner this weekend, so I guess it's my chance to tell them I'm gay, and I'm dating my best friend. I won't hide who I am any longer, and I certainly won't hide my boyfriend. Shane and I have come so far this year, and nothing can stand in our way.

He means everything to me.

It's inevitable that my parents will find out about us, and if I don't tell them first, I'll risk a scene at the symphony. They absolutely *cannot* affect my performance or my chances at a professional set in an actual New York City orchestra. I've worked too hard for this.

Professor Goldblum said it's a secret, but he wanted to give me a heads-up because of my anxiety and let me know that there will be scouts watching. This is an opportunity of a lifetime. These scouts will offer all sorts of opportunities, from orchestra auditions to graduate applications.

"God. I'm already sweaty," I complain, getting ready for another confrontational dinner with my parents.

And this time I get to tell them I'm gay. Yay.

"It's going to be okay," Shane insists, sitting on the end of my bed, waiting for me to finish getting ready.

I smooth out my baby-blue button-down and khaki Bermuda shorts while I stare at myself in the full-length mirror hanging over my closet door. This feels like déjà vu. This feels like exactly what I told myself I wouldn't worry about. But they're still my parents, and that little boy inside me still longs for their approval. I close my eyes for a moment and take a deep breath.

"Seriously. Come here," Shane murmurs, holding his palm out. I place my hand in his, and he tugs me over to where I settle between his spread thighs. "I've got your back, baby. *Always.*"

I'm taller than him in this position, so I stare down at my boyfriend, brushing his dark, messy hair off his forehead. I smile, leaning down to press my lips to his. "I know. Thank you. The only reason I'm not running around freaking out is because you're going to be by my side the whole evening."

"Am I your emotional support Shane again tonight?" he deadpans, and I giggle, nodding enthusiastically.

"Yep. And don't forget, my bodyguard, too. Those stairs are dangerous."

"And now I'm your boyfriend." Shane kisses me deeply, pulling back before we get carried away. "Are there any more titles I should strive for?" He raises a dark brow, smirking at me with his sexy, kiss-swollen lips.

Husband.

The intensely intimate word crash lands into my thoughts like a space capsule making impact in the middle of the ocean.

"We'll see," I murmur, my adrenaline spiking and heat

rushing to my cheeks, as if he can read my mind. "But you're doing exceptionally well in all of your current positions. Don't worry." I lean forward and press my mouth to his, kissing him affectionately.

"Good to know," he chuckles against my lips, reaching around to squeeze both of my cheeks.

We get lost in the kiss, melting and merging into each other like the colorful strokes in a Monet painting. "Ready to leave?" Shane asks, out of breath from our impromptu make-out session. "'Cause if you stay on my lap for even a second longer, we're gonna end up twenty minutes late with wrinkled clothes." He bites my lower lip, sucking on it while he encourages me to grind against him.

"*Okay. Okay,*" I say breathlessly, giggling as I swing a leg over and hop off his lap. "Let's get this shitshow over with."

Dinner's going as well as can be expected so far. My parents haven't brought up school or dating because they've been so busy talking about themselves the whole time, bragging about the newest multi-million-dollar home they closed on and the skilled staff they've built.

Blah. Blah. Blah.

"That's great, Dad," I say hollowly. "Sounds like you've got a really good team working for you."

"Drive, determination, and commitment will take you a long way in this world, son."

I nod, taking another bite of the chicken marsala but not really tasting it. "Mhm. For sure," I murmur, agreeing with him even though I'm hardly listening because all I can focus on is finding the right opportunity to come out. My heart is racing, and my face and hands are starting to get all tingly.

With a shaky hand, I reach for my glass of ice water. Shane doesn't miss a beat, noticing my nerves and placing his hand on my thigh under the table. He gently strokes my bare leg, attempting to settle some of the anxiety.

"You should consider working at the office this summer," my father says, setting his knife and fork down. "You can shadow me and your mother. Get your foot in the door." He takes another sip of whiskey, peering at me way too intently, as if he's looking for a reaction or a reason to argue.

My parents have been trying to get me to work at their real estate firm during the summer for a couple years now, but I'm just not interested. And he knows that. "Dad..."

"*I know. I know.* You're too busy with the violin and hate the thought of being stuck in an office all summer with your old man."

I don't respond because he's not wrong. I'm nineteen and in college. We live at the beach, for fuck's sake, and I have no intention of spending my summer days under artificial fluorescent lighting, doing something I hate.

"Speaking of violin," my mom suddenly says, and my heart nearly jumps out of my chest at what she might say. "I've been meaning to let you know that we won't be able to attend your performance at the end of the semester. The firm is sponsoring a fundraiser on the same night, and you know we can't miss something like that. It's too important."

Shane squeezes my thigh under the table, offering me his silent support.

"Of course," I murmur, pushing food around my plate at

this point. I'm actually relieved they aren't coming, but it still doesn't explain the slight ache in my chest.

"The offer of a summer job extends to you as well, Shane," my dad says with a smug superiority that rubs a lot of people the wrong way. As if the job offer is some sort of huge privilege. He completely ignores the topic of my concerto, immediately steering the conversation back to him and his business. My mom gives him a quick side-eye, clearly unhappy with the idea of seeing Shane in the office every day.

"Thank you, Mr. Livingston. I appreciate it, but I've been working at Coastal Cuisine for a while now, and I'm happy there," Shane replies respectfully.

"Ahh, yes. With Glenn. He's a good man," Dad says, recognizing the company name.

Shane nods, and we all continue to eat in silence.

When my mom finishes picking at her food, clearly irritated with something or someone, she pushes her plate away. "*Tobias,*" she practically snarls, spitting out my name like a curse.

"Hmm?" I ask with wide eyes, chewing a bite of chicken and swallowing it with an audible gulp.

"Once again, we thought you were bringing a girlfriend over for dinner, but no. Here you are. With Shane." Her blonde brows furrow, and she leans against the back of the chair, folding her arms across her chest. "*Again.*"

Here goes nothing.

"Well, actually . . ." I say, my fingers wrapping around the new pendant Shane gave me and sliding it back and forth on the chain. I drop it and grab my water, taking a nervous sip and stalling while my parents stare at me in anticipation.

My mother's inquisitive eyes dart down to the necklace

I was just fidgeting with, then over to Shane's forearm that's resting on the table. His matching wolf tattoo and the new purple butterfly next to it are in plain sight.

Her brows crease, and I recognize the very moment she puts it all together before I even have the chance to tell her. "*No,*" she breathes, holding a hand over her mouth as if she's devastated by the revelation. "You're..."

She can't even say the words.

I feel his eyes on me, but I can't look at Shane right now. I'm completely embarrassed by what's happening, even though I'm not surprised by it.

"Yes, mother. I'm gay, and Shane is my boyfriend," I tell her matter-of-factly, without flinching or looking away. With Shane by my side—supporting me and loving me—I no longer feel the need to completely panic over their reactions. Whatever they may be.

I sit up straight in my seat, correcting my posture and squaring my shoulders.

I know who I am, and I know I love Shane.

I've loved him for years.

Nothing can change that.

Shane reaches over and grabs hold of my hand under the table, squeezing it for reassurance.

"Can't say I'm completely shocked," my dad admits with a shrug, taking another bite of his asparagus. "There was this time when you were younger, and you only wanted to wear princess nightgowns to bed. Your mother indulged you. I told her not to—"

"*Matthew!*" Mom hisses, giving him a death glare. "This is serious. What will everyone at the country club think? *Church?*" She takes a deep breath, rubbing her forehead. "*My God.*"

I huff, completely irritated by her response. "That's

what you're worried about, Mom?" I roll my watery eyes because I don't care what her shallow friends think or the church, but I can't deny that it hurts deep down knowing that she's only worried about their feelings when they've got nothing to do with my life *or* this family. It would be nice for my mother to support me for once, but I really shouldn't expect anything more from her. It's only setting myself up for disappointment.

My dad, however, shocks me by speaking up and defending me in his own self-centered way. "Actually, honey, the club manager's daughter is a lesbian. I'm sure he will be very supportive of us."

She ignores him, aiming her fire at Shane next. "*And you . . .*" She eyes him up and down, making me extremely uncomfortable, but Shane only stiffens his spine, ready to take the blow. "The last thing I'd expect from *you* is to be gay."

Is that supposed to be some sort of insult?

Like always, Shane doesn't falter. "I've loved your son for a decade. It doesn't really matter what you think, because with all due respect, Mrs. Livingston, I'm not going anywhere. And I'll treat your son better than anybody else could—guy or girl."

"I beg your finest pardon—" Mom gasps, pressing her hand to her heart and literally clutching her pearls.

"Now, now. Let's all just take a deep breath," my dad says, holding his hands up and trying to play the mediator for some strange reason. I guess he doesn't want any drama to take away from the buzz he's got going on. "Let's not escalate this any further, Renée."

"Don't you *dare*, Matthew," she spits at him. "You can't tell me you're happy about this? Our only son is a *gay violinist* instead of a successful real estate agent who's dating a beautiful, southern belle ready to birth our grandchildren."

"A lot of families have to deal with this. It's not uncommon, Renée," my dad reasons, finishing off the last of his drink. "There's always adoption."

"I cannot believe you right now, Matthew," Mom growls, wrinkling her upper lip and baring her teeth.

"Honey," my dad pleads, "it's not the end of the world. I promise."

"*Stop!*" I shout, unable to bear sitting at this table and listening to them talk about me like I'm not even here. "Can we just agree to disagree like we do with everything else about my life?" I can once again feel myself retreating into my shell like a hermit crab. I'm ready for this evening to end. I don't even want to stay for dessert, I'm so uncomfortable.

"I can respect that," my dad says, "but just know, I don't disagree with you at all. It'll just take some getting used to on our end." Then he changes the subject as if trying to move on from the inconvenience of me coming out. "So, Renée, what's for dessert?"

"I don't think we were done with this discussion yet, Matthew," she says sharply, side-eyeing him with a pointed glare.

I stand from the table, interrupting this ridiculous conversation. "It's not a discussion. I was simply letting you know," I say bluntly, despite the heat rushing to my cheeks and the drum pounding against my ribs.

"Toby's right," Shane says, standing next to me and grabbing my hand to imbue some of his strength and resilience into me. He squeezes my fingers tightly, letting me know he's got my back. "Respectfully, Mr. and Mrs. Livingston, it's not your choice *or* your decision who your son is attracted to and dates. And it certainly isn't your choice who he falls in love with." He turns to me, whispering into my ear, but I'm sure they both hear. "I think it's time for us to go, butterfly."

My mother scoffs, rolling her eyes in disgust. "This is all your fault. You've poisoned my son since the day you met him. Public school was the ultimate mistake all along." She storms off into the kitchen before we can say anything back.

"Listen, boys. I'm sorry for her reaction. I think she may be in shock and slightly triggered. But nonetheless, please get home safely. I'll try to talk some sense into her over dessert." He chugs his drink back, shaking his head and smacking his lips as he fights the burn. "There was a time in college when I experimented with a man, and if I'm being honest with myself, I think about him often. *Renaldo,*" Dad purrs, and I nearly gasp in shock at his confession. "Your mother knows this, and she's always held some sort of resentment toward a man she's never met."

He's clearly drunk and spilling secrets that I really hope he doesn't remember.

"I'm goin' to make another drink," he slurs, waving us off. "Have a good night."

We're left standing in the empty dining room alone, nothing but the repetitive ticking of the grandfather clock in the corner.

"Let's go, Tobes," Shane murmurs, wrapping his arm around me and hugging me tightly. "Let's get the fuck out of here."

It's Sunday morning, and I can't seem to shake off last night's dinner with my narcissistic parents. I was hopeful that a good night's sleep might blur some of the details from my brain, but I can still picture my mother's disgusted eyes. The only thing she's worried about is her own reputation, as if my being gay might tarnish it.

It's bullshit, and it's hurtful.

After my dad's awkward, drunken revelation, I can see why she's so bitter and he's so absent.

I will never live in a loveless marriage where passion is dead and resentment thrives.

The only reason I haven't completely cut them off is that I still need help paying for college, but dealing with them definitely isn't good for my anxiety.

It's become a routine of sorts—coming to the dock when I need to forget about my problems or take my mind off of things. Maybe *routine* isn't the right word, more like a coping mechanism. But if I can forget about my mommy-daddy issues *and* practice violin, then it's a win-win to me.

Shane's at home, opting to study for his finals and give me some privacy. He said if I wasn't back in two hours, then he'd come looking for me. But I didn't want to talk about it last night, and I don't want to talk about it today. I'd honestly like to pretend that the entire dinner never even happened.

Towering cypress trees surround the lake, and morning sunlight shines through, shimmering against the calm surface of the water. Sitting cross-legged at the end of the old dock, I rest my folded arms on the bottom slat of the railing, propping my head up on them and staring into the distance in an attempt to clear my mind.

I take a deep breath of fresh air and close my eyes for a moment, allowing my other senses to take over. The cool breeze caresses my skin, and the warmth of the sun hugs my face. Seagulls and mourning doves sing and chirp in the trees above me, their melodic songs only interrupted by the occasional splash of a turtle or frog.

My happiness is my own, and no one else's.

I repeat the mantra two more times before I open my eyes, stand up, and unclasp my violin case to get warmed up.

Today won't be a "Pink Pony Club" kind of day, but instead a Ludwig van Beethoven day. I need to practice as much as possible, and I decide to start with the second movement—the adagio—since it's the most expressive and passionate. I could really do with an emotional purge right now. The lingering negative emotions from my parents have got to go.

Something about this particular part of the arrangement brings tears to my eyes, like I'm releasing all the anger, grief, and sorrow inside of me and opening up to love and happiness instead. It's a metaphor for my life right now, and boy, does it hit close to home. I get lost in the music and in the movements, releasing everything built up and everything I've repressed.

My parents don't deserve my worry or concern, and they certainly don't deserve *me*. It's their loss that they won't be there to see me blow everyone away at the symphony.

Loud, slow clapping startles me, and I spin around, finding my boyfriend watching me from the other end of the dock, giving me a flashback to the last time we were here together, and I came out to him. Two months later, and now he's my boyfriend.

I almost can't believe it.

"Was that a sneak peek for the symphony next week?"

Shane asks, slowly walking to me and making the wood creak under his weight.

"Yeah," I murmur, packing up my violin. "I'm ready to get it over with, honestly. It's kinda a lot of pressure."

"You're gonna do amazing, Tobes. Everyone who matters will be there to support you. Your friends, your boyfriend, and your grandparents."

"I actually never heard from Gran and Bo," I tell him, bringing back some of the stress I just got rid of. "I told them about it when I was down there for spring break, but I never sent them an official invite. My last text didn't even go through. You know how spotty their cell service is."

Shit.

That just opened a whole new can of anxiety worms.

He must see the panic on my face. "Don't stress. Text me their contact info. I'll handle it. You've got enough on your plate right now."

"Thank you so much," I breathe out in relief, looping my arms around his neck.

"That's what boyfriends are for." He slips his hands into the gap in my overalls, caressing my lower back between my cut-off shirt and underwear. His long fingers creep lower, brushing over the top of my thong and making him groan when he feels bare ass. Shane kisses my forehead tenderly, pausing his groping to check on me first. His dark eyes stare intently down at me. "Wanna talk about last night?"

"Not really." It was an embarrassing disaster, and I'd rather forget it ever happened. "Just promise me we won't ever become one of those bitter old couples filled with resentment and regret. *Please, Shane.* We can't ever let that happen to us."

"I promise. We won't," Shane says matter-of-factly,

peppering zealous kisses all over my face. "Of course, we won't."

"Okay," I say softly, trusting his words.

"Wanna go home and fuck?" he asks with an arched brow, his hand fully sinking down to squeeze and knead my ass.

My lip quirks at his candidness. I love how comfortable he's gotten. "Yeah."

Shane pops my G-string and hoists me over his shoulder, making me squeal loudly. "*Shane!*" I cry with a laugh, gripping onto his waist while hanging upside down. He grabs my backpack and violin case with one arm, keeping me steady with the other.

He stomps over to the passenger side door like an angry caveman retrieving his spoils and bringing them home to ravage. He opens the door and gently sets me down before going back for my bike and carefully lifting it into the bed of his truck.

I need something to take my mind off of everything because practicing the violin in my favorite spot wasn't enough to do the trick.

I need Shane.

I need my safe space.

We're barely in the door before we're going at it like two horny teenagers who finally have the house to themselves. We stumble toward the kitchen, our lips locked together as we continue to make out passionately.

"Spencer and Jake aren't home," Shane breathes into my mouth. "I want you right now. Right here." He nips my bottom lip. "Wanna hear you scream my name."

"*Yes.*" I tip my head back, moaning as he presses wet, open-mouthed kisses down my neck.

"Let's get you out of these," Shane murmurs, pressing the buttons and releasing the shoulder straps on my favorite blue jean overalls. They fall to the floor with a thud, leaving me standing before him in nothing but a cut-off white T-shirt, lacey thong, and fuzzy purple socks.

Shane steps back, staring at me in wonder. "*So sexy,*" he whispers, licking his lips like he wants to devour me.

My stomach flips at his compliment, and I step out of the fallen overalls in eager anticipation. Without warning, Shane drops to his knees and presses his face to the soft, sheer fabric cradling my dick. He inhales deeply, and my face gets hot with arousal.

"*Mmm,*" he hums, squeezing my bare ass.

Ever since Tate introduced me to wearing thongs, and Shane bought me a box full of pretty lingerie, I've enjoyed wearing them under my everyday clothes. It's like a naughty little secret that only I know about.

And Shane.

He mouths my dick through the thin lace, and the wet heat of his mouth has desire pulsing through every cell in my body. I whimper, thrusting my hips forward and silently begging for more. He carefully stretches the fabric down, allowing my hard cock to pop out of the top.

Shane licks around my sensitive crown, tonguing my slit and driving me wild. When he finally swallows my full length, I bite my fist and stare down at him in awe. Seeing a big, strong man on his knees and sucking me off has my orgasm racing down my spine. Before I get there, he pops off and pulls away, leaving me panting and my thighs shaking.

"*Shane!*" I cry out in utter devastation, yanking on my curls. "I was so freaking close."

Instead of giving me what I want, Shane stands up with a cocky smirk. "I know." He casually strolls over to the kitchen island, as if he didn't just cruelly edge me with his mouth. "Bend over the counter," he commands, slapping the cold, hard marble with his palm. His tone is dark and possessive, and his eyes are two bottomless pits I'd willingly dive into.

"W-what?" I gasp, glancing at the front door as if our roommates are going to walk in at any moment. A small thrill shoots through me knowing there's a chance.

"You heard me, butterfly. Shirt off, but leave the underwear and socks on, and bend over," he repeats with a little more force that makes my desperate cock twitch.

Shane smirks as I scramble to obey, bending over and presenting my lingerie-clad ass to him. He slips a finger under the G-string, running his knuckle along my crease and making me whimper.

"You like that?" he asks, pressing against my hole the next time he brushes over it.

"*Mhm. Yes,*" I moan. "More."

Shane's fingers disappear, and I whine at the loss of his touch before I hear a packet of lube being torn open. He pulls my thong to the side, holding it there while cool liquid drips down my crack. "You're so beautiful in this color," he whispers, praising me sweetly while he drags his fingertips across the lace fabric encasing my sac. He continues exploring my body, traveling up my taint until he gets to my hole, tracing soft circles around and around.

"*Oh God,*" I moan as he gently works one then two fingers inside, stretching me open and getting me ready to take his cock. When he adds a third and grazes my prostate,

I have to fight off the orgasm. "Okay. I'm ready," I pant. "Fuck me, Shane. *Please.*"

He continues to hold my thong to the side, teasing me with his wide cockhead. He slowly rubs against my hole, adding more and more pressure until I'm whimpering and whining and begging.

"So needy for me." He pushes forward until his crown pops in, making me cry out. He doesn't give me but a second to acclimate before he's sinking the rest of the way into me. A garbled scream tears from my throat at the sudden intrusion.

"Fuck, baby. The sight of my dick disappearing into your ass while you're wearing something so soft and pretty is the hottest thing I've ever seen." He pulls back, leaving only the tip inside before thrusting into me again.

"Oh God," I grunt at the impact.

"Not gonna last long," he grits out through a tightly clenched jaw.

"Me neither," I moan as he picks up his pace, and we find our rhythm together.

Shane tilts his hips just right, jabbing into my prostate on every thrust.

"*Ungh!*" I shout, gripping onto the sides of the island for purchase while my fluffy socks slip and slide against the hard floor. "*Mmf! Oh my God!*"

"You like that?" he grunts, increasing his pace until he's ramming my prostate at warp speed.

"*Harder, Shane, harder!*" I chant, pushing off the island and rocking backward to meet him aggressively. He grabs my hips with both hands and yanks me back as he thrusts forward. His strokes are hard, deep, and unforgiving.

Just what I need.

"Shane!" I cry out, pinching my eyes shut as his cock pistons in and out of me without losing rhythm.

"That's it. Say my name, baby."

"Fuck me, *Shane*," I groan into the counter.

"Louder," he grunts through gritted teeth, digging his fingers into my hips and making me see stars.

"*Shane!*" I holler, the moisture in my eyes building with every slap of skin against skin. "I love you," I cry, my voice shaking as I drag the words out. Pressing my cheek to the cold marble top, I surrender to the orgasm building inside of me as we chase our release together.

"Come for me," Shane demands, and it's like a switch goes off.

I cry out, clamping down around his cock and squeezing his length while I paint the side of the kitchen island with my jizz. My release triggers Shane's, and he explodes inside of me, a rush of warmth filling me up.

Shane collapses on top of me, his full weight pressing me into the countertop. "I love you too," he whispers into my ear, breathing heavily.

He slips out of me, and I carefully stand up, feeling his cum dripping down my leg and into my fluffy socks.

"Need to get cleaned up. But first, we need to take care of that." Shane nods toward the island, smirking at the mess on the side like he's proud of himself, while I just feel guilty.

First the bathroom sink and now the kitchen island.

I really need to stop coming on communal surfaces.

"I can't believe we only have a week of school left. Sophomore year has really flown by," I say with a yawn as we lie in bed together after cleaning the kitchen and showering.

"It has," Shane agrees. "But it's been good. Particularly the second half."

I smile thoughtfully. "Were you serious about getting our own place? Because I was," I ask vulnerably.

Without a single pause, Shane answers. "Very serious. In fact," he says, leaning forward and reaching for the laptop on the nightstand. "Let's search for apartments right now."

"Really?!" I squeak, my stomach flipping upside down at the thought.

A loud fart blasts through the door, followed by the sounds of Jake and Spencer's laughter echoing down the hallway.

"Deadass," Shane grumbles, shaking his head at how obnoxious our roommates can be.

I burst out laughing because the timing couldn't have been more poetic.

"Okay. Let's do it. Let's go apartment hunting."

CHAPTER THIRTY
SHANE

After a disastrous dinner with Toby's parents, for some reason, I decide I'm going to tell my mom about us. Just to get it over with, and so she can't ever claim I was hiding it from her.

"Hey, Shaney," she says in greeting.

"Hey, Mom. How you been?"

Oh, you know, back workin' at the flower shop, but I did just sell my first painting! It's not much, but it sure is exciting."

"That's good, Mom. Congrats. Buck been treating you right? Or do I need to pay him another visit?"

"Buck and I are done. I met someone new. Someone who really treats me right. His name is Corey, and I'd like for you to meet him."

I close my eyes and pinch the bridge of my nose. I'm glad that asshole is gone, but I just wish she wasn't immediately on to the next guy.

"Honestly, Mom, I'm glad Buck's gone, but I'm not sure when I can stop by. Semester's almost over, and I've got a lot going on with work and school. I was actually calling to tell you something, if you have a minute."

"Of course, honey. What is it?"

"I'm seeing someone . . . a boy."

"*Oh?* A boy? So you're . . ."

"I'm bi, Mom, and Toby is my boyfriend."

I can hear her sharp intake of air through the phone, but I can't tell if it's good or bad. Considering how much she adores him, I'm hoping it's good, because we don't need any more parental drama.

"Well, look at us, Shaney. Got ourselves a coupla boyfriends," she laughs, making light of the news. "Who woulda thought?"

"As long as you're happy, and he treats you right, Mom. That's all I've ever wanted for you."

"I could say the same for you, but I already know you're happy," she replies. "You've always been happiest around Toby. Even as a young boy. And don't think I didn't notice how protective you were over him around that jackass, Buck."

There's an extended silence over the phone, and I let her words settle in.

"I am happy. I love him."

"Aww, that is so sweet, Shaney! As soon as things settle down for you two, we've got to do dinner together. *Oh!* Like a double date!"

I think I'd rather gouge my own eyes out.

"Sure, Mom."

I don't invite her to the symphony, especially now that she comes with an unknown plus one. She's just not stable or trustworthy enough to count on not making a scene. I wouldn't risk Toby's big day. Because the kind of scene my mom likes to make usually involves the police being called.

It's half the reason I quit soccer in middle school, with the other reason being I couldn't afford all the gear.

"Corey is so sweet and thoughtful, I think you'll really like him."

I have no plans on meeting this mystery man of the month before he inevitably gets the boot, but I placate her nonetheless. "Glad to hear it." My mom is almost as self-centered as Toby's parents, and even less involved in my life. "Well, I'm off to work," I say, wrapping up the conversation, so I can make one last phone call before I leave the house.

"Let's plan that double date soon. Talk to you later!" Mom hollers, hanging up before I have a chance to reply.

I shake my head and pull up my contacts, tapping on Toby's grandparents *again*.

He knows not to get his hopes up because I haven't been able to get a hold of them, but I won't give up. There's still time.

I absolutely have to get Gran and Bo here.

"I'm going to be late!" Toby hollers, hopping around on one foot while he tries to put a sock on. "And if you're late, you can't play. *Even me!* Professor's rules. My parents would love that, huh?" he laughs sardonically.

The orchestra's end-of-the-year symphony and concerto starts at six for the public, but Toby has to be there an hour and a half early to warm up.

"Come here," I murmur, holding my hand out. I glance down at my other wrist, noting that he has forty minutes before he needs to be inside the auditorium. "You've got plenty of time," I reassure him, straightening his tie and adjusting his collar while he peers up at me with wide, terrified eyes. "Listen. You got this, okay? You're incredible with that bow, and you've practiced more than I've ever seen you practice before. I'll be in the audience, with all of our friends, cheering you on. The only family you need is the one we've chosen."

"Thank you," Toby murmurs, wrapping his arms around my ribs and giving me a hug. He takes a big breath of air, slowly releasing it.

"That's it. Just relax, baby." I rub his back softly, trying to comfort him without wrinkling his shirt.

Toby shakes the nerves out of his hands before rubbing small circles on his chest. "These heart palpitations sure aren't helping me relax," he chuckles dryly. "Especially knowing there are quite a few philharmonic scouts watching. Tonight could literally make or break my future as a professional violinist."

"*Tobes*. I heard you practicing on the dock. You've got nothing to worry about. I don't know anything about classical violin, but I do know I got goosebumps. You're gonna kill it, butterfly."

"But what if—"

"No. No buts," I say, cutting him off.

"No butts?" Toby mock-pouts, sticking out his bottom lip exaggeratedly. "I'm not sure how this relationship is gonna work then."

"Only your butt," I growl, grabbing a handful and pulling him closer to me.

He closes his eyes and takes a deep breath, releasing it through his mouth. I can tell his nerves are really getting to him, so I grab his hands and sit us on the bed.

"I made something for you," I murmur. "Thought it might help your nerves during stressful events." I reach under Toby's bed and pull out the little pouch I hid there while he was taking a shower. "It's an anxiety toolkit."

"An anxiety toolkit?" he parrots, looking confused yet intrigued as he holds the clear pouch up to examine the contents.

"Yeah. Just some stuff that I thought might help if you feel a panic attack or anxiety coming on." Unzipping the small pouch, I pull out the items one by one. "You've got a cold pack that you can break and shake to activate, a couple different sour candies for a distraction, a stretchy fidget toy, some gum, and Tylenol in case you get a headache after." I think I covered most of it, but he'll have to add his own prescription. He takes a pill every morning, but I know he has another for panic attacks that he only takes in an emergency because it knocks him out.

"Shane . . ." Toby's golden eyes shimmer with barely restrained emotions. "I've never been so seen or so heard by anyone in my entire life. I love you."

"I love you too. Now, go break a leg."

The entire crowd stands when the conductor bows, cheering and whistling like I've never even heard them do for our basketball team. The symphony was amazing, and Toby's concerto closed it strongly. I am *so* fucking proud of him. There wasn't a dry eye in the house during his emotional adagio movement, and as I look around the auditorium, many still have tears.

As soon as the door to backstage opens and Toby steps out, our friends rush over, surrounding him with hugs and compliments.

"You were incredible," I say, congratulating him. "Had

the whole audience mesmerized. I'm so fucking proud," I murmur, handing over the fresh bouquet of sunflowers I picked out for him.

"Thank you." He closes his eyes and smells the bouquet, humming at the scent. "I can't believe it's finally over, and if I could, I wouldn't fix one thing."

I chuckle at his candor. "Because you're a professional, baby." Kissing his forehead quickly, I step to the side and allow him to see who else is here to support him.

Toby's sharp intake of breath lets me know he sees them, but other than that, he doesn't move.

"Gran and Bo are here," I murmur under my breath, and that seems to kick him into gear.

"*Oh my God!* I can't believe you're here!" Toby shouts, rushing over and giving his grandparents a big group hug.

"So sorry you couldn't get a hold of us, dearie. We were on an Alaskan cruise, and wouldn't ya guess it. No cell service! But this young man over here didn't give up," Gran says, smiling fondly at me. "We finally got in touch through email, and we landed late last night straight from Juneau. So if my hair looks a little rough, that's why." Gran pats her gray curls, chuckling warmly.

"Alaska?! You came all this way for me?" Toby asks them in astonishment.

"Of course. Wouldn't miss it," Gran says simply.

"Darn tootin'," Bo adds, making me smile.

"And you arranged all this for me?" Toby asks, staring up at me with glistening eyes.

"It's nothing. Really. They're important to you. And you're important to me." I lean down and give him a peck on the lips, forgetting that we're standing right in front of his grandparents, and no one's pre-warned them yet.

"Ohhh. Is this new?" Gran asks with a sneaky little

smile. "Seems we have a lot to catch up on since spring break, grandson."

Toby blushes, chuckling awkwardly. "Yeah. It's new." He clears his throat into his fist a few times. "Um. Gran. Bo. I'm gay, and Shane's my boyfriend."

"Well, isn't that lovely. You both look so happy. Thank you for sharing with us," Gran says sweetly, clapping her hands together and smiling at the two of us.

"We will always support you," his grandfather adds. "There's nothing you could say or do that would make me love you less."

Toby's grandparents are the kindest people I've ever met, and I have no idea how his mom could be so mean compared to them.

Gran grabs hold of both of Toby's hands, squeezing them lovingly. "I think you've smiled more tonight than you did the entire week you stayed with us. We were a little worried, honey. It's great to see you so happy and thriving."

Toby hugs his grandmother tenderly, resting his head on her shoulder. "I'm very happy. Thank you. Mom sure wasn't," he mumbles.

"Well, I'm sorry to hear that, although I can't say I'm too surprised. But we won't talk about that on such a joyous occasion. It's time to celebrate!"

"Yes! We'd like to take all of you out to dinner," Bo declares. "Our treat. We can talk more at the restaurant."

"Don't threaten me with a free dinner," Tate purrs, making the old man blush. Daija subtly elbows Tate's arm, mouthing *tone it down*, while Toby distracts his grandparents with more hugs.

"That's so nice," Spencer says respectfully. "Thank you, sir."

"Yeah. Thank you, Bo," Toby adds, followed by the rest of us.

"Excuse me, sorry to interrupt," Professor Goldblum suddenly says with an impatient, excited smile. "Mr. Livingston, I have some very important people I'd like you to meet."

Toby's smile slowly grows until his dimples pop out and all his teeth show, lighting up the entire auditorium. "The scouts."

CHAPTER THIRTY-ONE
TOBY

The symphony and concerto went better than I could have hoped for, despite all the anxiety leading up to it. Having all my friends, my grandparents, and my amazing boyfriend there supporting me and openly being proud of me meant more than any of them could have realized. My professor was thrilled with my performance, too, and introduced me to a couple different scouts that approached him to inquire about me.

We all had dinner on the pier at The Crab Shack before my grandparents hopped on another flight out of here. For being in their seventies, they sure do have a lot of fun. I'd like to think that'll be Shane and me one day, retired and traveling the world. Even though their stay was quick, it was special.

Not only was it an incredible evening, but the following morning, I was contacted by the Brooklyn Classical Orchestra, offering me an internship for the summer. As in, moving to New York City, getting an apartment, and living there for two and a half months. This is something I've always dreamed of, but I told him I'd have to get back to him. He understood that it's a big decision and told me to take a few days and let him know at the beginning of the week.

Shane and I just started dating, and that's another dream come true, so the thought of moving to a different state for the summer is unbearable. I feel stuck between two possibilities—being with Shane and playing violin in New York City—both of which I desperately want for my life. Being faced with such a huge decision is crushing me and dragging me down from the high of last night.

Sniffling, I squeeze Shane's jean jacket that I never gave back, hugging it tightly to my chest. It still smells like him. *Safe.* Like citrus and bergamot. *Like Shane.* Another tear drips down my cheek, the jagged path feeling like the slice of a razor blade. I can't say no to this opportunity, but I can't be away from Shane for that long.

I need to talk to him.

As if conjured by love and tears alone, Shane knocks lightly before slipping inside my bedroom door. "Hey."

Sniffle.

"Hi."

"What's wrong? You sick?" he asks urgently, hurrying over and perching on the edge of the bed. He brushes my curls back and feels my forehead with four fingers and then his wrist.

"No. It's not that. It's nothing bad."

"Then why are you crying?" His brows furrow, and he uses his thumb to wipe away a new streak of tears, glaring at the droplet as if it's the one who hurt me.

"Because..."

"Why, Toby? Talk to me," he pleads, ready to fight my enemies for me. Even the invisible ones.

"Because I got an opportunity to move to New York City

for the summer and intern for a huge orchestra, but that would mean I have to move away for two and a half months and be all alone," I blurt out in one breath. "I wish you could go with me," I add without truly believing it's even an option.

"Are you inviting me?"

"What?" I sniffle, wiping my nose and sitting up to face him.

"Are you inviting me to New York?" he asks again, staring at me with a blank expression I can't read.

"Uh. *Yeah?*" It comes out like a question instead of an answer.

"I just got you; I'm not letting you go, Toby. *You're mine.* I'm coming too."

Tears of joy instantly well up, spilling over when I throw myself at him. "Oh, thank God! I didn't want to do that alone!" I cry out, excitedly sharing more of the details. "They'll provide the apartment, subway pass, and a living allowance. It'll be a small studio, but we only need one bed anyway."

"You could sleep on top of me, and I wouldn't mind."

I giggle, my mood instantly lifting and my mind running wild with all the possibilities this summer will bring, from new apartment décor to weekend getaways to the Jersey Shore. "What about your catering job?"

"Glenn will hold my position, no problem. He already told me I'll always have a job with him. Besides, working at a restaurant in New York City for the summer would look incredible on my résumé."

"Not to mention all the money we'll save without having to pay rent," I add.

"That too. We can delay our apartment move-in date to early August, before the semester starts."

This plan is coming together and making more and more sense as we talk through it. Campus housing comes completely furnished, so we don't have any furniture to pack up; it'll just be a few boxes of belongings. I'm sure Jake and Spencer won't mind if we store them at the house while we're gone, so we don't have to get a storage unit.

"I'm getting really excited. I'm going to call the scout back and let him know I accept."

"And I'll call Glenn. Then I'm going to get online and start looking for sous chef positions in Brooklyn."

"I can't believe we're really doing this!" I squeal, squeezing his neck in a tight hug and smooshing our cheeks together.

Shane pulls back, kissing me passionately on the lips before cradling my face between his rough palms. "Every second we're together, my love for you is carved deeper and deeper into the very core of who I am. Your outline is etched into my soul like a vinyl record stuck on repeat. I need you, Toby. And I can't fucking live without you."

Shane's eloquent words do funny things to my insides, and I chew on my bottom lip.

"You deserve all the good things in this world, baby. And I'll do everything in my power to give them to you."

"But what do *you* want?" I ask hesitantly. I need to make sure that he'll truly be happy in New York.

"I want a future with you, Toby. I want to build a life together. You're my happy place, and you always have been. I'd follow you anywhere."

I throw myself at him, feeling like the luckiest guy in the world to have such a kind and thoughtful boyfriend. "I love you. My sexy stalker."

EPILOGUE

Toby

Our apartment in Brooklyn is seven hundred and fifty square feet with one bathroom and a cute little balcony. We have a tomato plant that's thriving out there, too. Miss Edna, our next-door neighbor, gave it to us as a welcome-to-the-building gift. You should see her porch; it's an urban garden like I've never seen before. Our bedroom, living room, and kitchen are all in the same area, so there really isn't any privacy, but it's perfect. It's ours.

We've been in Brooklyn less than a week, and we both already love it, seeming to fit right in. The city is bustling and truly never sleeps, filled with artists hungry for work and amazing food joints on every block. Glenn set Shane up with a job at a swanky new French bistro on Fifth Street called La Belle.

I'm not talking to my parents right now, so as far as I know, they aren't even aware I'm in New York. But they haven't stopped the direct deposits into my account every month. Bo and Gran made it very clear that I could always reach out to them for help if my parents decide to take things further and cut me off financially. I'd only do that in a last-ditch effort because they're retired, and I don't want to take any of their hard-earned retirement money away from them when it has to last.

My phone buzzes while I organize the orchestra's supply room. It's not the most glamorous part of my internship, but if it's what they need from me, then I will alphabetize the cleaning products and rearrange the toilet paper every day if it means I get a chance to practice on stage with them.

I check who's calling before I answer and see that it's Shane. "Hey, babe," I say with a smile.

"Wanna meet in the park for lunch?" Shane asks, the sound of clinking dishes and people shouting in the background nearly overpowering his deep voice. "I miss you."

Brooklyn Bridge Park is our go-to meet-up spot. Shane always packs the food, and we lie out on a blanket, enjoying the sun and a little slice of nature in the middle of the city. Afterward, we walk along the water and take in the expansive views of the Lower Manhattan skyline.

"I miss you too. That sounds great," I say, setting the last roll on top of my toilet paper pyramid.

"I'll bring lunch. Meet me at our bench at noon."

"Okay. See you then. Love you."

"Love you too." Shane ends the call, and I slip my phone back into my pocket, wishing lunch would hurry up and get here.

Two hours of organizing sheet music later, and it's finally time for lunch. I grab my messenger bag and rush out of the door and down to the subway station a block away. It was a little daunting to manage at first, and I had to call Shane to come find me on more than one occasion, but I've gotten the hang of it now.

I'm at the park before I know it, smiling as a panoramic view of the East River and Lower Manhattan comes into view. The midday sun sparkles on the water's surface while cars zoom across the bridge, completely oblivious to this little slice of heaven down below.

I see him as I get closer to the water's edge.

My boyfriend.

Dressed in all black and still wearing his chef's coat, Shane is perched on our favorite bench, facing the water.

"Hey," I say, ghosting my fingers over the back of his neck as I walk around and join him on the wooden bench, giving him a quick peck.

"Hey. How was your morning?" he asks, digging into the brown paper bag he brought from La Belle.

"Can't complain. I'm in New York," I respond with a smile, accepting the wrapped sandwich he hands me. "You?"

"Busy, but same. I'm really happy, Tobes. The happiest I think I've ever been." He rests his hand on top of mine, squeezing gently.

"Me too," I murmur, biting back the tears and facing the extraordinary view in front of us. "Me too."

I hold up the handmade sign with Tate and Daija's names on it, bouncing on my toes in the middle of the airport.

I'm so excited, I can hardly contain myself.

Shane surprised me by having my best friends visit for the weekend.

"Ahh! There they are!" I shout, holding the sign above my head and waving it to get their attention.

They squeal when they see me, running over with their luggage flying behind them.

"*We missed you!*" they both shout in unison, enveloping me in a group hug.

"I'm so proud of our baby gay," Tate says, pressing a hand to his heart. "All grown up and in the big apple with his boyfriend."

"Our little hatchling has flown the coop," Daija teases, wiping a fake tear off her cheek.

Warmth fills my heart and my face.

"Sooo," Tate drawls with a mischievous little smile. "Do you still use your fake ID? Because you know we would fuck shit up in NYC, honey."

Shane side-eyes the three of us, and we burst out laughing. "Absolutely not," he growls, folding his arms across his chest and furrowing his dark brows. "I've got a reservation at a respectable cocktail lounge in SoHo."

Tate loops his arms through mine and Daija's, smiling up at Shane innocently. "Well, that sounds like fun, too."

We take an Uber back to the apartment since Tate and Daija have luggage with them. It's a tight fit, but they're staying with us both nights and sleeping on the couches. I give them an extremely short tour, and then we start the logistical nightmare of four people getting ready to go out for the night. It's not ideal, but we make it work.

I step out of the bathroom, freshly showered and completely dressed.

"Fit check!" Tate yells way too loudly, making Shane glower at him.

"*Oh my God!*" Daija squeals. "The outfit is giving, and

the body is tea!" She twirls her finger, indicating I should do a little spin.

I indulge my friends and turn around slowly, showing off how great my ass looks in these tight white jeans. My linen shirt is unbuttoned at the top, revealing smooth, tan skin. I make eye contact with a dark, possessive stare, and electricity crackles along my skin, fueling the desire growing inside me.

"Alright, you two! No hanky-panky tonight when we're all sleeping in the same room," Tate teases with a snicker.

"Oh, shut it," I say weakly, swatting at him with a laugh. "Wouldn't you like that?" I tease right back.

"Babe. You know I would. That's some dream porn right there."

"*Oh my God!* Tater tot! Stop it!" Daija laughs, shaking her head. She's sitting on her heels at the kitchen table with a portable makeup mirror, painting on the perfect winged liner. She's wearing a bright red romper with gold necklaces, bracelets, and beads throughout her braids. She looks incredible as usual. *Jake would die.*

"You look beautiful, Daija. You should send Jake a pic," I say, effectively changing the subject from Shane and I fucking.

"Ohhh. Yesss," Tate agrees. "Lemme take it."

"Fiiine. One sec," she mumbles, peeling off her lip tint and applying the gloss. "There. All done." She smacks her lips, slips into her stilettos, and hands her phone over.

"Pose for me!" Tate hollers.

I quickly slide the curtains open, a burst of sunlight brightening the room, and an incredible view of the city filling the backdrop.

Daija poses a few different ways while Tate snaps a million shots.

"One of those will be good," he proclaims, handing the phone back. "You're gonna make that poor boy nut in his shorts."

The entire room erupts into raucous laughter, even Shane.

I have a feeling tonight's going to be one to remember.

"It's been an absolute blast this weekend," Daija says with a frown and a hug. "Shane, thanks for planning everything."

Tate sighs. "What she said. I never want to leave. This gay was made for the city."

"Thank you guys for coming. I had so much fun." I don't know why I feel so emotional when we'll see them back at school in another month. Shane throws an arm around me, pulling me into his side.

"Sure you don't want us to ride with you to the airport?" Shane offers, always in protector mode.

"We'll be okay. Thanks, though," Daija says with a sweet smile, wheeling her suitcase across the sidewalk and over to the waiting car. "I really do love it here. The vibes, the atmosphere, the people. Everyone we met was so inspiring."

"I just thought of something," Tate suddenly says. "You know what the perfect future would be?"

"Are you plotting ways to move to New York?" I ask with a smirk.

"*Duuuh.*" He rolls his eyes and fluffs his curls. "So, I have a plan. A *business* plan. Get this—a one-stop shop wedding service. Daija and I will be the event planners, Shane the caterer, and Toby will provide the music. Think about it! *It's perfect.*"

I glance around and see the wheels turning in everyone's heads.

That's actually not a bad idea at all.

We developed such a comfortable routine here that our tiny little studio in Brooklyn feels like home now. The only reason I can stomach leaving and going back to Crescent Bay is because we're moving into our new apartment off campus as soon as we land.

We left our vehicles at the house while we were in New York, so we took an Uber from the airport to our new apartment and stopped at the leasing office to pick up the keys. Jake and Spencer are coming over later to bring our boxes and one of the cars. I don't care if we won't have our new furniture delivered for two days; we can sleep on the floor in a pile of blankets for all I care. I'll be happy as long as I'm with Shane.

"Home sweet home," Shane whispers into my ear, wrapping his arms around me from behind as we step into the foyer of our brand-new and completely empty apartment.

"*Home sweet home,*" I repeat softly, my smile slowly growing as I peer around at our future. "I love you," I tell him earnestly

"Love you too, butterfly," he murmurs, and it still feels like a dream to hear it back from him sometimes.

My best fucking friend.
Forever.

ACKNOWLEDGMENTS

First, thank you to all my amazing readers, your support means everything to us indie authors. Every review, comment, and recommendation is truly appreciated.

My ARC team and Chaotic Creatives' influencers, you all are incredible and so supportive. Every time I see a new edit, review, or recommendation posted on social media, it brings a smile to my face and makes my day. The content you all create is seriously impressive and so appreciated!

Thank you to my two lovely beta readers, Jamie and Lane, who helped me get through all the heavy lifting and fine-tune this story before editing. You both are so important to me as friends and top-tier beta readers.

My editor, Katie, it was once again such a breeze to work with you, and I truly appreciate your attention to detail as well as the explanations. It is so helpful, and your positivity is so encouraging. I'm excited to continue this series with you!

And finally, a huge shoutout to my PA, Ari, and the entire Chaotic Creatives team! Ari, I couldn't do it without you. Your support and friendship are irreplaceable, from managing my social media and book tour, to designing yet another perfect cover, all while making me laugh. Thank you for all you do!

ABOUT THE AUTHOR

Charli Meadows is an obsessive reader, avid Bookstagrammer-turned PA, and now an author herself. Lover of all things romance, she plans to write a little bit of everything but make it sweet and spicy.

You can usually find Charli working her boring corporate job or at home spending time with family, drawing, and tending her plants. When she's not reading, writing, or daydreaming about books, that is.

ALSO BY CHARLI MEADOWS

The Loyal Boys

Cali Boy

Bad Boy

Lost Boy

Unlucky 13 - Shared World

Shattered: A Black Diamond Novel

Elemental Desires - MM Fantasy Romance

Oleander

Flame - TBD

Best Bros Forever

The Bro Pact

The Bro Date

Made in United States
Orlando, FL
25 September 2025